SWAMP KILL

Juan heard it a second before he felt the massive vibrations through his feet. It sounded like a huge bulldozer running full speed through the jungle.

He turned toward the sound, raised his rifle, and waited.

It exploded from the undergrowth. The size of an elephant, with skin as thick as an armadillo's, a huge bear-like head, and a long, muscular tail tipped with two-foot spikes. It came at him fast, its eyes glinting with murderous intent.

Juan fired. Fired again.

The creature stopped, then with amazing speed, pivoted, and swung its tail at Juan's head. The man's head split like a melon.

The monster snuffled at the dead man. To make sure, it dug its claws into Juan's belly, spreading bloody entrails over the ground to mix with the thick swamp mud.

CARNIVORES

PENELOPE
BANKA
KREPS

ZEBRA BOOKS
KENSINGTON PUBLISHING CORP.

ZEBRA BOOKS are published by

Kensington Publishing Corp.
475 Park Avenue South
New York, NY 10016

First Printing: July, 1993

Printed in the United States of America

This book is for my daughters
Kim and Tracy

Chapter One

Ben Torry, Chief Ranger at Everglades National Park, found a man's leg bobbing around in a cluster of cypress knobs at eight-thirty in the morning. He found a head five minutes later. After losing his breakfast over the side of his flat-bottomed boat, he fished the remains out of the water and headed back toward the Ranger Station.

"Fuckin' gators," Juan Degas said under his breath after the last of the reporters had left.

Ben ignored the young ranger. It was the first alligator attack in the Glades in more than six years. He hoped it would be another six before he had to see something like that again.

"Fuckin' gators," Juan said a little louder.

Ben frowned at him. The man's attitude pissed him off, but he held it in. "That one six years ago. The guy got too close to her nest."

"So?"

"This isn't nesting season." He shook his head. "Alligators would rather run than fight. Unless they're protecting the nest. A croc will attack a man for no reason, but not a gator. Something's wrong here."

Juan shrugged. "You hear about it all the time. People get attacked in their backyards."

Ben shook his head again. "Those are the gators that people are stupid enough to feed. They think it's great to have a gator hanging around their pond or whatever, and they toss it food scraps. The gator loses its fear of humans, and one day it decides it's hungry, and bites the hand that feeds it. The gators in the Glades are wild. They don't usually do this."

"Usually."

"Yeah. Usually."

One week later, Harvey Sprague and Emil Brandon, both in their late twenties and out for adventure, paddled a canoe toward Shark River Slough. Three days in the Glades was a yearly ritual for them, ever since they'd graduated together from Las Flores High. They laughed at the guided cruises; that was for tourists. They were woodsmen . . . well, swampmen. . . .

"About what? Six more miles?" Harvey said over his shoulder to Emil.

Emil studied the islands on either side of the shallow river. "About. Maybe less."

They stopped at the same large, reasonably dry island every year to have lunch before paddling the rest of the afternoon toward one of the raised platforms erected by the Park Service, where they would spend the first night.

Bliss, Harvey thought as he paddled easily along the river. Not that he'd ever use that word out loud; it sounded too wimpy. . . .

"Hey. What the hell is that?" Emil asked softly.

Harvey turned his head again to see what his friend was looking at. Emil pointed to the left.

Gator, was the first thing Harvey thought, but then he changed his mind. One of the rare Florida crocs? No . . . not quite.

"Hey!" Emil said again, this time louder.

The reptile had left the bank and was coming right at them. Fast.

"JESUS!" Harvey yelled. "GET OUT OF ITS WAY! GET OUT OF ITS WAY!" He dug the oar in and pulled hard, looking for speed. *What the hell* is *that thing?*

Emil matched him, and the canoe leaped forward.

A dozen strokes, and Harvey dared look back. It was gone. They took a dozen more to make sure, then let the canoe drift as they searched the water surface for any sign of the creature.

"Shit," Emil said. "That fucker was fifteen feet at least. Never seen one that big. I can't believe it. . . ."

"Did you see its snout?"

"What?"

"Its jaws," Harvey said. "It looked like a croc's jaws, but different teeth. Longer. The teeth, I mean."

"I don't like this." Emil looked around nervously. "Crocs are mean suckers."

"And its nostrils were up by the eyes. That's really weird. Gators and crocs have nostrils at the end of— What was that?" He looked at Emil sharply. Had he felt the bottom of the canoe bump on something?

"We hit bottom," Emil said calmly. "We—"

It came up out of the water like a gray geyser, an inch from Emil's face. Harvey had a good look at its teeth before he found himself underwater. He came up screaming.

9

"EMIL! EMIL!" He sucked in air and water, trying desperately to see through the roiling froth of river and mud that tried to drag him under again. He heard the sound then . . . high-pitched and eerie. It took him several seconds to realize it was Emil. The turbulent water turned pink. The sound stopped. So did the turbulence.

Harvey struggled to his feet in the waist-deep water, his feet slipping on the muck of the riverbed. He gagged and spat, and wiped the silt from his eyes. "Emil . . . ," he said, and looked out over the now calm river. Emil stood farther out, shoulder-deep. The canoe bobbed a few feet away.

"Get the canoe," Harvey gasped. "EMIL!" He waded toward his friend. "EMIL!" Why didn't he move? Why didn't he get the damned canoe? Why did he have that look . . . ? Harvey stopped three feet from Emil.

Emil's eyes were wide and shocked, and staring right at him. His mouth was open, and a thin trickle of blood ran down his chin and dripped into the water. He didn't blink. He didn't reach up to wipe away the blood.

Harvey fought through his growing dread to take the few more steps to reach his buddy. When he put a hand on Emil's shoulder, he watched with a strange and sudden sense of detachment as the top half of Emil rolled over in the water. There was no bottom half.

Chapter Two

Dr. Evan Tremayne, psychiatrist on the staff of the Las Flores Medical and Psychiatric Center, walked down the hall to room 3B. The patient had been transferred from County General in south Florida after the doctors there had determined that he was physically unharmed. His mental condition was something else, and LFMPC had inherited him.

Every staff member at the hospital knew Harvey Sprague's story by now. Cases this sensational were hard to keep quiet. The young man had shown up at the Everglades Ranger Station two days ago, babbling about a monster that had attacked his canoe. When Ben Torry, the Chief Ranger had calmed the man somewhat and had gone out to look at the canoe, he'd found the upper half of a body, neatly covered with brush, lying in the bottom of the battered craft. He'd assumed that it was another alligator attack (one had occurred the week before), but Sprague had insisted that the creature that had attacked them was not an alligator. Then Sprague had retreated into a silence that he refused to break. Not even his hysterical parents had been able to bring him out of it. So here he was. At least now he was responding to questions with nods and shakes of his head, Evan thought. His guess was that it was simple shock, and that he was now beginning to come out of it, and no permanent damage had been done.

"Morning, Harvey," Evan said as he entered the room.

Harvey sat in a chair near the window and turned at the greeting. "I'm not crazy," he said.

Evan sat on the edge of the hospital bed and smiled. "Nobody said you were. As a matter of fact, you seem pretty normal to me as of this moment, but before I let you go home, I'd like you to talk about it."

Harvey seemed to consider this, then said, "I'm having nightmares . . ."

"Not surprising," Evan said.

"I can't believe he's dead, you know?"

They talked for almost an hour. Evan led Harvey through his feelings, steering him toward a beginning of acceptance and understanding. And finally Harvey said, "It wasn't an alligator, Doctor Tremayne. Or a croc, either."

"What was it?"

Harvey shook his head. "I don't know."

"Could you draw it?"

"Yeah," he said. "I could do that."

Evan showed the drawing to several colleagues. They all said a poorly drawn alligator or crocodile, and one intern said it looked like a gavail, a kind of reptile found in India. All related, Evan decided, and had almost dismissed the whole thing as Harvey Sprague's imagination when the coroner's report on Emil Brandon came to his attention.

"Inconclusive?" he said aloud, and went down to see the man himself.

"Are you sure?" Evan asked.

The old man peered at him over his wire-rims. "Sure as shootin'. You want me to tell you how many alligator attacks I've seen? Plenty in my time. Some on people, most on animals. Alligator will clamp on to you, shake you up, roll you over, drag you under, drown you, then gnaw away. Makes a mess of it. This poor guy was nipped in half neat as you please. Like a hot knife through butter. No alligator is going to take a grown man's body and cut it in two as nice and neat and fast as this. Uh-uh."

"So what did it?"

"Don't know. Burnham's been hot on my ass to put something beside 'inconclusive' down on my report. Says for me to put gator cause it's simpler and won't make any difference to anybody anyway. Won't do it. It'd be a lie, and I don't give a goddamn what he says."

Evan grinned. The old man was one of the few people brave enough to go against the hospital director. Burnham was publicity-shy, and this case looked as if the sensationalism and mystery behind it gave it the potential to cause a lot of it. "What about the attack last week?" he asked, sobering again.

The coroner shrugged. "Didn't see those remains myself. Not much to see if I have the story right."

"What does this look like to you?" Evan asked, pulling Sprague's drawing from his pocket.

"Hmmm." The old man took the picture and studied it carefully. "I'd say croc, but . . ." He brought it closer to his face. "Teeth are wrong. Nostrils should be at the

13

tip of the snout, not back by the eyes. . . ." He handed it back to Evan. "What's this about?"

"Could an animal like this do the kind of damage we saw on Emil Brandon's body?"

"Yep. Easy. But not likely."

"I don't get you."

"If I remember a bit of a couple of courses I took in paleontology some years back just for kicks, this looks to me like an ancestor to modern reptiles. Haven't been around for about a hundred million years or so."

Later that afternoon, Evan sat at his desk with the picture spread out in front of him. According to the coroner it was impossible. But so was what had happened to Emil Brandon. Paleontology. The study of prehistoric forms of life through fossil remains. Jake Van Gower.

Evan reached for the phone.

Chapter Three

Lydia Matthews knelt in front of the shrieking pack of children and held out her arms. The leader, her dark hair flying in undisciplined ringlets around her face, launched herself straight at Lydia and wrapped arms and legs still chubby with baby fat, around her mother's neck and waist. Caught off balance, Lydia steadied herself with one hand on the hot sidewalk and hugged the grinning child with her other arm.

Children of varying ages swarmed around them, more or less mimicking the ritual with their own adults as the Las Flores Day Care Center released most of its charges to their working parents.

"Mommy! See what I did!" Jenny Matthews waved a sheet of manila paper in her mother's face. Smiling, Lydia let the child slide out of her grip and took the paper as she stood up, wondering how much longer her body could stand Jenny's daily assaults. The child was getting too heavy for her to lift as easily as she had when the greeting had established itself—when Jenny was only two. Right after Greg died. Lydia forced her thoughts away from that and focused her attention on Jenny's drawing.

"It's Duke, Mommy! See it? It's Mr. Winslow's Duke!" Jenny jumped up and down with excitement, anxious for praise. Drawing was her favorite part of the day, and she knew she was good at it—Mrs. Olivera said so.

Lydia smiled at the picture and ruffled the child's curly hair. "So it is," she said. "And it's a wonderful drawing, sweetie! You get better every day!" But privately, Lydia wondered. A month ago, when Lydia's freelance photography assignments had piled up at a gratifying rate and she'd been lucky enough to enroll Jenny in the Center's summer session, Jenny's pictures had been better. Better than the average six-year-old's pictures, anyway. And it wasn't just mother's pride, she told herself; Jenny had inherited his talent. Greg had been an artist, and a good one. His work had just been accepted for a one-man show at Trevor Galleries when the car accident . . .

"Do you really like it, Mommy?"

"Yes, darling." Lydia tore her thoughts away from Greg and the ever-present threat of depression, and concentrated on her child. Jenny always wanted more than simple praise—she wanted a blow-by-blow discussion of the merits of her work.

But this? Duke was their next door neighbor's dog—a sleek, snappy German Shepherd, and Jenny, an animal lover, had drawn pictures of him before; stylized but accurate renditions that left little doubt as to what it was. A dog. This picture looked like a watermelon with a hump and horns.

"Mrs. Matthews?" Margarita Olivera touched Lydia's arm.

"Yes?" Lydia looked up and smiled at the teacher

who had walked up behind her while she studied the drawing.

"If you have a free minute, I'd like to speak to you."

She was smiling back at Lydia, but there seemed to be a serious squint around her eyes, and Lydia's heart did a little bump. Jenny had taken her father's death with seemingly little trauma, but then she'd been only two years old when it had happened, and now Lydia found herself occasionally worrying over if and when a delayed reaction might set in to mar her daughter's equanimity. She stole another glance at the strange picture as she and Jenny followed Mrs. Olivera back into the classroom.

The Las Flores Day Care Center was a one-story, white stucco building with an orange Spanish tile roof; a style common to the west central Florida area that Lydia and Jenny had lived in all their lives. The main playroom was sunny and large with sliding glass doors that looked out over a chain-link-fenced backyard filled with swings, slides, monkey bars, a sandbox, and dozens of brightly colored toys that had been scattered and discarded by the departing children at the end of the day.

Mrs. Olivera and Lydia threaded their way through the small desks and chairs toward the teacher's private office while Jenny made a dash for the doors and presumably the monkey bars, her favorite pastime besides drawing.

Lydia's eyes skimmed over the Disney characters that danced across the pale yellow walls of the playroom, and she glanced quickly at the blackboard where letters of the alphabet were printed boldly in pink chalk. Dozens of childish pictures were taped at random along the lower part of the far wall, and she wondered if any of them belonged to Jenny.

Margarita Olivera held the office door open for Lydia to pass in front of her, and Lydia was glad to see that the window in the room looked out over the backyard—she could keep an eye on Jenny while the teacher said whatever it was she had to say. Her hands felt clammy and she wiped them on her jeans before taking a seat opposite the teacher.

"This may be nothing, Mrs. Matthews, but . . ." Mrs. Olivera smiled reassuringly, and Lydia tore her eyes away from Jenny, who was now happily hanging by her knees from the top of the monkey bars. She tried to smile back at the woman, but it felt stiff, so she gave it up.

Margarita Olivera was a sturdy-looking woman who Lydia guessed was in her late fifties. A few gray hairs stood out in stark contrast against the coal black of the rest of her hair, and she wore it cut short in a style that flattered her face. That face, usually kind and gently amused with life, was frowning slightly now, and Lydia took a deep breath and waited for the bad news.

The teacher shuffled some papers on the desk in front of her, not meeting Lydia's eyes. "As I say, this may be nothing," she repeated, then seemed to find what she was looking for, and looked up at Lydia. "But when Jenny first came to us, she was relatively quiet and obedient. Compared to a lot of the others, that is. You know how rambunctious children this age can be." She gave Lydia a conspiratorial look. Lydia nodded.

"Lately however, she's been showing some unusual signs of aggression that just don't seem to me to be a part of her normal behavior pattern."

"How do you mean?"

18

Margarita sighed, always reluctant to tell tales on her charges. She genuinely cared for all the little ones; that was what put her day care center in such demand in Las Flores. Good child care was as hard to come by in this county as it was anywhere else, and the retired teacher had a reputation as a treasure. "Jenny has initiated several arguments with her classmates in the past two weeks. Fistfights, actually. She——"

"What!" Lydia half rose from her chair, then sat down again. This was the last thing she'd expected. Her Jenny was sweet to the point of being placid. How many times had she run inside crying over a childish slight, never willing or able to stand up for her rights against her playmates? Why, she'd never raised a hand in self-defense, let alone in aggression!

"Please, Mrs. Matthews." Margarita held up her palms with a placating gesture. "Don't be alarmed—this is a common phase in childhood. It's just that her change was so sudden, I thought that I should bring it up in case there was a connection to some problem at home—something I should be aware of and perhaps we could work out together. I don't mean to pry into your private life, but Jenny is such a sweet girl, and——"

"Yes, yes." Lydia glanced out the window at her daughter and then quickly back at Margarita. "You've caught me off guard. I didn't expect—that is, you know her father was killed in an automobile accident three years ago, but . . . that is . . . could she be reacting this way now . . . I mean . . . there may be a connection, but . . ." She let her voice trail off, not sure how to express her worries to this woman.

"I know of course that you're a single parent," Margarita said softly. "It's in Jenny's records. And I doubt that her sudden behavior change has anything to do with your husband's death three years ago, but then I'm not really qualified to say that since I'm not a psychiatrist. I thought perhaps there might be some other . . . newer problem . . . ?" She folded her hands on the folder in front of her and looked sympathetically at Lydia.

"No," Lydia said. "No. There aren't any problems." Now that the initial surprise was over, she began to regain her usual composure. "Please. Tell me exactly what's been going on. What did Jenny do?"

Margarita appraised the woman in front of her. She'd thought, given Mrs. Matthews' delicate good looks and trim figure, there might be a new man in her life, one who might have triggered feelings of resentment and jealousy in the child. But if that were the case, surely the mother would be aware of it—and she wasn't sure how much she could pry without seeming indelicate.

"Last week, one of the boys was playing with a toy . . . I don't remember what it was, but it isn't important," she began, "and Jenny suddenly left the monkey bars, ran over to the boy, and snatched it from him. Naturally, he tried to grab it back."

"So?" Lydia said. Even though the act was unusual for Jenny, it didn't sound as if it was any big deal.

Margarita sighed. This was hard for her. "So she attacked him . . . like . . . an animal. She scratched and bit at the boy—not enough to require any serious medical aid, but there was a little blood—"

"I don't believe this."

"And the most frightening part was the . . . growling."

"Growling?" Lydia felt anger rising in her, anger directed at this woman telling lies about . . . no, she caught herself. Mrs. Olivera wouldn't . . .

"Jenny sounded like a wild thing, Mrs. Matthews.

20

And it took three of us to get her off the boy, a boy considerably taller and heavier than she is, by the way."

Lydia stared at the woman. "What else?" she asked, her voice weak. "You said more than once, didn't you?"

Mrs. Olivera nodded. "I let that one go as an isolated incident. And since the boy's mother didn't make a fuss either . . . her boy is something of a bully and I think she's used to these things, so . . ." She took a deep breath and looked Lydia straight in the eyes. "But today . . . well, Jenny did the same thing after yanking Peter Barnes off his swing for no apparent reason . . . and Mrs. Barnes wasn't quite so understanding. I promised I'd speak to you . . . which I would have anyway, but . . ." She shrugged helplessly and dropped her eyes from Lydia's to rummage in the folder.

"And these . . . I want to show you these." The teacher silently held out a sheaf of papers to Lydia.

"JENNY" was scrawled across the bottom of each page in capital letters, and if it hadn't been for that, Lydia would never have guessed who'd drawn the pictures. She sucked in her breath with shock. Stick men galloped across the pages. Some of the heads were oversized and ugly, as if they wore vicious masks of hatred and evil. Most of the figures held a wand . . . or a spear of some sort; some lay flat, with outstretched arms and legs held stiffly out from their sides; others surrounded figures on their knees; one showed a masked stick figure piercing another with his spear.

Lydia felt sick. What was this? Jenny had never, never drawn anything like this before. She looked up at Mrs. Olivera, too stunned to form a question. Her eyes searched the woman's face for an explanation; surely she had one. She was a professional with these children, wasn't she?

21

The teacher remained silent, waiting.

Lydia turned her head toward the window and stared out at her daughter. Jenny hung from the top of the monkey bars with one hand, swaying slightly. She stared back at her mother with blank eyes.

Chapter Four

Bett Wilson cracked the eggshell expertly on the side of the bowl and let the slick, raw insides plop on top of the pound of ground round that sat waiting to be transformed into her secret meatloaf recipe. The yolk slid over the mounded meat and bumped the side of the bowl, breaking the fragile membrane and spreading a yellow ribbon of viscous liquid between the red meat and the edge of the bowl. Saliva filled her mouth and she swallowed several times, then broke another egg and popped it quickly in her mouth. It slid easily down her throat and she forced back the urge to do it again.

I'm going to die of cholesterol poisoning before I'm twenty-seven, she thought. The strange cravings had started when she was twenty-one and planning her marriage to Raymond. She'd chalked it up to nerves brought on by the frenzied prenuptial activities, an increased need for protein or something, she'd reasoned. But it hadn't stopped, even after five years of a relatively stress free life, and she'd learned to live with it . . . only lately though, the cravings seemed to be getting stronger.

She dug three fingers into the raw meat and brought

the glob up to her nose, inhaling the bloody smell of it before stuffing it into her mouth. An almost sensual feeling of satisfaction flooded through her as she chewed slowly, savoring the taste.

Lots of people do this, she rationalized. She took another Ping-Pong-ball-sized chunk of meat and jammed it into her mouth before she'd even swallowed the first. And another.

Stop! Stop it! She dumped spices and a can of tomato paste quickly into the bowl and thrust her hands into the mess, roughly kneading and squeezing the mixture through her fingers. She could smell the spices now, and the sharp, earthy scent of tomato; the craving faded.

For a while, right after the marriage, she'd thought she was pregnant, but after many months and no missed periods, she'd given up on that explanation. And there hadn't been any children. No children at all, not even a miscarriage. Even after five years of trying.

Stop thinking about that, she scolded herself, mentally pushing aside the familiar ache to hold a child, feed it, smell it. It was harder now, it got harder every day. Probably because my biological clock is running out of time, she thought. Maybe she should talk to Ray about adopting again.

She molded the meatloaf into a Pyrex dish, then splashed a dash of cognac, her secret ingredient, over the top of it before shoving it into the hot oven.

She shut the oven door and sighed. Sometimes she felt her entire life was spent pushing aside deep, unresolved needs that burned in her, most of which she didn't understand. Except for the need for a child, of course. That was normal. . . .

* * *

T.G.I.F. Ray Wilson thought as he swung the dark blue Buick into his driveway. His eyes swept over his property as he waited for the automatic garage door-opener to do its work, and he made a mental note to trim the pyracantha that was threatening to swallow the spare bedroom window—and fertilize the roses, and naturally—mow the lawn. Always have to mow the lawn on Saturday. Fact of life in summertime.

He grinned, looking forward to the chores. He loved yard work. After five days of high-power pressure as a customer service manager for Nakemco, a progressive chemical company based in southwest Florida, he was ready for the mental relaxation and physical exertion of playing with his own private piece of the earth. He eased the car to a halt inside the garage and hopped out, his almost endless supply of energy still bubbling strong in spite of a full work week that would have left a lot of men exhausted and grumpy. But weekends with his beautiful Bett—and his anticipated yard work—overrode any feelings of flagging energy he might otherwise have felt.

The smell of something good in the oven hit him as he walked in the kitchen door, and he inhaled appreciatively. He patted his belly reflexively and followed his nose toward the smell. At five-foot-seven, he was beginning to put on a little extra weight around the middle—easy to do at his height—and his wife's cooking was responsible for it. Another reason to redouble his activity in the yard, he told himself. He was only thirty-two—too young to let himself go to pot. He chuckled at his own self-derogatory pun and peeked in the oven. Meatloaf—one of his favorites.

"Can't wait, huh?"

Ray closed the oven door and turned around with a

wide grin. Bett, as usual, had "freshened up" just before he came home, and he could smell the sweet scent of her favorite Jungle Gardenia perfume as he hugged her.

"Can't wait for some of you," he said with a mock growl, and leaned down to nuzzle at her neck. Bett made him feel tall, made him feel loved. He hummed "The Second Time Around" and waltzed her around the kitchen.

His first marriage had also been a happy one—Ray was a nice guy, easy to get along with. His Dora had been a journalist, and a good one. The sniper's bullet that had ripped her out of his life while she was covering the senseless event had nearly destroyed him too.

In the nine months after her death, he'd skipped meals, started drinking too much, let his appearance go to hell, and nearly lost his job. And didn't care.

Then Bett Brownerly, a young computer programmer at Nakemco, saved his life. She'd bullied, prodded, yelled, and finally loved him back to life. His marriage proposal had had one stipulation; he wouldn't allow her to work. No matter that computers posed no dangers equivalent to cameras, tape recorders, and potential killer bullets—he wanted her at home—safe. She agreed.

They had a happy marriage.

Chapter Five

She paused a few feet from the great nest of grass and weed stalks that she'd carefully concealed on a high rise of land, and cocked one eye toward her single nestling. She'd built the nest as she usually did, but now it lay partially collapsed and sagging under the weight of her one baby. A nest usually lasted through several breeding seasons, but her practiced eye told her that once again this year's nest would be useless for hatching her next clutch of eggs.

The Florida sandhill crane had laid two olive gray, brown spotted eggs when the nest was new, but only one had hatched. The newly emerged first chick had seized upon the other egg and devoured it almost before the sun had dried his leathery, gray body. And it hadn't run from the nest shortly after hatching as she always expected her chicks to do; it refused to fend for itself. Now nearly twice the size of its mother, it looked down at her and shrieked for the Pig Frog that dangled lifelessly from her beak. She flapped into the air and dropped it down into the nestling's demanding, snapping maw. It wasn't necessary to shove the frog deep into this one's throat. Or sensible. Not since dozens of tiny, sharp teeth had sprouted like seeds along the edges of its massive hooked beak.

The crane settled into the marsh next to her nest and cast a quick look around for possible predators. There were none, and she relaxed a little.

Now the nestling shrieked again and spread short, featherless wings out into the hot, humid air of the Everglades. The crane understood; "Feed me more" was the demand. Obediently, she soared away over the swamp, searching for more food to satisfy the insatiable appetite of her young one. It was the third year in a row that she'd hatched and struggled to fulfill the constant hunger of such a strange and vicious offspring. But she didn't remember that.

Chapter Six

Ranger Juan Degas cut the motor on his boat and let it drift as he searched the banks for his prey. On the seat in front of him was his own Remington model 870, 12-gauge shotgun, loaded and ready to kill. If his boss, Ben Torry, knew that he was out here to deliberately slaughter any gator he came across, he'd have shit fits. But if the Chief Ranger was going to be such a soft-assed wimp about all this, Juan would do the job that had to be done himself!

Ben's idea of action had been to deny all Backcountry Use permits until further notice. It would cost the Park in revenue, and he'd had some opposition, but that's the way it had gone down. In Juan's opinion, it wasn't enough, and he'd said so. But Torry had insisted that to go out and randomly kill every gator they could find was irresponsible, since the animals were essential to the ecosystem of the Glades. A couple of isolated, freak accidents, he'd argued, incidents that were unlikely to repeat themselves if they took some reasonable, temporary precautions. Bullcrap, Juan had said to himself. And now here he was.

He hadn't seen one gator yet, not in the entire three

and a half hours he'd been out here. Not that unusual. Lots of times the tourists complained because they spent big bucks on the guided cruises and hadn't had even a glimpse of the usually shy animals.

He started the motor again and headed deeper into the Glades. Maybe a few more miles in . . .

An hour later, Juan was about ready to give up. He'd have to make fast time to get back in when he was expected. As usual, when any Ranger went out, he left a log of his planned route, and an estimated time of return. If you were late, they came looking for you. He'd followed the rules. He just hadn't mentioned the extra-curricular activity he'd had in mind. He turned the boat in a lazy arc, deciding to quit. He could always come back tomorrow.

As he chugged past a large island to his right, a flock of snowy egrets from its interior rose into the air in a flapping, screeching mass. What the hell . . . ? he thought. What had spooked them? Curious, he pulled in and stepped out into the muck at the island's edge. He anchored the boat and reached for his rifle. No sense taking any chances.

It was tough-going at first. The vegetation was thick and he almost went back twice. But he flailed his way farther in, cursing the tangle of tropical shrubs and vines. Finally it thinned, and he walked more cautiously, remembering to look down for snakes. It took a few more minutes for Juan to realize that he was on a trail.

The trail was wide, and in moments he was standing in a thirty-foot wide, almost-round clearing that had multiple trails branching off in every direction. The ground was packed solid in the clearing, and where the trails led off into the jungle, trees with at least four-inch-diameter trunks had been snapped in half and pushed aside like children's discarded pick-up-sticks.

"What the fuck . . . ?" Juan said. He'd never seen anything like it. Campers, he wondered? Not likely. There were no signs of people; no dead campfires, no cigarette butts, no empty beer cans. . . .

He heard it off to his left a second before he felt it through his feet, a rumbling and vibration that sounded like somebody was driving a big truck or bulldozer around on the island. He turned toward the sound with his rifle lifted at ready and waited.

They came out of one of the trails—two of them. Juan blinked. They looked something like armadillos, but they were the size of rottweilers. And the heads were wrong. Bearish.

They stopped about twenty feet from him and stared at him. Juan stared back, wondering vaguely why the rumbling hadn't stopped. One of them turned away, and Juan gasped. The long thick tail that he hadn't been able to see before, dragged along the ground. At its tip was a fist-sized knob covered with three-inch spikes.

It exploded from another trail as Juan carelessly let his guard down for a few seconds to watch the extraordinary creature and its twin lift those lethal-looking tails and disappear back into the brush.

But he heard it. Without thinking, he spun and fired.

What was coming straight at him was the same creature—but this one was the size of an elephant. It came at him silently, its eyes glinting with the murderous intent of any animal protecting her young.

Juan fired again. It stopped in its tracks, and Juan felt relief beyond imagining—until he realized why it had stopped. With amazing speed and grace for its enormous

31

size, the creature pivoted and lifted its tail. There was no way Juan could duck the spike-covered basketball that flashed down toward his head.

The huge creature snuffled at the thing she'd just killed. She contemplated it dimly for a few moments, then just to make sure, she raked her long claws deep into its belly, spilling and spreading its insides over the ground. Finally satisfied, she turned and hurried off after her children.

Chapter Seven

The search party found what was left of Juan after spotting his boat moored at the large island. The media were having a wonderful time of it.

DEATH IN THE EVERGLADES! KILLERS IN THE GLADES! THIRD MYSTERIOUS DEATH IN GLADES! MONSTERS IN THE SWAMP!

Evan went down to see the coroner again.

"They went over my head, Evan. Sent the remains to Tallahassee for the 'experts' to look at. They didn't believe me." He sounded disgusted.

"This man was mangled," Evan said. "On dry land. Not like last time."

"There's nothing in the Glades that could do the damage I saw. Nothing big enough."

"Bear? Panther?"

The coroner shook his head. "His head was disintegrated. Nothing but a few bone fragments left, and they had a hell of a time finding them. Panther and bear are rare out there, and even so, they run from man. Any-

33

way, the claw marks in that fellow's belly would make bear claw marks look like kitten scratches."

"So what did it?"

"Damned if I know. And that's just what I put in my report. Caused quite a stink around here." He grinned.

"What the hell is going on?" Evan asked more to himself than to the coroner.

The coroner shrugged.

Evan wished he had gotten a hold of Jake Van Gower. He made himself a promise to try again that night.

Chapter Eight

It wasn't coming out right. Jenny shoved the offending piece of paper out of her way. It slithered across the shiny surface of the dining room table and hovered in the air for a split second before floating in an erratic path to the floor. She ignored it.

Maybe a different color, she thought. Black. She pulled a fresh paper from the stack on her left and rummaged through the box of Crayolas with her other hand, anxious to start over again. She had a picture in her head of what she wanted, but every time she tried to do it on paper it escaped her.

Black. She grabbed the crayon and leaned over her drawing paper with determined concentration. The form she wanted was clear in her head, and she pressed hard with the crayon, drawing a heavy arched line over the top half of the paper. Her tongue protruded slightly from between her teeth as she humped up the right side of the line, then drew it down again at a forty-five-degree angle. This was the hard part, when the image she held started to fade, and she tried to clamp her mind around it. Pointy knob, she thought. Pointy knob. The crayon kept moving. There! She was past the spot that had always baffled her, and she sat back and stared at what she had so far. It wasn't quite right, but . . .

"Jenny? How're you doing, honey?"

Her concentration broken, Jenny glared up at her mother. "Mo-m! Now you made me forget!"

"Sorry, I—"

Jenny snapped the crayon in half and threw it on the floor. Tears burned in her eyes and a sob of frustrated anger cut off the rest of her mother's apology. Then she was out of her chair and running toward her room, the precious picture in her head destroyed.

"Jenny . . . ?" Lydia stood in the dining room and listened to the unmistakeable sound of a door slammed in anger. Baffled by her daughter's behavior, she began cleaning up the mess Jenny had left. Should she go after her right now or let her cool off awhile? These temper tantrums were something new lately, and she wasn't quite sure how to handle it. Jenny had always been so placid. . . .

She looked at the drawings, searching for clues, half afraid of what she'd see. But they were nothing like the ones Mrs. Olivera had shown her yesterday—thank God. Then again, they were nothing like anything Jenny had ever done before, either.

Lydia picked up the drawing that had dropped to the floor and put it alongside Jenny's other pictures. There were four of them, and she'd seemed to be struggling for the same effect in all of them—hard, curved, disconnected lines that showed none of the airy, delicate lightness that usually showed in Jenny's work. And compared to the almost prodigal mastery of form and perspective that the child had shown in the past, Lydia thought, these attempts were almost . . . primitive.

She gathered the drawings together and dumped the

crayons back into the battered shoe box that served as Jenny's art supply box. Then she carried them down the hall and bent to leave them outside her daughter's bedroom door. Nothing but silence radiated from Jenny's room, and she thought, hoped, that Jenny had decided to take a nap—to sleep off her disappointment at having her artistic mood destroyed.

She took one last look at the drawing on the top of the pile that lay on the floor before she went into the kitchen to start dinner. With a small pang of sorrow, she suddenly realized that it looked more like a typical five-going-on-six-year-old's drawing than anything Jenny had ever done. Maybe all the early signs of talent had been a fluke; there was no such thing as inherited talent. Could Jenny have lost it? Just like that? If so, she could certainly sympathize with her frustration and anger. But it didn't explain the strange, evil-looking pictures she'd drawn at the day-care center.

Sighing, Lydia pushed the questions out of her mind and concentrated on rummaging through the refrigerator for salad makings.

Jenny wasn't asleep. She heard her mother pause outside her door, but she was still too mad to get off her bed and go talk to her—or apologize. She knew she'd *have* to apologize for her rotten behavior sooner or later, but she just didn't feel like it yet.

She squeezed her eyes shut and tried to get her picture back, but she couldn't do it. Why was it so important anyway, she wondered? Usually if something was too hard for her, she forgot about it and drew something else. It was a stupid picture, she decided. A lot of the pictures she drew now were stupid. She couldn't seem to help what her hand did anymore.

A tiny sound outside her window distracted her from her fading anger, and she jumped off the bed to look. A huge live oak grew no more than ten feet from her window, and some of its branches spread toward the house and swayed over the roof. Others swept almost to the ground, forming a leafy canopy that Jenny sometimes liked to hide under and play make-believe. Plenty of times her mother had had to hire Mr. Sanderson, who did what she called "odd jobs," to go up and cut away the branches that might crash through the house during the next storm. But she wouldn't let him cut down the tree. That was because birds and squirrels lived there, and she, Jenny, had cried a lot every time her mother said that they should maybe cut it down.

Now she pressed her nose and palms against the glass and peered out at the tree. She smiled and tapped her fingers against the window. The nest was still there, and the babies were okay.

A pair of mockingbirds had built the nest only a few feet from her window, and she'd watched them while they patiently brought a seemingly endless supply of sticks and twigs and bits of grass and fluff to the tree. Eventually they transformed the bits of stuff into a comfortable resting place for the three greenish blue, red-brown splotched eggs that the mother laid. Then the mother bird just sat there—forever, Jenny thought— until one day when she looked out the window, the mother bird was gone and it looked like the nest was empty! Alarmed, she had tried to pull the window open for a closer look, but it was too hard and she ran downstairs for her mother.

Lydia had photographed the industrious birds and the

eggs in the nest, planning a series on the mockingbirds' development for *Natural World* magazine. As a freelance writer and photographer, her work in the nature field was well known and respected. Disappointment had shown on her face as well as Jenny's when she followed her daughter to the bedroom window.

As Lydia had put her hands on the window sash to open it for a closer look, an adult "mocker" suddenly soared into the nest, an unidentifiable insect clamped firmly in its beak. Instantly, three tiny, bright yellow beaks lifted from the concealing fluff in the nest and yawned wide.

Jenny had laughed and clapped her hands at the sight of the begging beaks wobbling around on the weak, skinny necks, and Lydia, grinning, had hushed her and drawn her away from the window. "Don't frighten them," she'd said. "You must always watch quietly. Respect nature, Jenny." And Jenny did.

Now, it was the insistent cheeping of the little nestlings that had distracted Jenny from her anger, and she smiled at "her" birds through the window.

But something was wrong. The two adult birds swooped and shrieked at something at the base of the tree, and Jenny flattened her face against the window and peered down at the ground.

A cat! Mrs. Haverstrom's cat! She watched in horror as the cat, ignoring the hysterical birds, slowly clawed its way up the tree toward the nestlings.

Jenny yanked at the window, but like the last time, she wasn't strong enough to open it. Frantic, she banged on the glass and yelled. The cat kept coming.

Fear for the safety of the little birds flooded through her and she froze, heart pounding, with her upper body pressed against the window. And the cat inched its way toward the nest.

Jenny felt dizzy; a warm, black fog seemed to swirl around her, dimming her peripheral vision, and she clutched at the windowsill for support. A roaring in her ears cut off the sound of the birds, and the window wavered out of focus . . . and disappeared. She stumbled for balance and put her hands over her ears against the noise. Frightened for herself now, she turned, still holding her ears, and tried to run for her mother. She never took a step. Walls, floor, ceiling, furniture . . . snapped out of existence with a deafening bang, and she spun back toward the nonexistent window, screaming.

Jenny stood in a deep green jungle. Silent now. In front of her, a huge cat crept toward the tiny child who sat playing quietly in a shaft of sunlight. A fierce protectiveness toward the child exploded in her chest at the sight of the menacing animal, and she growled a warning.

The great beast hesitated, then turned and snarled back at her, the two long fangs that curved down from its jaws glinting in the smoky light.

She held a pointed stick. Shrieking in defiance, she raced toward the cat, the stick held in both hands high over her head. The cat leaped at her. She felt the point of her weapon sink into its soft underbelly.

And she was Jenny again . . . staring through the window at Mrs. Haverstrom's calico cat. The cat stared back at her, frozen in midclimb, its eyes wide with surprise and fear. Jenny growled again. The cat leaped from the tree, twisting its body in the air and landing feet-first on the ground in an amazing performance of feline agility. Then it streaked out of sight. It never looked back.

Jenny stood at the window for a few minutes, her dilated eyes gradually coming back into sharp focus. The dizziness faded. She watched the mother or father bird, she couldn't tell which, land on the nest and poke around at its babies. The babies opened their mouths wide, begging for food.

Suddenly she remembered the cat! Where was it? She pressed against the window again, searching the ground for any sign of it. It was gone. Funny . . . she didn't remember seeing it leave. Maybe the mother and father birds had chased it away and she'd just missed it. Yes, she thought, that must be it.

Jenny waggled her fingers in a friendly good-bye to her birds and skipped toward her bedroom door. It was almost dinnertime she was sure, and she was hungry.

Chapter Nine

Can't breathe. Suffocating. Run! Run!

Bett jerked awake and sat up in bed. Sweat drenched her nightgown, and her heart beat wildly. The content of the nightmare slipped away from her immediately, leaving only the terror behind.

She sat trembling, forcing the fear back into the dark place where it had come from. Only a dream only a dream only a dream, she told herself over and over again. But she wished she could remember it. If she could, it might give her a clue as to what was causing them—them, because this wasn't the first time. But she couldn't grasp even the slightest shred of the bad dreams once she opened her eyes. And they were becoming more frequent. At least twice a week now, and it was taking longer and longer to get over the terrors once she was fully awake.

Gradually she stopped shaking and looked over to the side of the bed where Ray lay sleeping peacefully. She wouldn't tell him this time. He was beginning to worry about her and she didn't want that. He'd had enough misery in his life, and she'd be damned if she'd be responsible for causing him any more.

She wiped a damp strand of long blond hair off her forehead, then lifted the rest of it off her neck to let the cool night air get under the tangled mess. Must have tossed around a lot to make all these knots, she thought, marveling at how Ray could have slept through all her thrashings. She tried to comb her fingers through the knots. It hurt, and she stopped. Maybe she should cut it short for the summer.

Her nightgown stuck to her body in clammy folds, and she dropped her hair and eased out of bed, careful not to wake her husband. She still felt as if she couldn't breathe properly. She peeled the gown over her head and put on jeans and the pink blouse she'd worn that day and had tossed on a chair before going to bed. She still felt too hot and clammy to struggle with underwear. Besides, who would see her this time of night . . . or know that she wasn't wearing anything underneath, anyway?

Quietly, she left the bedroom and walked out through the kitchen slider into the backyard.

A soft breeze whispered through the screened-in lanai and made tiny ripples sparkle on the surface of the pool. Bett took several deep breaths of the jasmine-scented air and walked to the edge of the water. She felt better now that she was outside—much better.

She looked up through the screen at the sky. The night was clear and filled with stars, and the moon was almost full. She wished she knew more about astronomy. It would be fun to say, "Oh yes . . . there's Orion," or, "There's Capricorn" to an admiring audience. Or even to just one child. Her child. And he'd be so impressed with how smart his mother was. She smiled to herself and made a half-hearted promise to take a book out of the library and study up on it . . . just in case. . . .

A dull ache started in her left temple, and she lifted her hand to massage it. Damn! she thought. This was part of the pattern. First the nightmare and then the headaches. She hoped this wouldn't be a bad one. She could never tell at first, and the severity of the headaches didn't necessarily mirror the severity of the terrors of the nightmares. If they did, this would be a bad one.

Aspirin, she thought. Take it right now before it gets any worse. She turned back toward the house and shrieked at the sight of a dark shadow moving toward her from the kitchen door.

"Jesus, Bett! It's only me!" Ray hurried forward and put his arms around his wife, reassuring her.

"You scared the hell out of me!" Half angry at Ray for scaring her, and half embarrassed by her overreaction, she returned the hug and buried her face in her husband's shoulder.

"Another nightmare?" he asked softly while he lightly stroked her hair.

She hesitated, debating, then sighed and said yes. She wasn't going to lie to him.

"Headache?" he asked.

"Not bad yet."

"Good." He held her away from him, then bent down and kissed the tip of her nose. "Come back inside. I'll get you an aspirin."

"And some tea?"

"And some tea."

They sat at the kitchen table, two cups of steaming tea in front of them. Bett wrapped her hands around the cup, her earlier night sweats having given way to intermittent chills. Also part of the pattern. If I weren't so

44

young, she thought bitterly, I'd think I was going through menopause. The headache had spread to the right side now, and she prayed for the aspirins to kick in and do their work before it got any worse.

"Are you okay?" Ray looked at his wife with a frown of concern.

"Mmmmm," Bett said.

"That's pretty noncommittal."

"Sorry. I'm okay, I guess."

Ray reached across the table and put a gentle hand on her wrist. "I'm getting worried about all this, Bett. Please see Dr. Colby. Just make sure—"

"Okay! Okay!" Bett jerked her hand away from him, spilling a little of her tea on the table. She felt sudden tears filling her eyes and angrily wiped them away. The headaches always made her bad-tempered, and she hated herself for it but she couldn't help it; she couldn't . . .

Ray quietly got up for a sponge, and when he started to wipe up her mess, she reached up for him, wrapped her arms around his neck, and let the tears go.

He stood there holding her until they stopped.

"My guess is that the headaches are a result of the tension that you experience during your night terrors, Mrs. Wilson." Dr. Colby folded his hands on his desk and watched Bett, his expression sincere and intense.

You guess? she thought as she stared back. Well, at least she had a new, scientific name for her nightmares. Night terrors. Great.

". . . not really my field," he was saying now. "I can give you some medication for the headaches, but to get to the cause of your problem, well . . ." He rummaged

45

through a Rolodex. "I can give you the name of someone . . . he's a psychiatrist over at—"

"A psychiatrist?" Was this man saying he thought she was crazy?

Dr. Colby looked up quickly at the sound of shock in her voice. "He specializes in the mind; yes, Mrs. Wilson. And he's very good with sleep problems, which is the important point here. Most sleep problems he deals with are children's, but you'd be surprised how many adults have a dysfunction in that area too."

Bett's worried expression didn't change, and he hurried on. "He'll test you first for any physical problems. . . . EEG, PET scan and a few other simple tests, then probably—"

"Do you think I'm losing my mind?" May as well hear it straight out.

"No," Colby answered. "But I think you have a problem. Most people who experience night terrors wake up screaming, and they can also become physically violent when in that state. Or they can start sleepwalking. Your night terrors haven't progressed to that point yet, and I don't want them to . . . not any more than I'm sure you'd want them to. But I'd prefer that you see a specialist. As I said, it isn't my field. So . . ." He sat back and looked at her, waiting for her decision.

Bett wished Ray had come in with her to talk to the doctor. She didn't know what she wanted to do. Ray was out in the waiting room. If she could just talk to him first. . . .

"Look, Mrs. Wilson." Colby glanced surreptitiously at his watch. "Why don't I just give you a prescription for the headaches, and the name and phone number of the man I'd like you to see. Then you can discuss it with your husband and make up your mind about it at your leisure. I'm not asking you to decide right this minute."

"Fine," Bett said, but her voice cracked and she cleared her throat. "Fine," she repeated, in case he hadn't understood her.

He gave her a quick, tight smile, then bent his head to write on a white pad.

Bett glanced at the slips of paper as she hurried out into the waiting room toward Ray. One was an unintelligible prescription. The other said, "Dr. Evan Tremayne" and had a phone number scrawled under the name.

"Because I just don't want to, Ray!" Bett slammed a head of lettuce on the cutting board with a little more force than was necessary, then pulled the loosened core out with a quick twist of her wrist.

Ray kept his back turned to her while he flipped the sputtering pieces of bacon over in the frying pan. "Bett . . ."

"No. Listen, hon," Bett interrupted him before he could talk her out of it. Her voice was coming out in a little girl whine, and she made a conscious effort to sound more mature, as if it would lend weight to her decision. "I just want to try the medication for a while . . . then if it doesn't work, I'll . . . I'll . . ."

"See Dr. Tremayne?" he finished for her.

She jabbed a knife into a bright red tomato. The skin squashed in a little, then parted neatly under the blade. "Yes," she said shortly.

Ray pushed the lever down on the toaster and turned to put his arms around his wife, but the tense set of her back and shoulders made him hesitate. Why was she fighting this? She seemed to feel that there was something shameful about seeing a psychiatrist, and he was surprised at what he considered to be an old-fashioned attitude.

But maybe the medication was all she needed. Maybe he was worrying over nothing. Maybe he worried about her too much.

The toast popped up. Ray ignored it and put a tentative hand on his wife's back. "How about a swim after lunch?" he asked in an effort to change the subject, ease the tension.

Bett's shoulders relaxed. She gave him a smile that made him feel better immediately. "Sure," she said.

Chapter Ten

Evan leaned back in his chair and stretched his arms over his head. It had been a long day. He was ready to go home and relax, maybe catch up on some paperwork. . . .

The intercom on his desk beeped, and he punched a button and said, "Yes."

"Dr. Van Gower here to see you." The nasal voice of his receptionist sounded annoyed; it was time to go home.

"No kidding! Jake?" Evan was surprised. He'd left countless messages on Jake's answering machine in the past few days, and hadn't expected more than a call back whenever Jake finally made it back home.

"No, sir," the receptionist answered tightly. "I'm not kidding."

Evan sighed. The woman was efficient and loyal, but took everything everybody said literally. She drove him crazy. "Send Dr. Van Gower in and go home, Linda," he said. "I won't need you anymore tonight."

"If you're sure, Dr. Tremayne . . ." She let her voice trail off hopefully, and when Evan said he was really sure, she clicked off and buzzed open his door for Dr. Andrew "Jake" Van Gower.

The man who leaped through the door grinning wildly, his arms flung wide in greeting, was enough to raise doubts in most people's minds about his sanity—especially in receptionists who worked for psychiatrists.

"EVAN! OLD BUDDY!"

Evan was caught in an exuberant bear hug, then released and pounded repeatedly on the back.

Van Gower was six-foot-four and had the physique of a slightly overweight linebacker, but moved with a grace and energy that reflected regular daily exercise. Sun-bleached-blond hair hung slightly below his ears and contrasted vividly with the deep tan that shaded almost to chocolate in the creases and wrinkles that years in the sun had permanently etched on his face. At exactly Evan's age, he looked five years older.

Evan pumped the big man's hand enthusiastically and grinned up at him. "You old son-of-a-bitch! I didn't expect to hear from you for months! Your answering machine said you were digging old dinosaur bones someplace in Montana!"

"Was! Where do I get a drink around here?" He threw himself into one of Evan's black leather armchairs and looked appreciatively around the office. "Nice digs," he said, then laughed at his own pun.

Evan pulled a bottle and two glasses from a small cabinet in a corner of the room. He rarely drank after work himself, but kept a bottle of Scotch on hand for guests. And Jake was the best guest he'd had in months, he thought as he looked at his good friend with genuine pleasure.

Jake was a paleontologist and had befriended the quiet, studious Evan Tremayne when they'd shared a dorm room at the University of Pennsylvania. The friendship had held together through the years in spite of their diverse fields of interest and the long periods of silence that frequently hung between them due to the paleontologist's need to work in places where there was frequently little means of communication.

"How long has it been?" Evan asked, handing Jake a Scotch-on-the-rocks. "Two years?"

"Two and a half." Jake downed half the drink in one swallow and sighed contentedly. "How are Laura and the kids, or shouldn't I ask?"

Evan busied himself with pouring his own drink. "The kids should be here for the summer in a couple of weeks. I'll tell you how it is then." He ignored the reference to his ex-wife, and Jake didn't press him.

"On vacation?" Evan asked, smiling. "Or did my messages intrigue you enough to have you hot-foot it down here?" He sat on the couch across from his friend and sipped his drink after briefly raising it in the big man's direction.

Jake returned the gesture with his half-empty glass. "Business. And your messages." He jumped to his feet and went to the cabinet to top off his drink. When he turned back toward Evan his face was serious. "We've tried to keep it away from the press . . . don't need reporters tramping in there mucking up the evidence . . . if there really is any."

"What evidence?" Evan asked, instantly interested.

"One of our people took his wife and kids on one of those boat rides through the Everglades a couple of weeks ago. You know . . . typical tourist stuff. Then they stopped off at a Seminole Indian reservation for local color . . . where they wrestle alligators and sell jewelry and blankets?"

51

Evan nodded, wondering what his friend could possibly be getting at.

"This Seminole kid comes up to him. About nine or ten, he thinks. Tries to sell him some paintings his father had done." Jake sat back down in his chair and leaned toward Evan, his face showing signs of growing excitement. "Most of it was the usual stuff . . . indigenous animals, subtropical landscapes, Indian faces with lots of 'character' . . . you get the picture?" He grinned.

"Yes, but—"

"One was different." Jake paused for effect, and Evan kept silent, waiting.

Satisfied that he had the psychiatrist's full attention, Jake inched forward in his chair and stared into his eyes. "You know what an Archaeopteryx is."

"Yes," Evan said. "Supposedly the first species of bird. So the man had an interest in paleontology and he expressed it in a drawing. So what?"

Jake waved an impatient hand in Evan's face. "Second species. Proto Avis was first, but that's not important. My friend questioned him. The guy didn't know paleontology from astrophysics. He draws from life."

"Oh, come on, Jake!" Evan laughed, searching the man's face for signs of a joke. It wouldn't be the first time Jake had sucked him in. But Jake wasn't laughing with him. And what he was saying was beginning to ring some bells. "If I recall from your endless babblings on the subject, Archaeopteryx lived during the Jurassic Period about a hundred and fifty million years ago."

"Close enough. Didn't know you were listening."

"I listened. But I can't believe *you're* listening to something as bizarre as—"

"Why not!" Jake shouted. He jumped to his feet

again and began to pace. "The man I was listening to is a respected—"

"Did he see it too? In life?"

"No, dammit!" Jake was getting agitated. "But if he's right . . . if there's just the slightest *chance* that he's right . . . this will be the biggest thing that's happened since man discovered fire! My *God*, Evan! A living fossil! *Think* of it!" He threw his arms wide and grinned at the psychiatrist, his usual, happy, exuberant nature breaking through his frustration over his friend's skepticism.

"I have to admit it's mind-boggling," Evan said. "But how could something like this happen? And why now?"

"Don't know. That's why I'm here. I'm meeting a colleague in the Everglades tomorrow, and we plan to find out."

"I have something to show you," Evan said. "And I admit I was playing a bit of a devil's advocate there for a minute."

"The dinosaur picture you were yapping about on the phone?"

Evan pulled a piece of paper from a desk drawer and handed it to Jake. "Actually it's just a drawing."

Jake glanced at it. "Thecodont. You say a guy *saw* this?" He wasn't laughing anymore.

"Yeah. I admit the guy who saw it was probably in shock. The thing had just attacked his friend. My thought was that it was just a mixed-up picture of a croc or gator, but it was the coroner who hinted that it might be something else."

"It sure is."

"You recognized it right away."

Jake studied the picture more carefully. "The guy's a good artist. I'd like to talk to him."

"Sounds as if this thing could tie in with your bird."

"What else do you know?" Jake asked.

"Well, this might not tie in, but—" Evan told him about the Park Ranger, Juan Degas. "Could a thecodont have done that to him?" he finally asked.

"Who the hell knows?" Jake answered.

"Right." Evan stood up and stretched, then smiled at his friend. "And I thought paleontology was dull. Come on . . . I'll treat you to dinner and you can spend the night at my house. Just promise you won't keep me up all night yapping about dinosaurs in the swamp and flying fossils in the suburbs."

"You got it."

"Seriously," Evan added. "I'm glad you're here. If anybody can make sense out of this mystery, it's you, and I admit the whole thing intrigues me. So you can yap all you want."

Jake grinned. "Good. Because you wouldn't have been able to stop me."

They left the building, Jake still favoring Evan with a running commentary on the awesome attributes of Archaeopteryx, and Evan wondering if all this was true about living fossils in the Glades, how on earth it could all have gotten started.

Chapter Eleven

Had she seen them, the armadillo wouldn't have recognized her great-great grandchildren. Four years ago her twelve offspring, all developed from a single fertilized egg that had waited several months before firmly implanting itself in her uterus, had been born kicking and screaming into the dark burrow.

They'd been difficult from the beginning. Refusing to heed her warnings to hunt only at night, they'd scrambled away from her and out into the daylight long before her instincts told her they were ready to leave her side at all. And they'd refused all offers of succulent vegetation that she'd urged on them, preferring to hunt and feed on small animals that they were surprisingly adept at capturing.

Then one day, when they were at least three times her size—but still, to her, her babies—they'd left the meadow. They'd lumbered off to the south, heading in a straight line toward the huge swamp that wasn't far from their home. She'd watched them for a long time as they left her, afraid to follow. When they finally disappeared from sight, she forgot them and scurried back to her burrow.

She had no way of knowing that others of her species had given birth to similar strange offspring, nor that an ancient instinct deep in their brains was driving them to the same place that her children were going. She didn't know that these solid-armored throwbacks to a time long past would interbreed and strengthen their mutant genes. She didn't know that in a short amount of time her grandchildren would be nine feet long, roaming the depths of the Everglades and fighting for territory with mighty swings of the spiked, macelike club that grew at the ends of their tails.

Chapter Twelve

She was so uncomfortable! Jenny sat up and kicked the light blanket to the foot of the bed, irritated by the way it clung to her legs. Minnie Mouse stared up at her from the pillow, one leg bent back and under her black felt body in a grotesque position. Jenny straightened the leg and patted Minnie's pink dress back in place.

The night around her seemed heavy and stale, as if she were breathing somebody else's used air. And it smelled bad. She could smell her sweaty feet. She could smell the waxy, sweet odor of her crayons even though she had the cover on the box. She could smell what her mother had cooked for dinner—fish (it smelled old now), and wilted spinach, and the heavy odor of buttered noodles. Her nose was stuffed with the smells and she covered it with her hand, trying to block them out. No good. She pinched her nostrils shut and tried breathing through her mouth, but that didn't help; the odors just ran down her throat and made her feel sick to her stomach.

As her eyes adjusted to the dark, shapes took a clearer form and became more recognizable—her white-painted dresser; a small vanity table with a pink ruffled skirt, and a triple mirror (she was only allowed play makeup, but she spent hours in front of it, imitating her mother); two bookshelves—one filled with Golden Books and Dr. Seuss, and another jammed with dolls and stuffed animals. And it all seemed closer to her than she remembered, as if the room had somehow shrunk.

She felt confined. Trapped. Her heart beat faster and she gulped in a breath of rancid air; almost choked on it. Whining softly, she scrambled out of bed and ran for the bedroom door. The doorknob was slippery in her hands, and she struggled with it for a few seconds, fighting back the sense of panic that was making it harder and harder to breathe. She had to get outside! Finally the door squeaked open and she gathered her long nightgown up in one hand and tiptoed down the hall. She didn't want to wake her mother. Her mother would make her go back to bed, and she wouldn't be able to stand it!

She paused outside Lydia's bedroom door, listening. A soft rustle, her mother turning over in bed. A little cough. Then she could hear breathing—even and shallow. Jenny padded down the hall and out the back door.

Heavy rainclouds rolled across the sky, blocking out the moon and starlight. Humidity hung heavy in the air, unrelieved by the cool wind that blew in ahead of the storm and whipped Jenny's dark curls around her face. She plucked a strand of hair from her mouth and took a deep breath. Another. She felt the fresh air clean her lungs, and she sighed with relief. The panic in her flowed away into the night and she ran around the corner of her house toward the big oak tree. It didn't seem strange to her that she had no trouble seeing in the dark.

Jenny ducked under a low-hanging branch and leaned against the rough bark of the trunk. She was tired now and wanted to sleep. She looked up at the leafy canopy that arched protectively over her head and smiled. A small hop up, and her hands grabbed a branch. She swung her legs toward the tree and gripped the trunk with her toes, then scrambled up into the bottom crook and looked down from her perch. Not high enough. She climbed, careful not to disturb the nest as she passed it.

At about fifteen feet up, the main trunk divided in two, forming a wide natural platform. Dead leaves and Spanish moss had settled in the curve, and Jenny gave the debris a cursory fluff with her hands before settling herself comfortably in the middle of it.

Night sounds drifted around her—insects, frogs, and the distant cry of a loon. At peace now, Jenny closed her eyes. When the storm hit, she slept right through it.

A clap of thunder shook the house and rattled the windows. Lydia jerked awake. Still slightly disoriented as she struggled up from a fuzzy sleep, her first thought was for Jenny. Thunder terrified Jenny. She jammed her feet into a pair of slippers and hurried down the hall toward her daughter's room. Flashes of lightning illuminated the night with split seconds of light. Thunder crashed and rumbled in counterpoint. A typical Florida thunderstorm. It looked and sounded like war.

"Jen?" Lydia peeked into the darkened room, hesitant to turn on the lights in case if by some miracle the storm hadn't awakened the child. Usually by now Jenny would be in bed with her, burrowed safely under the blankets and pressed against her side for comfort and safety.

No answer. A sudden feeling of dread prickled the

hairs on the back of Lydia's neck. Flash. An instant of light, but enough to show her Jenny's empty bed.

"Jenny!" Lydia snapped on the light, refusing to believe what she thought she'd seen. The constant glow of harnessed electricity verified what its wild cousin had hinted at. Jenny wasn't in her room.

Lydia left the light burning and ran back to her own room. Could she have passed Jenny in the hall and not seen her? No. Empty. On impulse she flung open the closet door. "Jenny?" No answer.

Frantic now, Lydia ran through the house screaming her daughter's name and banging open doors. Her voice carried over the thunder in rising hysteria. And the thought kept pushing at the back of her mind and she kept pushing it back. Kidnapped. Kidnapped.

Every light in the small, stucco ranch house was on now. There was no place else to look. Lydia forced herself to stop running through the rooms over and over again. She stood trembling in the living room, trying to think. There was no way she could believe Jenny would voluntarily go outside in a thunderstorm, day or night. Not alone. That left only one terrifying possibility. But how could a kidnapper get in? All the doors were locked. Weren't they?

She walked on trembling legs to the front door and tried the knob. Locked. Time seemed suspended as she walked into the kitchen and reached out to turn the handle on the back door. It opened easily and rain whirled into the kitchen, soaking the front of Lydia's nightgown and leaving little puddles on the floor.

Her mind numbed with fear now, she pushed the door shut against the storm and reached for the telephone.

* * *

The young police officer sat at the kitchen table with Lydia and wrote Jenny's description down on a lined yellow pad. His partner, older and showing signs of a beginning paunch, searched the house, poking into all the places that Lydia had already poked into. Now, apparently finished with his search, he stood in the kitchen slapping his flashlight against his palm.

"Ma'am?" He spoke softly to her, and she turned pained eyes on him. "There's no sign of a struggle, ma'am."

"I didn't hear any . . . but the storm . . ."

"Yes, ma'am. But the point is . . . the little girl would have made a ruckus, don't you think? If somebody was trying to kidnap her?"

Lydia stared at him, not sure what he meant.

"Point is," he said as if reading her mind, "it's my guess she might have wandered off before the storm started and just holed up somewheres when it got rough. To get out of the rain, I mean."

"She's never—"

"Yes, ma'am. But kids can do the damnedest things sometimes . . . you can take my word for it." He grabbed his black rain slicker off the back of a kitchen chair and shrugged into it. "C'mon Buddy. Take a look around outside," he said to the younger man.

Lydia leaped to her feet, the initial shock of Jenny's disappearance giving way to a nervous and driving urge to do something, anything, to help. "I'm coming with you." She ran to the hall closet for her raincoat. They waited for her.

The rain wasn't coming down as hard now, even though it had tapered off into a fine, misty drizzle that still had the power to soak through clothes in less than a minute. A hint of dawn struggled near the horizon, making it easier to see than it had been when the police officers had first arrived, but they snapped on their flashlights anyway. Lydia trudged after the men, ignoring the puddles that hadn't been absorbed by the sandy soil yet. Her slippers were soon beyond repair. Her eyes followed the flashlights, looking hopefully from one to the other, straining to see and identify every dark lump that came within their searching beams.

"What's that?" The young one. His flashlight was pointed up into the old oak tree. Lydia pushed past him and peered up into the branches. *Jenny.*

Relief, confusion, and fear swam in Lydia's mind as she stared up at her sleeping child. She opened her mouth to call Jenny's name, but the young officer put a cautionary hand on her arm.

"Don't," he said. "If you startle her awake she might fall. Do you have a ladder?"

Lydia nodded her head toward the aluminum toolshed in the corner of the yard and he sprinted for it.

In a few minutes they had the ladder in place. It reached far short of Jenny, but the climb toward her looked easy enough after that point.

The young man inched his way toward the sleeping child. When he was close enough, he reached out and closed a strong hand around her arm.

Jenny's eyes flew open. "ONDO! NA TAM!" She tried to yank away, her face a mask of terror.

But he had her.

"ONDO! NA TAM!" she shrieked again.

He wrapped one arm around the tree trunk and pulled the screaming child close to his chest in a bear hug. Her back was to him, and she clawed at his hands and hissed and spit at him over her shoulder—the terror changed to rage.

"Jenny! JENNY!" Lydia yelled at her struggling daughter. "STOP IT! STOP!"

Jenny didn't stop. But a six-year-old was no match for a healthy young male, and he dragged her kicking and screaming down the ladder.

When they reached the ground, Lydia grabbed Jenny's face in her hands and forced the child to look at her. "Jenny. Jenny. It's Mommy, honey. Look at me."

Jenny stopped fighting and stared at her mother. There was no sign of recognition in her eyes, but she seemed to calm down at the sight of the female reaching out to her. Suddenly she held out her arms.

Lydia eased the child from the officer's grip.

Jenny wrapped her arms and legs around her mother and clung to her like a little monkey. "Ba na," she whispered. "Ba na." She put her thumb in her mouth and buried her face in Lydia's neck.

Lydia carried the soaking wet child into the house.

Morning. Jenny sat at the kitchen table shoving overloaded spoons of cornflakes and bananas into her mouth. Lydia kept one cautious eye on her while she talked on the phone with her mother.

"No. Nothing. She doesn't remember anything . . . I did, but . . . No. She seems fine now, but . . . Uh huh."

"I'm done, Mom. Can I go out?" Jenny was already sliding from her chair.

"Stay in the yard, Jenny. Wait a minute, Mother." Lydia stretched the phone cord over to where her daughter stood, knelt down to her level, and held her arm to get her full attention. "I mean it. Don't wander off. Do you understand me, Jenny?"

"Okay." Jenny danced from one foot to the other, anxious to be outside. "Can't I go get Sally?"

"I'll call her mother as soon as I stop talking to Grandma. You wait for her in the sandbox."

"I want to go on the swings."

"Then go on the swings," Lydia said curtly. She'd been awake all night checking on Jenny constantly, and her patience had suffered for it. "Just don't leave the backyard." She shook Jenny's arm for emphasis.

"Okay." Jenny pulled away from her mother's restraining hand and ran out the kitchen door. She let the door slam behind her and Lydia winced.

"The point is," she said back into the phone, mentally chiding herself for picking up the policeman's speech mannerism so quickly, "that she's been acting so strangely lately that I don't think I want to leave her with you while I go on assignment. . . . No, no, Mother." Lydia sighed. "I'm not insinuating that you and Dad aren't competent. What I'm saying is that I don't want to give you any added problems with . . . Yes." She put a hand on the side of her head and rubbed it. She was getting a headache. "Look . . . I'll think about it, okay? I have two days until . . . Yes . . . Okay, Mother . . . Yes. I love you too."

Lydia poured herself a lukewarm cup of coffee and swallowed two aspirin with it before she remembered to call Sally's mother.

Sally was eight, but she liked to play with Jenny. Jenny was easy to boss around. She flipped her blond ponytail back over her shoulder and looked down her nose at the chubby younger girl who sat in the sandbox.

"Now we're going to play house and I'm the mother

and you have to be the father," she said imperiously. "And I just came home from work and I have to spend quality time with the baby while you start dinner." She reached down and snatched a Raggedy-Ann doll from Jenny's arms.

Jenny felt a fingernail tear as the doll was yanked away from her, and she stuck the finger in her mouth and glared at Sally.

"WELL?" Sally shouted. "Start dinner!" She kicked a red plastic pail toward Jenny and pointed at the far corner of the sandbox. "There's the kitchen."

But Jenny didn't move. She couldn't. Her head was spinning and she felt sick to her stomach. The air shimmered and darkened around her, and her body felt hot and clammy. She closed her eyes and sobbed—a tiny animal sound of distress.

Sally's voice sounded far away. "What's the matter with you?" she was saying. "What's the ma . . ."

Jenny couldn't hear her anymore. Frightened, she opened her eyes. And immediately felt better. She was safe. The jungle pressed close around her, protecting her. The sounds of her tribe fishing in the creek nearby reassured her that she wasn't alone, and she turned her head toward the voice that she suddenly heard not far away from her.

A woman stood a few feet away. The woman had her baby. *Her* baby. Growling, she slowly got to her feet. The woman backed away.

"Ag da," she said, motioning with her hands for the woman to give the baby back.

The woman clutched the child to her breast and took another step back.

"AG DA!" she shouted, and growled again to make sure the woman knew she meant it. The woman turned to run. It was a mistake. She was on her in a second, pulling her hair, screaming, scratching, and biting in a frenzied maternal rage.

Then someone was pulling her away. Someone shouting at her in a strange language. An aching pressure filled her ears, and her vision faded from gray to black. Dizzy. Her limbs went slack.

Floating.

"Jenny! Jenny!"

Loud voice now. Somebody shaking her. Her head hurt. Somebody else crying. Sally? Why was Sally crying?

"Jenny! Please wake up! Oh my God! Jenny!"

Jenny opened her eyes. "What?" she said to her mother.

"There isn't a thing physically wrong with her, Mrs. Matthews. Every test we've done is negative." Dr. Gerald Galviston sat with Lydia in the Central Community Hospital waiting room. "But the nightmares she seems—"

"What nightmares?"

"About the jungle? And the baby? She didn't tell you?"

"No."

"I see. Well." The doctor steepled his hands and blinked at Lydia. "I'm not a psychiatrist, Mrs. Matthews, but my guess is that Jenny is identifying with the baby in her nightmares, and someone trying to steal it may symbolize an unconscious fear of separation or abandonment . . . you did say her father died . . . ?"

"Yes." Worst fears come true, Lydia thought.

"Well, like I said . . . I'm not a psychiatrist, but since

66

there's nothing *physically* wrong with Jenny . . ." He waited.

"You want her to see a psychiatrist."

"Sleepwalking, nightmares, aggression, stress to the point of losing consciousness . . . what do you think, Mrs. Matthews?"

"Yes."

"Good." Dr. Galviston slapped his hands on his knees and got to his feet. "I'll make the call for you. There's a good man over at Las Flores Medical and Psychiatric Center."

"Can I see Jenny now?"

"You can take her home . . . but go sit with her in the waiting room while I make your appointment." He turned and hurried down the hall, leaving Lydia sitting there staring after him.

"Wait!" she called out to his back. "The psychiatrist! What's his name?"

"Tremayne," Galviston called back over his shoulder. "Dr. Evan Tremayne!"

Chapter Thirteen

Bett held the cookbook opened flat with her elbows and studied the timing chart. Her hands were slick with butter from the stuffing, and she held them up like a surgeon waiting for rubber gloves.

"At fifteen minutes a pound ... that's, let's see ... one hour and about forty-five minutes," she mumbled to herself and abandoned the cookbook to reach for the kitchen twine. The pages fluttered, losing her place as she cut off a piece of the string with a greasy paring knife and tied it around the roaster's legs. She debated tying down the wings too. May as well do it right, she thought, and picked up the ball of twine again. And suddenly stood very still.

The kitchen wavered around her, shimmered, closed in on her—then snapped away with a sudden crack of sound that forced her to her knees in fright. The daylight tunneled away in a yellow whirlwind, leaving her behind in the cold dark. So cold. She closed her eyes and screamed—thought she screamed. She couldn't hear herself.

Warm again. Sunlight found its way through the thick tangle of leaves overhead and dappled the ground around her, heating her naked body. No. Not quite naked. A thin strip of leather circled her waist. A few soft, brown furry pelts hung from the thong and dragged in the decaying leaves of the jungle floor where she sat.

Her fingers flew, swiftly tying intricate knots in the long, tough grasses that she whipped one by one from the pile by her side. She was the best in the tribe at this task, and took great pride in her skill. Her mate brought in more fish from the rivers than any other man, and it was because of her that this was so.

Her one regret was that Too-nee, her eldest daughter, could not seem to learn the skill. She'd tried and tried to teach her, but the child's fingers refused to learn the patterns. Instead, the girl would whine and cry to follow her father, begging to pick up the spear or the bow and join him in the hunt.

She thought of this now, and her face flamed with the shame of it. Doga, her husband, didn't seem to mind the child's strange behavior though, and she marveled at his patience. Other men would have scolded the girl until she realized her place, but Doga would take her away privately, away from the eyes of the others, and let her play with a broken spear that he no longer had any use for.

Suddenly a shout of triumph rang through the trees and she looked up to see Doga approaching her, a new kill draped over his shoulder. She smiled at him, her heart filled with pride. The tribe would eat well today.

Doga shouted again and she looked at him curiously. His face did not show the pleasure she thought should be in it. He dropped the kill and knelt beside her, worry and fear in his eyes. He shouted her name again and her heart beat faster. Her hands trembled and dropped the grasses she was holding. What was wrong? Confused and frightened, she covered her eyes with her hands, not understanding, and not wishing to see his distress.

"Bett! Bett!"

The voice was far away.

"Bett!"

Closer. Louder. Insistent. Someone shaking her. She moaned, pulling herself up from a dark hole, fighting the nausea that suddenly rolled over her.

"Bett!"

The nausea left as quickly as it had come and she opened her eyes to see Ray's face inches from her own, his expression twisted with the same fear and worry she'd seen on . . . on . . . whose face?

"What are you doing?" Ray whispered. "Get up, honey . . . come on. Are you okay?"

Doga. It tried to slip away. She held on to it.

"Bett, please talk to me." Ray eased her into a kitchen chair. She didn't resist. He ran to the sink and filled a glass with water—brought it to her and held it to her lips.

She had the fleeting thought that he didn't know why he did that, but it just seemed to be the thing everybody did when they didn't know what else to do. Then everything came back into sharp focus. "Ray?" she said. "Ray? What happened?"

He put the glass of water on the table and took her hands, rubbing them. "I don't know, hon. You have to tell me. When I came in you were sitting on the floor and . . ." He looked down at the string that lay in a heap at her feet. "You were playing with this." He picked it up.

She looked at it curiously, then took it from him and held it up with both hands. It unrolled and dropped in graceful folds into her lap—a beautifully crafted, intricately knotted and woven net.

She remembered. "I did this," she said. "But it was some kind of grass, not . . ."

"What?" He stared at the net, then at his wife.

"I dreamed . . . I think I was dreaming. . . that I was sitting in a jungle and making this thing." She ran her hands over it, confused and a little frightened because she didn't know how it had happened for real. But a part of her, somewhere deep inside her brain, something slowly crawling out into the light—puffed up with pride.

Not again! Not again!

Bett sat up in bed, heart hammering, cold with sweat and shaking with fright. This time she didn't remember. This time she screamed. And she knew it was time to get help.

"Some of your symptoms are classic night terror symptoms, Mrs. Wilson . . . Bett," Evan said. "The accelerated heart rate, intense fear, perspiration, rapid breathing, screaming, the inability to remember the dream that caused the terror. But some of it . . ."

He picked up the net that lay on his desk and draped it over one hand, admiring the workmanship. "Can you do this again for me? Now?"

"No."

Evan glanced up at the woman who sat calmly regarding him from the chair on the other side of his desk. Most people with relatively minor disorders who faced a psychiatrist for the first time were nervous, embarrassed, or defiant. But the tiny, blond woman in front of him radiated an almost eerie inner calm. Real or forced, he wondered? His gut instincts warned him that this was going to be a tough one.

Her blue eyes were steady on him. "My husband insisted I see you, Dr. Tremayne. And . . . I agreed that I need a little help. I assume there's some medication you can give me that will cure my nightmares?"

It wasn't a challenge, just a simple question, and Evan hated to disappoint her.

"I'm afraid it isn't that easy, Bett," he answered. He dropped the net back on the desk. She was obviously reluctant to talk about it and he didn't want to press her. "Night terrors in an adult usually indicate some deep mental trauma. And medication would only relieve the symptoms, not cure the problem. I can give you Diazepam for some temporary relief, but it won't eliminate the underlying cause of your night terrors."

Bett took a deep breath. She had to ask—get it out in the open. "Could it be physical? A disease or something? Or a . . . a brain tumor?" An instant of fear flashed across her face, betraying the fiction of her calm, and then disappeared.

Evan caught it. "Are you worried about that?" he asked.

She hesitated. Looked down at her hands. Looked back up at him. The calm demeanor was cracking. "My aunt Teresa died . . . I loved her . . . she . . . ." Now the grief in her eyes was unconcealed, and she just stared at him.

"It's highly unlikely that your night terrors are brought on by a brain tumor," Evan said gently. "Will you tell me more about your aunt Teresa?"

"I like him, Ray," Bett said. "He's . . . kind."

They sat at the kitchen table sipping iced tea. Ray squeezed the last drop of juice out of his piece of lemon and dropped the rind back into the glass.

"I'm glad, hon," he said.

"We talked about Teresa."

Ray watched her carefully. When he'd questioned her reluctance to see a psychiatrist, she'd told him the whole story about her aunt Teresa—a story she'd only hinted at before. Bett's mother had died in childbirth when Bett was three. The baby, a boy, had died too, and her father had then more or less given Bett to his sister to raise while he spent more and more time on the road with his job.

Teresa had been childless, and she'd lavished a true mother's love on the little girl—until Bett was eighteen. Then Teresa had gone mad. She'd vacillate between sitting motionless for hours in front of a blank wall, and endless weeping. After a few months of this, she began to sneak out of the house at night. In the mornings, when they realized she was gone, Bett and her uncle would go searching for her. They'd find her blocks away, begging nickels from strangers—or sleeping in the park—or trying to force her way into someone's house, convinced that she was where she belonged.

They put her in a psychiatric hospital forty-five minutes from home and visited her every day, waiting, hoping, for any sign that the psychotherapy she was undergoing was curing her.

Then they discovered the brain tumor. Teresa died on the operating table. Bett blamed the psychiatrists. The courts didn't. "Why didn't they find it sooner?" she'd asked. "They let her die while they talked," she'd said. "Never trust a psychiatrist," she still said. Until now.

Ray had been more frantic over Bett's nightmares than he'd let her believe, and after hearing her story, the fact that he'd persuaded her to see Tremayne at all was astonishing. Now, hearing her say that she *liked* him was a miracle. He closed his eyes and said a little prayer of thanks to whatever powers that might be listening.

"He says brain tumors aren't hereditary," she was saying now. "But he says that maybe my worrying about it is making things worse, so we're going to do the tests, EEG and CAT scan, and I forget what else, right away. To make me feel better. I asked if he would and he said yes. He says that maybe my fears, because of Teresa, are causing me most of my problem. Maybe. And we're going to explore that too. And other things. He didn't exactly say what, but just talking about Teresa made me feel better, and he seems so nice . . . not like the others. I think I trust him."

She looked at him with hope, and a little fear, on her face. She was talking too much and too fast and she knew it. But *God,* she was nervous!

Ray took her hand and brought it to his lips. He kissed her fingers. "I have a good feeling about all this, hon," he said. "Everything's going to be okay."

"I know," she whispered. She felt the pressure of tears forming behind her eyes. Fear, relief, or self-pity, she wondered? Right now her emotions were too confused for her to really tell.

Chapter Fourteen

She lay in the shallows, her huge head resting on the bank, her tail swaying and bobbing in the gentle flow of water that lapped against the rest of her body. She kept one yellow eye on the mound of mud and dead vegetation that blended into the underbrush about ten feet from where she lay.

It was time. She roused herself and crawled slowly toward her nest. A dozen or so tiny animals in her path hesitated at the sight of her, then dodged around her and laboriously dragged and flopped themselves toward the safety of the water.

A cooter had laid her clutch of eggs in the alligator's nest, and now the tiny hatchling turtles raced for their lives. But she ignored them.

The alligator stood motionless by the mound. She'd built it earlier than usual this year, as she had for the past few years. Immediately after her April mating, she'd begun the three-foot high and seven-foot long nest, instead of waiting the two months that she usually did. Then she'd carefully scooped out the center and laid fifty-three leathery eggs. Now, old instincts whispered that it was too soon, but newer, stronger instincts shouted "now!" Her tiny brain struggled with the decision.

But the sounds that had triggered her desire to approach the nest were insistent, and she finally began to dig into it. She stopped once or twice, listening to the faint cries of "chee-ohw, chee-ohw, chee-ohw" that signaled the birth of her babies.

Then they were free, wiggling from the mound, blinking their eyes in the sun and racing to her for protection. She gathered one of the ten inch-long hatchlings gently into her mouth and carried him to the edge of the water where he would wait for her. They would all stay with her for one to three years, at first riding on her great head when they were tired, then merely staying close to her side while she basked in the sun or hunted through the hundreds of miles of water that nurtured and provided easy prey for them. The last few pods had stayed only a year, then the ten-foot-long youngsters had gone their own solitary ways, leaving her in peace.

It took many trips to get all her babies in the water, and she watched them paddle and play in the shallows, their black, yellow-banded bodies flashing in the dappled sunlight. Except for a few. A few of them were bright green with a speckled pattern of brown spots peppering their bellies, and their nostrils sat far back on their heads, close to their eyes, instead of at the tip of the snout where they belonged. And rows of sharp, bony plates covered their backs; it had made them awkward to carry. Now these few huddled together, avoiding the rest of their siblings. It took almost an hour of gentle urging for her to integrate them with the group, but she finally succeeded, and the new family glided silently out into the Everglades.

Chapter Fifteen

June was a hell of a lousy time to go poking through the Everglades, Jake decided. He slapped at another mosquito that had found its way into the Research Center offices. Missed. It whined away and he lost sight of it. The creatures were obviously bent on extracting the last bit of blood from every human foolish enough to stray into their territory. Which was everywhere. Outside had been unbelievable, and he blessed the foresight that had made him stuff a can of insect repellent into his backpack. Not that it had saved his tough hide from all of them, but he cringed to think of what his short sprint from the jeep to the Research Center door would have been like without it. And now he was going to spend *days* out there in mosquitoland. Wish I could get a few more cans of juice before we leave, he thought miserably. He looked hopefully around the long hall of the Research Center, but there were no tourist accommodations here—no vending machines, or souvenirs or postcards for sale. Or insect repellant. Nothing but discreetly lettered office doors.

"Jake! Hello, Jake!"

The cheerful voice belonged to Dr. Ralph Jenner, the

fellow paleontologist who'd first run across the remarkable drawing of Archaeopteryx and called Jake in on the hunt. Ralph was short, thin, and balding, and he ran a handkerchief across his sweating head as he hurried down the hall toward his friend. He was grinning like a kid at Christmas.

Trailing behind him was a man Jake didn't know, but who he guessed was an administrator from the National Park Service.

"We have our Back country Use permit," Ralph said. "And this is Dr. Krells." Ralph motioned to the middle-aged man. "He's from the Park Service, and has given us the use of a small pontoon boat for our expedition, in addition to getting us the special permit. There seem to be some unexpected restrictions in effect, but they were waived for us. This preliminary trip will be only one overnight, and if we don't find what we're looking for we can return for more supplies and rent a bigger, more comfortable boat for a more extended stay."

Dr. Krells grinned up at Jake. "Archaeopteryx, huh? If I didn't know your reputations, I'd say you people were pulling my leg. We have our people out there all the time doing full-time environmental research and nobody's ever seen anything that even remotely resembles what you say you're after."

Ralph drew himself up and bristled at the implied criticism. "Does your extensive research include daily travel to every remote area of the Everglades, Dr. Krells?"

"Of course not. That's impossible. The Park area alone is about one and a half million acres, and that covers only about one seventh of the Everglades, but . . ."

"And perhaps your people are all trained paleontologists and would instantly recognize Archaeopteryx if it flew in their faces?"

Dr. Krell's smile disappeared. "Now look, I'm not saying—"

"What kind of research are your people doing out here?" Jake asked. The last thing they needed to do was antagonize the authorities in the Glades, and Ralph's legendary temper and his passionate feelings and opinions about his work could spark him into heated arguments at the slightest provocation. He and Jake had argued over some of the finer points of paleontology more than once, and the man was, in Jake's opinion, a stubborn, hot-headed, narrow-minded, brilliant son-of-a-bitch. And if he said Archaeopteryx was out there, then by God, he'd bet his life that it *was* out there. But he could certainly understand the skepticism on Krell's part.

Krell turned to Jake, obviously relieved to escape a confrontation with the angry little man who stood glaring at him. "We do some interesting work here, Dr. Van Gower."

"Jake, please."

"Jake. We have five areas of study. Hydrology— which is vital because water is so important to the Everglade's delicate ecosystem . . ." Krell started warming up to his speech, drawing them in to what he had to say. "Then we have groups who study wildlife, plant, marine and fire ecology.

"Dr. Bostwick from our Wildlife Survey department will be anxious to hear any results you find on your expedition, by the way." Krell turned to a bulletin board crammed with papers that hung in the center of the hall and ran his finger down a list of names on a pink sheet. "Dr. Thurman, Jane Thurman, will be in tomorrow afternoon when you get back. I won't be here, but her office is the third door on the right." He waved a hand toward the doors that lined the hall to his left.

"Yes, yes . . ." Ralph pointedly looked at his watch. "Time enough for consultations later. We should move on."

Jake shook hands with Krell and followed Ralph to the door where he braced himself for the onslaught of mosquitos that he knew were lying in wait for them.

"Go back to the road you came in on," Krell said, following them, "and make a left. Go down it to the Great Hammock Trail. Your guide is already out there. He came in about an hour ago. And please . . . don't swim, don't take any unnecessary risks, and listen to the guide's warnings and instructions. You're going to be out of the mainstream waterways and we don't want to lose any of you." He grinned as if he'd just made a joke.

"Shark and barracuda," Ralph said.

Jake glanced over at him. "What?"

"The waters are filled with shark and barracuda. And alligators and an occasional Florida crocodile. That's why we can't swim." He didn't smile.

"Oh," Jake said.

They went out the door into the early morning heat—and the mosquitos.

The half mile down the Great Hammock Trail was a half mile into another world. A slight drop in temperature as they entered the damp, jungle-like environment was an immediate relief from an already scorching early-morning sun, and Jake and Dr. Jenner gazed up

80

through the branches of the massive mahogany trees in silent appreciation.

Ahead of them near the water, a stocky, dark-skinned man stood near a sixteen-foot pontoon boat that bobbed gently in the water. "Dr. Jenner?" he asked, his black eyes jumping from one man to the other in quick appraisal.

"Yes." Ralph stepped forward and held out his hand. "You're our guide?"

"Charlie Jones," the man said, then briefly shook hands with Jake as an introduction was made. "Park Service briefed me. Boat is ready. Bedrolls and provisions too. Stow the rest of your gear in the back. There's room behind the four parrot cages."

"This is marvelous!" Ralph said, waving his arms to encompass all the flora crammed in around them. "Look at those paurotis palms! Magnificent!"

Charlie gave him a blank look, then turned on his heel and walked back toward the boat.

Jake gave Jenner a quick grin before dog-trotting back to the car for the rest of the gear.

After loading the extra provisions, Jake went over a nautical chart with Charlie. "Here's where the bird was spotted, we think," he said. "Somewhere between here and Barracuda River to the northwest."

Charlie grunted and nodded. "Some easy water. Some not so easy. We'll do a turn here." He pointed to a spot on the map. "Make a narrow loop like so, and stay at Soames River Chikee at nightfall."

"Chikee?" Jake asked.

"Yeah. Wood platform built high over the water. Has a roof. Chemical toilet. Open sides. Safe sleeping."

"Sounds primitive."

"Yeah. It is." A faint smile. "Let's go."

They glided out into the shallow water. Jake reached for his binoculars and his insect repellent.

Ralph craned his neck back toward the trail where masses of ferns, orchids, and bromeliads covered the ground or hung in delicate aerial gardens from the trees. It was clear to Jake that the older man, whose interest in botany almost equaled his passion for paleontology, could have stayed on that one half-mile trail for hours.

A few small hammocks on either side of them as they boated out into the wilderness echoed the exotic flora of the Great Hammock Trail, and Ralph unzipped a camera from a waterproof bag, slipped on a wide-angle lens, and snapped a few pictures. Then they were out into the Coastal Prairie, and Charlie navigated a narrow channel through the sea of tall saw grass.

Curious, Jake reached out toward the sedge.

"Don't!" Charlie yelled, and Jake snatched his hand back and raised an eyebrow at the guide.

"Cut your hand to shreds," Charlie said.

Embarrassed by his stupidity, Jake put his hands in his lap. "Are you a Seminole?" he asked, trying to take attention from himself.

"Miccosukee. Mostly, anyway. My great grandfather was a white man. Jones. White man's name. You?"

"Me? Uh . . . English and Welsh . . . touch of Irish somewhere on my mother's side." He was beginning to get used to Charlie's abbreviated way of speaking and unconsciously mimicked it. "You know your way around the whole Glades?"

"Haven't lived long enough. Short way in you want to go is easy."

"Uh huh. If we're not successful on this trip, Charlie, are you willing to take us on an extended expedition . . . into some of the remote areas?"

Charlie was silent. The boat puttered into a swampier expanse. Far ahead, Jake imagined he could sense a change in scenery, almost smell the beginnings of the vast, ancient, mangrove swamp. Way too soon, he thought, but his anticipation was high.

"Hundred dollars a day," Charlie said. "Not counting the boat rental."

"A hundred . . . ? I'll talk to Dr. Jenner." Jesus, Jake thought.

"Some risk now," Charlie said without sounding the least bit afraid. "Rogue gator out here. Surprised you got a permit."

The attacks Evan told me about, Jake thought, but said nothing. For the first time he wondered just how great the danger out here really was.

A long time later, the little boat carried its passengers into a primeval world.

Chapter Sixteen

"Nightmares are common in Jenny's age group, Mrs. Matthews. Most children outgrow them."

Evan and Lydia stood looking through the one-way mirror into the "playroom" where Jenny and a young female therapist laughed over a comical cow that the little girl had drawn for her new friend. The cow had wings on its feet and was gaping in surprise at a bird that flew complacently through the air near its face. It was a "typical" Jenny picture, one that showed no sign of the strange, dark impulses that had been cropping up in her work lately.

"Are you saying that there's nothing wrong with her?" Lydia asked. She watched Jenny grab a new piece of paper and an orange crayon. The therapist sat back in her chair, folded her hands in her lap, and watched the child with obvious interest.

"Not exactly," Evan said guardedly. "I'm just saying that the nightmares aren't our main problem . . . though they could be, probably are . . . an indication of inner stress. The sudden change in personality, the aggression, the sleepwalking, and the blackout she experienced concern me more right now."

The small spark of hope that Lydia had grabbed at died, and she turned away from the window to face the psychiatrist. "What do we do now?" she asked.

Evan shoved his hands in his pockets and rocked a little on his heels. "Well," he said, "first we have to realize that Jenny is going through a difficult stage right now. She's at an age where her central nervous system is taking a giant leap toward maturity, and she's beginning to experience reality-based thinking . . . which at times can be confusing for her."

"I don't understand. What . . . ?"

"For instance . . . a child younger than Jenny will play house and *believe* she's really the mommy. That's nonreality-based thinking. At around Jenny's age, a child begins to realize that she really isn't the mommy . . . it's just pretend.

"She's also beginning to learn value judgments . . . to develop a conscience. She's learning which feelings, thoughts, and actions are acceptable and which ones aren't. All of this is usually automatic, and the transitions seem so natural that the child usually grows and develops without the parents even being very much aware of the wonderful and complex processes going on."

Lydia frowned. She thought she knew what he was getting at, but . . . "And sometimes it isn't so automatic . . . so easy? Is that what's happening to Jenny?"

"Maybe." Evan suddenly put a hand on Lydia's back and steered her gently toward the door of the observation room. "Let's go back to my office. Jenny will be fine in there with Miss Norville."

Lydia settled into the chair in front of Evan and waited while he shuffled through a stack of papers on his desk.

"I have a schedule here somewhere," he mumbled. "I want to give her a WPPSI as soon as possible."

"What?"

Evan grinned up at her, but his smile faded when he saw her tense expression and he mentally kicked himself for being so obtuse. He'd been concentrating on the child and the symptoms her mother had described, and had obviously forgotten to say all the comforting things the woman needed to hear. He leaned back in his chair and put the smile back on his face.

"Please don't look so worried, Mrs. Matthews," he said softly. "I have every confidence that we can help Jenny. Her problems aren't life-threatening, and we've dealt with these minor dysfunctions many times before." He stressed the word minor, and he watched Lydia unclench a little.

"WPPSI," he said, "is the Wechsler Pre-school and Primary Scale of Intelligence test. It's for children between the ages of four and six and a half, and it measures perceptual motor abilities and verbal and nonverbal reasoning. It should give us a good general idea of where Jenny is at in her development, and point out any problem areas that may be causing her stress."

"I see. But didn't Dr. Galviston's report rule out any physical problems?" Lydia asked.

"The EEG ruled out epilepsy, yes. He thought at first that Jenny's aggression toward her playmates and her blackout in the backyard indicated a psychomotor seizure, but the EEG and the fact that Jenny was alert after the episode ruled that out."

Evan could see Lydia relax as they talked. Uncertainty and fear of the unknown were, he believed, the worst things for frightened parents, and he'd found that

86

sometimes by relieving parental stress, the child automatically improved. Sometimes.

"You see," he continued, "people with psychomotor seizures are confused and disoriented when an episode is over . . . and they have no recall of the event. Jenny not only knew where she was and who you and Sally were, she gave a detailed account of a . . . a dream she'd experienced while in her unconscious state. Very curious."

Lydia frowned at Evan. She didn't like that last remark. It showed uncertainty and that made her nervous again.

Evan, evidently giving up on finding the schedule he'd been searching for, got up and crossed the room to a file cabinet. "I'd like you to fill out this questionnaire for me, Mrs. Matthews," he said. "It's a simple history . . . things like when did Jenny first sit up, stand, walk, talk. Diet. Injuries, infections, fevers. Any problems with her delivery. History of family illnesses . . . things like that."

"What do you think is wrong with Jenny, Dr. Tremayne?" She knew the question was premature, but she couldn't help it. If he thought she was an overanxious ninny, so be it.

But when he turned back to her he didn't look annoyed—just thoughtful.

"I can't tell you that yet . . . but I have a hunch." He hesitated and studied her for a moment, as if weighing the advisability of saying anything yet. Finally he gave a little nod to himself and crossed back to the desk, slapping the questionnaire against his palm. "Please don't hold me to it until I know more . . . a lot more. But I know you need some answers, and we can discuss and discard or reevaluate ideas as we go along if you like. I think it helps most parents to know where we're going at every step. Even if some initial evaluations are wrong. Agreed?"

"Yes," Lydia said. "Definitely yes." She suddenly realized that she trusted this man. He was going to help Jenny. She knew it.

Evan sat on the edge of his desk and smiled down at her. "Have you ever heard of Impulsivity?" he asked.

"No."

"Okay. In some children there's no delay between impulse and response . . . they just react to a stimulus without thinking of the consequences. This kind of reaction can be a result of emotional immaturity or simply an immature nervous system. And these kids are aggressive . . . they'll smack a playmate for the slightest infraction."

"Like Jenny did with Sally . . . and the boys at school."

"Yes. Has Jenny had any bed-wetting problems? Does she play with matches or have you caught her stealing?"

"What?" Lydia felt off balance at Evan's last questions. They were strange. Left field. "No!" she cried. "What does that have to do with anything?"

Evan looked disappointed. "Symptoms. Just further symptoms of Impulsivity . . . but if she hasn't showed any signs . . . Well, I may be on the wrong track."

Lydia's next question was interrupted by the sudden appearance of a white-coated young man who threw open the office door without ceremony and shouted at Evan, "Room three!"

Evan was on his feet and out the door before Lydia could leave her chair. "Stay there!" he shouted over his shoulder at her, and she obediently sat still. Was "room 3" Jenny, she wondered uneasily? She couldn't remember. And now he was gone and she didn't know where room three was, and she didn't know if she could trace her way back through the maze of hallways to find her, either.

Room 3 was a mess. Children's desks and chairs were overturned, their legs sticking up in the air or pointing sideways, and toys littered the floor.

The young woman who had been watching over Jenny grabbed Evan's arm as he flew into the room and held him back, silently nodding her head toward the child who sat crouched in a corner.

Jenny was hunched over a piece of paper, a black crayon in her hand. A fine sheen of sweat covered her face and dripped off the tip of her nose as she concentrated fiercely on what she was doing. She grunted softly and repeatedly as the crayon moved quickly over the paper.

"What the hell . . . ?" Evan whispered.

"I tried to take the crayons away from her," the woman whispered back. "I wanted to try some play techniques . . . you know, just for a preliminary evaluation. When I touched her crayon, her posture became rigid and her eyes dilated rapidly. At first I thought seizure, but . . . she . . ."

The woman hesitated and Evan glanced quickly at her. "What? What?" he said irritably.

"She saw me . . . I know she was aware of me . . . it wasn't like . . . and . . . and she snarled at me."

"Snarled at you?"

"Yes, sir. And then she trashed the place," the young woman finished with a slight tremor in her voice.

"Did you try to restrain her?" Evan asked calmly.

"Yes, sir." She silently held out an arm toward the psychiatrist. Four gouges ran from her elbow to her wrist. Blood seeped from the wounds and dripped on the floor.

Evan curbed his shock and spoke quietly. "Go. Have that taken care of immediately. I'll handle this."

She left without another word and Evan walked slowly over to where Jenny crouched in deep concentration. The crayon flew, and the child grabbed one piece of paper after another, filling each one with bold, black lines. There was no hesitation as she worked.

Evan knelt next to her. She froze, her eyes flicking sideways toward him. And growled.

The feral sound raised the hair on the back of his neck, but he held his ground. "Jenny," he said softly. "I won't hurt you. And I won't take away your pictures."

Jenny turned to stare at him. Her head moved in stiff jerks, as if the muscles weren't synchronized with her brain, and she dropped the crayon. Her eyes rolled back in her head and she crumpled into a heap on the floor, scattering and crushing her drawings underneath her.

Evan, his heart pounding, reached quickly for her pulse. As he touched her, her eyes flew open.

"Hi, Dr. Tremayne. Do you like my pictures?" she asked.

Jenny wiggled off Lydia's lap and began exploring the things on Evan's desk. Lydia reached out to restrain her, but Evan waved a hand. "Let her go. She can't hurt anything."

The child smiled at him and picked up a magnetic paper-clip holder. After a few moments she sat on the floor with it and contentedly dragged the little pieces of metal through different patterns, enjoying the way they clung and separated at her direction.

"I want to do an evaluation on Jenny," Evan said to Lydia, but he kept one curious eye on the child as she played. "We'll do several assessments . . . intrapsychic, interpersonal, and behavioral . . ."

Lydia half heard him. What was happening to her baby? She watched Jenny make a long string out of the paper clips. She looked so . . . normal! What was setting off these rages?

". . . doesn't seem to be hyperactive or distractable when she . . . ," Dr. Tremayne was saying.

What was he talking about? He didn't seem to know why Jenny wrecked room three. How was she going to handle this alone? Her stomach clenched and she blinked back tears. *Cut it out! Stay rational.* She shifted in her seat and cleared her throat, fighting for control.

"Mrs. Matthews?"

Lydia snapped her attention back to Evan.

"Can you bring Jenny back in tomorrow morning?"

"Yes. Of course." His eyes on her were kind, and she felt the knot in her middle loosen. He was going to help. He would. He would. She gave him a shaky smile.

"Good. Eight o'clock?" Evan got up and walked around the desk to shake her hand, and Lydia hung on to it for a moment longer than necessary, seeking—needing the reassuring contact. Evan took her hand in both of his and smiled down at her, but said nothing.

Jenny put the paper-clip holder carefully back on the desk and skipped happily to the door. Handshakes meant hello and good-bye. Suddenly she stopped, then turned and ran back to Evan. "Good-bye, Dr.

Tremayne," she said, and held out her own hand. Evan released Lydia's hand and solemnly shook Jenny's.

"Good-bye, Jenny," he said. "I'll see you tomorrow."

She gave him a genuine, open-faced smile before running back to the door, and he felt an unexpected surge of protectiveness toward her. Whoa! he told himself, surprised. Don't get emotionally involved. First rule. But there was something about the child. . . .

Dr. Harold Burnham, the director of Las Flores Medical and Psychiatric Center, stood amid the chaos of room 3 and gently smoothed out the drawings. His hands shook slightly. This was incredible. Impossible. The implications! Wait. Wait, he cautioned himself. Perhaps someone had a book . . . just copied . . .

He gathered up the papers and hurried toward Evan's office.

"Familiar, Harold?" Evan asked. He peered at Jenny's drawings again. "No. Now do you mind telling me what you're getting at? If you have anything that might help my patient, I'd certainly appreciate hearing about it." He leaned back in his chair and looked up at the old man.

The director had barged into his office about a half hour ago, asking . . . no, demanding . . . to know who had drawn the pictures he'd been waving around. Evan told him. And Harold didn't believe him. It had taken Miss Norville's corroboration to finally convince the man that a six-year-old child had drawn the pictures . . . and that no, she hadn't copied from a book.

The old man was now grinning wildly and shoving

the pictures back under Evan's nose. And he'd kicked Miss Norville out of Evan's office and slammed the door behind her.

"Harold, take it easy, will you?" Evan was surprised at the excitability the director was displaying. It was a side of him that he hadn't seen before. He'd had a previously untarnished image of the dapper, white-haired neuropsychologist as a perennially thoughtful, calm, unshakable pillar of scientific brilliance. Like Einstein. Maybe it was the hair, he mused. Anyway, even though his evaluation had been wrong, it was nice to see the guy had a human side. Stoic calm always made him uneasy, made him feel as if the person evidencing it was going to great lengths to hide himself from the world.

"How much do you know about art, Evan?" Burnham was asking now.

"Not much, I'm afraid. I never had the time—"

"Have you ever seen pictures of cave drawings?" Burnham interrupted. "Ever hear of Lascaux? In France? The primitive drawings of aurochs? Deer . . . horses . . . stags?"

"Harold . . ."

"No! No! Don't argue!" He got up and started to pace, and occasionally rushed back to the desk to pound at one of the pictures with a blunt finger. "If you don't know primitive art, you can't argue! I'm telling you these are almost identical . . . identical! . . . to the ancient drawings in that cave! Do you realize the possible implications here! Do you?"

Evan picked up one of the pictures and examined it more closely. He had to admit he hadn't studied them very carefully yet . . . although he'd planned to bring them home with him that night, along with several other case studies he was working on. Now he seemed to be looking at a potbellied little horse. Pregnant? The neck and head were thick and the feet were dainty. The mane stuck straight up in the air, didn't have the flow he would expect in a typical drawing of a horse. But . . . and he felt a thrill go down his spine . . . this was unlike any child's drawing he'd ever seen. There was a mastery of form and perspective in the primitive drawing that was beyond the skill of most adults. And if he couldn't trade knowledge of the Masters with even the most blatant neophyte, he could recognize exceptional talent when he saw it. And he was seeing it. In the scribblings of a disturbed six-year-old girl. Harold was right. This was extraordinary.

"Primitive genetic memory," Harold Burnham said with quiet awe. "This child is living proof of all my theories." He stroked one of the pictures reverently. "They won't doubt me anymore."

Evan tossed the picture back on the desk. "I'll grant you that these pictures are exceptional, Harold," he said. "But that doesn't prove a damn thing about genetic memory. She likes to draw. Her father was an artist. In that kind of situation she could have been exposed to all sorts of artistic works from infancy on. She could have been shown pictures of cave drawings when she was a few weeks old, for all we know . . . and for some reason her unconscious is expressing the memory now."

"The unconscious can express all it wants to . . . these are beyond the normal capacity of a six-year-old to recreate without there being unusual circumstances." Harold grabbed a drawing and shook it in Evan's face.

Evan ignored the picture. "Maybe she's a prodigy . . . nothing more. Although that's pretty unusual and impressive in itself, I admit. But I don't believe she's delving into latent prehistoric memories. For God's sake,

Harold, keep an open mind here. Don't be so anxious to prove your theories that you lose your scientific objectivity."

"Fine." Dr. Burnham sat in the chair opposite Evan and folded his hands in his lap. He smiled. "I'll take your advice if you will. Keep an open mind, Evan."

Evan couldn't repress his own smile. "Caught by my own words. Okay, Harold. But I want you to let me continue my own evaluation. If the child checks out to be normal in all psychological respects, I'll entertain the possibility of genetic involvement ... and I'll explain the research that you and Dr. Frankel have done to her mother. Then it's up to her if she wants to continue along these lines."

"That's fair enough. I would have insisted on it anyway. I agree that all other possibilities should be ruled out before embarking on this kind of testing."

"Good point," Evan said. "And don't forget it's expensive ... could be a stumbling block if insurance doesn't cover. She's a single parent and I don't know if she can afford—"

"If she agrees, I'll cover expenses myself," Harold said and rose to his feet. He reached out for the drawings.

Evan smacked his hands down on the papers and smiled benignly up at the director. "Ah, ah, Harold. These aren't any of your business until I'm through. Confidentially, you know. You shouldn't even have seen them."

Dr. Burnham drew himself up and tried to look indignant. "As director of this hospital, I'm entitled to know everything that goes on here." He relaxed and grinned at Evan. "And besides, you'd have to bring it up at weekly conference anyway. This is a teaching hospital, remember?"

"Yeah." Evan looked sheepish. "It's hard to get over the private practice habits. Here. You can take one." He held the drawing of the pregnant horse out to Burnham.

"Thank you, Evan. Keep me informed." He took the picture and practically skipped out of the office.

Evan laughed quietly to himself as he watched the old man go. Burnham's enthusiasm and dedication were legendary, and he genuinely liked the man. And wouldn't it be something if he were right, he thought.

Burnham's last words nudged at him. Weekly conference was tomorrow, and he hadn't even begun to formulate his reports. He liked the sharing of information that went on here, as opposed to the strict secrecy that went on in most private practices. Dozens of well-trained minds working on a problem brought fresh ideas to situations that were complex and occasionally subjective in a science that was less than exact. And because of this, there was less chance of error of judgment in any given case. But it did take up a lot more time this way, and he hated the extra paperwork.

Sighing, he reached for one of his reports. He had fifteen minutes to work on it till his next appointment.

Chapter Seventeen

Bett finished brushing her teeth and half filled a glass with cold water. She hesitated, looking at the pill in her hand. Here goes, she thought, and swallowed it. She hated the idea of pills. It suggested a weakness in her somewhere. But she hated the dreams even more. She'd begun to think of them as a mental cancer, and she was almost anxious to see Dr. Tremayne again—have him exorcise the badness in her.

She went to bed with a small sense of relief, instead of her usual trepidation. This time she would not be bothered by dreams—Dr. Tremayne had promised. . . .

She had a lot of help this time. The tribe was growing; there had been many successful birthings in the past year, since so many of the hunters had achieved their maturity and taken wives. Of course this necessitated the building of more sleeping platforms, but it was a thing of joy to do. And she, with her swift, competent fingers, was chief weaver of the thatched roofs that capped the new homes needed by the fertile couples.

The men had worked hard the past few days too,

placing and stabilizing the logs that held the sleeping platforms high above the ground. The main supports had been dug deep into the forest floor and braced for strength. Then smaller trees had been lashed together in a square and firmly secured flat to the posts, forming a raised platform that would afford protection from sudden flooding or, more importantly, the dangerous animals that prowled the night in search of prey.

The platform held more supports, one on each corner and one in the center of each side, and saplings were soaked and bent to arch gracefully between them. The intricate dome created by this technique was then covered with thatch, tightly woven to keep out the hot sun and most of the rain that tore through their land during the rainy season.

It was this pleasant chore that she did now. The women who helped her chattered and gossiped between themselves as they worked, but kept one eye on her for her approval or instruction. She enjoyed her status in the tribe, and took pride in never making the mistake of misusing her power. She felt that it was her kindness and patience, in addition to her skill, that kept her place as head-female secure.

. The only unpleasantness in her life was Zeb-Zeb, the wife of Chug. Chug was best-hunter, and his arrogance was mimicked by his chosen woman.

Of course she, Tepi, was the chosen of Doga, the best-fisherman, and she refused to defer to Zeb-Zeb. Not that the tribe expected her to do so, in fact would have frowned upon it. There was no named leader in their society; all worked for the good of all, and major decisions were decided by lot. If some thought it was time to move to a new hunting-place, for instance, they would tell their thoughts at meeting. Those opposed would speak then, and the tribe would carefully consider all the words said. Then the speaking-sticks would be brought out, and every member of the tribe would cast either a long stick or a short stick, depending on whose words seemed most sensible, into the center of the meeting-circle. The side with the most sticks of their chosen length would prevail. There was never an argument after the sticks were tossed.

The only thing wrong with the system that Tepi could see was that when a child had lived through six rainy seasons, he or she was given the right to throw a stick. And since she'd noticed that children always went the way of their parents, and couples were usually in agreement, those with the most children-of-age usually swayed the decisions.

But perhaps this should be so, she thought as she flipped and twisted the thatch into a strong mat. After all, without the children the tribe would soon cease to exist, so those who were mostly responsible for the continuation of the tribe should be mostly responsible for the decisions. The only problem was, she thought, those who were the most fertile were not necessarily the wisest.

She sighed. Her brain was tired from so much thought. And it was not a real concern of hers anyway. She had six children-of-age, four more than Zeb-Zeb. It was another reason for the woman to hate her.

"Tepi-mada?"

Tepi looked down from the platform at the sound of the childish voice. Her youngest, a girl child who had just come of age smiled up at her. She motioned with her hand, and Ja-nee shinnied up the nearest post and flopped herself down near her mother's feet.

Tepi gave the child a few strands of grass to weave, and the child's fingers immediately began manipulating the strands into a passable net. The holes were too big, but she was still young and inexperienced. Tepi smiled and stroked the girl's dark hair. She heard a few of the women make noises of approval at Ja-nee's work, and her thoughts turned to Too-nee, her eldest. They had never made those sounds for Too-nee. "Ja-nee," she said to the child. "Where is Too-nee?"

"With Doga-mada and the brothers," she said simply. She didn't look up from her work.

Tepi sighed. Doga would make a boy-child out of the girl yet, she thought. She stood for a moment and considered what to do next. She decided. "Where are Doga-mada and the brothers?" she asked Ja-nee.

"At Great Pond, fishing," she answered.

"Stay with the women," she told the child, then quickly climbed down the wood ladder to the ground—a more decorous route than her daughter had chosen.

It was far to go, to the Great Pond—but perhaps her unexpected arrival there would make a point to Doga. The point being that she was angered with her husband's actions and she wished Too-nee to be treated as a female from this time on.

Tepi had been walking forever, it seemed. She was tired. And disappointed in herself. The last time she'd accompanied Doga to the Great Pond, just out of curiosity to see her nets in use against the big fish, she had walked by his side with little effort. Of course that had been many seasons ago. She wondered if the walk was now an effort for Doga too. She hoped not. It would not be good if he were asked to remain in camp to help the women, or only allowed to fish the small waters. Such requests were made out of consideration for the elderly, she knew, but many men spent their last days sulking in the shade of the trees, their pride wounded beyond healing. No amount of teasing or prodding, or offers of choice meats would stir them from their self-imposed exile. She hoped Doga would not be one of these men when it was his time to leave the big hunts to younger men.

She couldn't go any farther. Perhaps a short rest was all she needed. She climbed up into the safety of a many-branched tree and settled herself into a crook made by two of the highest, sturdy branches. She was asleep almost instantly.

Bett drifted slowly up from sleep. Vague images floated and shimmered through her reverie, and she tried to follow them as they slipped, one by one, into the dark, concealing foliage of the jungle. She reached out a hand and called after them to come back.

A stab of pain shot through her outstretched hand and jerked her awake. The shadowy images disappeared as her eyes focused on reality—on the object she'd slammed with her hand—the steering wheel of her Buick.

Bett struggled to a sitting position and massaged her injured hand. She felt confused, disoriented. What the hell am I doing in my car, she wondered fuzzily. I'm still dreaming. Must be.

She looked down at herself in the dim, predawn light and giggled. She was in her nightgown. The white one with the pink flowers at the neckline. And she had shoes on. She picked up one foot to see better. Her black high-heels. Should be slippers, she thought . . . it would go better with the nightgown.

Suddenly her head cleared. She glanced out the car window in sudden panic. This all felt too real. Where in God's name was she? It looked like a parking lot! She strained her eyes into the dark. A mall. The La Citrona Mall, for Christ's sake! At least twenty miles south of Las Flores!

Shaking with fear, she fumbled for the car keys and thankfully found them still in the ignition. It took three tries for her to start the engine. Slowly, she drove out onto the deserted highway.

Evan tapped a pencil on his desk as he listened to Bett's rambling, often incoherent narrative of her som-nambulism. She broke down into tears twice, and he waited while her husband comforted her back to a calmer state.

Ray was grim-faced. He'd awakened before dawn and had spent two frantic, terrified hours before his wife finally appeared in the driveway, badly shaken and babbling about jungles and huts and children. He'd called the hospital's emergency service number, and they'd called Evan. After determining that she was physically unharmed and back in touch with real-ity, he'd told Ray to bring his wife in at seven o'clock that morning.

Sleepwalking was a common phase of night terrors, Evan thought as he listened to Bett, but Bett's amazing recall of the dream state during her episode was extraordinary, to say the least. The details she'd recounted were far beyond what most people could recall, and he wondered if she was embellishing or filling in fuzzy gaps—consciously or unconsciously.

Even more curious was that the dream made sense. There was a normal, logical progression to it that was abnormal to most dreams. Most dreams were erratic. Scenes and people were jumbled together in sequences that were incoherent and illogical upon awakening. This was too pat. And most intriguing—it seemed to be a continuation of the dream that Bett had reported in their last session.

Bett was finished. She sat gripping Ray's hand and staring at Evan. "What's happening to me?" she whispered.

Evan dropped the pencil on the desk and leaned toward them, clasping his hands in an unconscious pleading gesture. "We have a very advanced sleep lab here, Bett. Will you spend a few days with us? We'll continue our previously planned evaluations during the day, then hook you up to an electroencephalograph at night. Don't look so alarmed." Evan grinned at her. "It doesn't hurt ... I guarantee it. And it might give us some valuable insight into your sleep patterns."

"At this point I think I'd try anything," Bett answered, and Ray gave her hand an assenting squeeze.

"Good," Evan said. "Go home and pack some clothes and essentials for a few days' stay, then come back. We'll get started right away." Evan stood up and glanced at his watch, ending the interview. It was eight o'clock.

Bett and Ray left Evan's office. A woman and a little girl sat in the waiting room, and Bett heard the nurse

103

say, "You can go in now, Mrs. Matthews." The woman said, "Come on . . . , Ja-nee . . . Ja-nee. . . ."

Ja-nee . . . Ja—! Bett turned toward the child, held out her arms . . . and collapsed in a heap on the floor.

Chapter Eighteen

It was getting late and they hadn't seen a goddamned thing that even remotely resembled Archaeopteryx, Jake thought irritably. He glanced over at Ralph. Ralph seemed contented with the trip so far. He'd snapped about a dozen rolls of film, and he had a perpetual smile on his face. Sighing loudly, he raised his arms over his head and stretched. He was stiff from sitting in the boat all day and was even beginning to look forward to getting out and walking around on one of the damned chikees again.

"Gator, left," Charlie said, and Jake put his arms down and looked with disinterest at what seemed to him to be the zillionth alligator of the day. The first few had been interesting enough, but they never did anything more exciting than lie motionless on the mud flats or sink quietly underwater without a ripple.

Suddenly his attention sharpened. This one looked different, but it was too far away to see it clearly. Maybe it was a croc. Crocodiles were rare in the Glades—and dangerous. Good. A little excitement, he thought—and he raised his binoculars.

He adjusted the focus. Stopped breathing. "Charlie,"

he whispered. He dug his fingernails into Charlie's shoulder, never taking the glasses from his eyes.

"OW!" Charlie yelped. "Hey, man!"

"Follow it," Jake said. His voice caught on the "it."

"What?" Charlie reached up an pried Jake's fingers off his shoulder.

"FOLLOW IT! LEFT! LEFT!"

Startled, Ralph half stood in the boat, craning his neck and peering through his own binoculars to see what Jake was screaming about.

Jake watched the animal glide at an angle away from them. Charlie swung around and tried to head it off. Jake grabbed the side of the boat for balance. "Come on . . . come on," he said softly.

A long, narrow nose cut the water. But the beast's nostrils weren't at the tip of the snout like a gator's or croc's; instead, they sat far back on the head near the eyes. Jake readjusted the focus. Trick of light . . . must be, he thought. Or Evan's drawing had been accurate. He realized he hadn't believed it until this moment.

Suddenly it dove. Jake caught a glimpse of backplates glinting in the setting sun as the animal disappeared beneath the surface of the water. *Damn! Damn!* They'd lost it!

Charlie idled the motor, and Jake strained to see the spot where the animal had disappeared. Gone. He dropped the binoculars back on his chest and twisted around toward Ralph.

"Did you *see* it!" he shouted. "Ralph! Did you *see* it!"

Ralph looked stunned. "I . . . I can't be sure. . . ."

"Jesus, Ralph!" Jake was grinning so hard that his cheeks hurt. "It was a *thecodont!* A goddamned, living . . . breathing . . . THECODONT!"

"Well . . . ," Ralph said, then looked around as if the creature would magically appear again to verify Jake's claim.

"DAMMIT! I know what I saw!"

"Jake," Ralph said calmly. "Thecodonts have been extinct for about a hundred and eighty million years."

"Archaeopteryx has been extinct for a hundred and thirty million years, and you're out here looking for *it!*" Jake came back at him. "There's something I have to tell you," he added more calmly. "Something I didn't mention before because I didn't think it had much merit." He told him about the picture Evan's patient had drawn.

Jenner listened intently, and finally nodded his acceptance of Jake's story. "Some sort of Phytosaur, I'd say . . . ," Ralph mumbled. "Maybe later . . . maybe Rutiodon," he added, turning to look back out over the waterway with an intense expression of concentration.

"HAH!" Jake shouted. "Okay! We're together on this! Charlie, I think it went that way." He pointed to a darkening sliver of water to the left. "Let's go."

"No way, man. We head for the chikee. No way I'm getting caught out here in the dark with some prehistoric monster. I think you guys are nuts, but I don't take any chances. Uh-uh!" Charlie revved up the boat's engine and cut a straight line through the water.

Jake couldn't believe his ears. "Are you crazy! That could be the find of a century back there! A *millennium!*" He grabbed Charlie's arm. "Turn it around, man!"

Charlie shook off his hand and kept going. "Not in the dark," he insisted.

"He's right, Jake," Ralph shouted over the sound of the engines. "We'd never find it now anyway . . . not in

107

this weak light. And besides, we promised to keep to Charlie's safety rules, remember? Remember why we have a special permit? It's entirely possible that the creature we just saw was responsible for those deaths, and going after it under these circumstances would be foolhardy."

Jake grumbled under his breath all the way to the chikee. He consoled himself with the fact that they were at least in the ancient animal's territory.

The three men hauled the food, equipment, and sleeping bags up the chikee stairs, and Charlie handed out sandwiches, Taco chips, and soft drinks as soon as they were settled.

Cool breezes shifted and flowed through the open sides of the chikee as they ate and talked, the scientists excitedly throwing theories back and forth, and at one point Charlie got up and lit a Coleman lantern. And the night noises began.

"A hundred dollars a day is fine, Charlie," Ralph was saying now. "But we'll need a bigger boat . . . with its own portable toilet, if possible. I understand there aren't any chikees where we'll be going, and I don't relish urinating over the side of the boat, or squatting in the brush."

Charlie opened his mouth, but Ralph waved a hand at him. "I know, I know . . . that'll be extra. That's fine. Can't be helped." He took another bite of his ham and cheese sandwich and kept talking between chews. "I'll need a week or so to prepare . . . wire in some of my private funds. We'll want to be out here at least two weeks . . . have to stock up on food, camera equipment, collapsible specimen cages, tranquilizer guns—"

"Whoa!" Charlie said. "Check with Park services on all that! I don't want to lose my license for—"

"Already did. Already did," Ralph said impatiently. "All the necessary permits have been cleared ahead of time with the National Park Service through the Harcourt Research Institute of Paleontology. They're all aware of the possibly incredible ramifications of this expedition."

"What do you think you saw?" Charlie interrupted. "I couldn't follow your jargon. It just looked like an alligator."

Ralph looked pleased at the question and cleared his throat for one of his lectures. Jake groaned and Ralph gave him a sharp look.

"I'll keep it short, Charlie, since I don't want to bore my more learned constituent."

"Hey, don't leave anything out on my account," Jake grinned. "I was only kidding."

"Yes. Well." Ralph, appeased, turned his attention back to Charlie. "Thecodontians, which simply means by the way, 'socket-toothed' reptiles, were the direct forerunners of all the dinosaurs . . . and today's crocodiles. They were what we call archosaurs . . . latter members of the Diapsid or 'two skull hole' reptiles. They lived in the upper Permian through the Triassic Period, about two hundred and twenty-five million years ago, and they were carnivores. And they were rather formidable creatures. All the other reptiles that lived around those times were 'sprawlers.' The configuration of their legs allowed them to only plod along . . . not very efficient. A thecodont on the other hand, could stride from its hips instead of its knees . . . like a crocodile. It made them much faster . . . and deadlier."

Charlie leaned toward Ralph, obviously interested.

"And these thecodonts—they looked like today's gators and crocs?"

"Quite a bit," Ralph answered.

Jake left the two still talking and threw himself down on his bedroll. He turned his head away from the light and stared out at the primeval jungle that rang with the sound of insects, birds, and night-prowling animals that ruled the dark. How much different was all this from what it looked like millions of years ago, he wondered? He'd have to ask Ralph about the flora. He wouldn't be surprised if mangroves were around that long ago. They looked ancient enough to be part of a prehistoric landscape.

"Hey."

A dark form knelt next to Jake, his outline barely visible so far away from the lamplight.

"Yeah, Charlie?"

"This is big news, huh?"

"Could be."

"I get my name in the papers?"

Jake propped up on an elbow to get eye level with the Indian. "Only if we're the first ones to come out with the news . . . which means keeping your mouth shut while we prepare for the next expedition. No reporters yet, Charlie. Comprende?"

White teeth exposed. "You got it, man." He crept away, whistling softly to himself.

Jake eased himself into a comfortable, prone position and closed his eyes. What *were* the implications here? First a supposed sighting of Archaeopteryx, supposedly long extinct. And now this—a confirmed sighting of a thecodont. And he'd seen this one for himself. It made the first claim more feasible, didn't it? What the hell was going on? He was still running the unanswerable questions through his mind when he fell asleep.

Something chasing him . . . pawing at him . . . legs wouldn't run . . . closer . . . gripping his face . . . fight!

Jake bolted awake, his heart pounding. A dream! God! For a moment he was disoriented, not sure where he was. It came back to him in a rush, and he looked over at Ralph and Charlie, who were stirring restlessly in their sleep, as if they too were in the grip of bad dreams. Had something disturbed all of them? It was all he had time to think about before it happened.

The shriek that drowned out all the other night sounds was no more than five feet from Jake's ear. With an instinct born of pure and instant terror, Jake rolled away from the edge of the chikee. Something slammed down on the platform, the boards he'd been lying on cracked under the force of it, and Jake screamed. So did something else. Again. Louder.

"SCREEE-EEEEE-EEEK SCREEE-EEEK!"

"RALPH!" Jake yelled, but Ralph and Charlie were already awake. And they were screaming too, their screams almost drowned out by the maniacal shrieking of the thing that was trying to pound the chikee into splinters.

There was just enough starlight to see outlines. Jake threw himself at the Coleman lantern, catching it a second before it toppled off under the beating that the platform was taking. He fumbled matches out of his pocket and tried to light it. *Night thing!* his terrified brain babbled. *Night thing!* Scare it with light! He heard Charlie shout . . . heard the crack of a rifle. No! No! Don't want a wounded beast! Oh, God. He dropped the match . . .

hands shaking too hard. Horrible shriek! Charlie must have hit it! *"Don't shoot!"* he shouted. Another match . . . careful. There!

He turned the lamp on high and rolled over, holding it out in front of him like a talisman. And he didn't believe his eyes.

A massive, birdlike head weaved and bobbed over the edge of the chikee. It snapped an enormous, parrot beak in the air, obviously enraged by the shot that had drawn blood near its left eye. The blood spattered Jake's arms as he crawled to his feet and waved the lantern at the great head. He took a step toward the thing, his arms stretched out as far as possible in front of him. He was calm now . . . didn't know why. Shock, probably, a rational part of his brain said disinterestedly. Closer.

It snapped at him, but drew back. He could hear it stamping in the mud and water, and it let loose another horrible shriek.

"JAKE! NO!" Ralph screaming at him. "NOOO-OOO!" Charlie, screaming louder. Getting off another shot. *Don't worry, guys . . . I'll fix everything.* Another step.

SHRIEEEEK!

And it ducked.

Jake stumbled to the edge of the chikee and held the lantern high, expecting to see the creature hauling ass away from the light and the rifle.

It came up under the chikee. The night was filled with the sounds of cracking boards, people screaming and above it all, the high, angry screeching of the monster that was demolishing the platform.

The spot Jake was balanced on buckled, and he felt himself slipping toward the edge. He dropped the lantern and threw himself toward the center of the chikee,

112

his hands grabbing frantically for any hold. The boards were slick, and he went over the side. The warm water closed over his head as he splashed into the shallow river. He was up and scrambling in seconds, not sure which direction to take to avoid the stamping feet of the enraged bird. He wanted to scream again . . . didn't dare. If he was lucky, the damned thing didn't know he was down here yet!

He could see the shoreline, and he headed for it, praying that Ralph and Charlie would get away too. He didn't hear either one of them over the insistent squawks of the bird, and the thought came to him that as long as the thing was making noise, it wasn't eating.

It stopped making noise.

"Shit!" Jake said softly, and turned his head to see, ready to go back and fight if he had to. He saw a massive open beak swooping straight down at him.

Jake dove. His hands hit bottom in no time, and he knew it was no good. Not deep enough to get away!

It caught him by the shirt and belt, a surprisingly delicate grip that startled Jake almost as much as realizing he was nabbed. And then he was lifted, as easily as a robin pulls a worm from the ground.

The rifle shot cracked out through the now eerily quiet night.

The great bird jerked and leaped, and opened its beak to shriek again.

Jake hit the water a second time, and this time he was happy about it. The river bottom shook under the stamping of the huge beast, and then as suddenly as it had appeared, it fled, back toward shore and away from the frustration of dealing with prey that fought back. It shook its head and flapped seemingly useless wings as it crashed into the jungle of the near island. They heard one last, angry screech before everything dissolved back into the relative silence of a normal Everglades night.

"JAKE! JAKE!"

It was Ralph's voice, and Jake found himself laughing, silly with relief. "I'm okay! Charlie?"

"Hey! I saved your life, man!" Charlie's voice came back. He sounded as giddy as Jake felt.

The two men appeared from the backside of the demolished chikee, and together, the three of them waded toward the boat and clambered aboard. It listed badly to port, and Charlie cursed "the damned canary" steadily as he tried to inspect the damage by moonlight.

Finally he said, "Thing must've stepped on it. We can't use it like this. I can jerry-rig it as soon as it gets light. What in holy hell *was* that thing, Doc Ralph? Looked like a ten-foot parrot. Never seen anything like it. Another one of your theco-whatsits? I'll say one thing . . . you guys sure aren't boring me."

Danger had made Charlie voluble, and Jake and Ralph looked at him in surprise.

"More like seven feet, I would guess," Ralph answered. "Diatryma didn't exceed seven feet."

"This one did," Jake said, instantly accepting the older man's label. He'd come to that same conclusion himself. "Charlie's right. Hell, I'd guess that thing was over ten feet."

"Fossil records—"

"Are incomplete at best. Come on, Ralph. Just because we never *found* anything over seven feet doesn't mean it didn't exist."

Ralph considered this, then agreed. "Charlie, how long do you think it will take you to fix things?"

Charlie put his hands on his hips and looked toward shore. "If your monster doesn't come back and kill us first, I'd say a few hours, as soon as I can see well enough to work. Too bad we lost that lantern, Jake."

"Good," Ralph said calmly. "That will give Jake and me some time to explore the island. That is, if you won't need us."

"We have one rifle. I think we should stay together," Charlie answered. "To tell the truth, I'd like to get the hell out of here now."

"You said—," Jake began.

"Yeah. Can't. Even if this tub was in one piece, we couldn't likely navigate out of here at night."

"I suggest we all get some sleep," Ralph said. "I suppose we'll be as safe as anywhere else if we stay on the boat." He didn't sound at all sure.

"We'll take turns standing watch," Jake said. "I'll take the first two hours."

Charlie and Ralph settled themselves as comfortably as they could, and Jake sat with the rifle over his knees, watching the dark shadows on the island.

Chapter Nineteen

When Ralph touched him on the shoulder, Jake came instantly awake. His first thought was *danger*.

"It's light," Ralph said, and Jake relaxed. The night had passed safely.

Jake and Ralph waded out to retrieve what they could of their equipment from the wreckage of the chikee while Charlie took a hammer from the underbench emergency tool kit. The crushed side of the aluminum boat dipped crazily down into the water, and Charlie cursed mildly as he tried hammering it back in shape.

It didn't help Jake's mood any to think about the sharks and barracuda they'd been warned about as he kicked his way through the shallow water, feeling for submerged equipment with his feet. Then the thought of what they'd been up against the night before made the prospect of encountering sharks and barracuda seem tame. He almost smiled.

Those lesser threats stayed away, however, and finally, when Jake and Ralph had salvaged all they could, they went back to the boat and a disgruntled Charlie. Charlie was obviously unhappy.

"I dunno," he said to Jake, who had just tossed a

plastic cooler he'd found into the boat. "Looks pretty bad. But even if it doesn't hold up, we can probably limp in."

"Peanut butter and jelly," Ralph said, peering into the cooler. "The bread is soaked."

Jake waded to the side of the boat. "Well, that's all that's salvageable."

"They're insured," Charlie said. "Let's go."

"No."

Jake and Charlie looked at Ralph.

"I want to look around on the island first."

Charlie exploded. "No way! You're nuts! And my say-so is law around here, *mister!*"

"We can come back when we're better prepared," Jake said mildly.

Ralph, with a determined smile of conviction, jumped back into the water and waded toward shore. "You'll have to carry me on board, gentlemen!" he shouted over his shoulder. "And be forewarned, I intend to put up a fight!"

"Shit," Jake mumbled.

In the end, the two younger men followed Ralph to the island.

"An hour. Just an hour," Charlie said for the third time as they pushed their way through the tangle of palm, shrub, and vine.

They heard them before they saw them, a medley of hisses and barks that sounded like a pack of dogs squaring off with a pond full of alligators.

Feeling as if every ounce of common sense had deserted him, Jake crept toward the sounds. Ralph and Charlie, their faces mirroring Jake's with a combination of excitement, curiosity, and fear, followed close behind him.

There were nine of them in a small clearing, squabbling over the remains of a wild pig.

Jake heard the two sharp intakes of breath from behind him as he sank to a low crouch behind a thick stand of palmetto to watch.

The smallest was about four feet long from nose to tail tip, the largest over ten feet. The reptilian bodies were long and slim, the tail taking up half the body length. They walked on their hind legs, and did little hop-dances of aggression as they fought over the pig. The front legs were short in contrast to the back legs, and occasionally one would kick out at a herd-mate with a lethal-looking hind claw. But it was sham, Jake realized. They never connected.

It was the head that appeared most dangerous. Long and narrow, the jaws were crammed with sharp teeth. Even from the long distance between them, Jake could see the cutting, serrated edges of those teeth.

"Mother of God," Charlie whispered behind him. "What are they?"

"Coelophysis," Ralph whispered back.

"What?"

Jake turned around to look into Charlie's awestruck face. "Dinosaurs," he said.

Charlie looked back at the beasts. "Why aren't I more surprised?" He should have whispered.

A large Coelophysis raised his bloody snout from the pig and stared in their direction, then raised up high on his hind legs and bleated a warning cry.

Jake hoped like hell he was warning his herd-mates, and not them.

The herd was instantly alert.

So were the three men.

The reptiles moved cautiously toward the men, as if they were of one mind, heads high and tails whipping.

"Shoot over their heads," Jake said calmly to Charlie. Charlie did. They kept coming.

"Shit!" Charlie yelled, and his next shot hit one of the smaller dinosaurs square in the chest. It rocked back on its hind legs with a bark of surprise, but it didn't go down. Blood poured from the wound.

"Go for the boat," Jake ordered. "Run like hell and don't look back. And pray that these guys hate the water."

"Wait," Jenner said. "Look."

The largest dinosaur had turned to his wounded herd mate. In a lightning fast move, he grabbed the bleeding reptile by the throat and bore the smaller animal to the ground. In an instant the whole herd was on the victim. It was over without a struggle, and now the sounds of tearing flesh melded with the other jungle sounds of birds and frogs and insects.

"We always surmised that coelophysis were cannibalistic," Ralph said, never taking his eyes off the ugly scene.

"Let's go before they start looking around for dessert," Jake said.

The boat handled reasonably well, but Charlie kept at a slow pace to lessen the stress on the damaged pontoon.

"This is incredible, truly incredible," Ralph kept muttering. He looked thoroughly delighted.

"What's going on here, Doc?" Charlie asked.

Jake answered for him. "The impossible. These animals should have been extinct millions of years ago. I

119

sure as hell can't believe they've been here all along and nobody has noticed them till now, either."

"I would hazard a guess that some sort of reverse evolution has taken place here."

"It's a good theory, Ralph," Jake agreed. "It makes more sense than saying, 'Oh, look what we just now noticed!' But if it's true, what could have triggered it? These things just don't 'happen.'"

"I have absolutely no idea," Ralph admitted. "But I intend to find out. And I intend to bring back and study some live specimens."

Chapter Twenty

She'd had fun today. Playing all those games. And everybody talked to her. All day. She never once had to be by herself. She liked Dr. Tremayne. Her mother liked him too. She could tell. But it was hard to tell if he liked her mother back. She knew he liked her, Jenny. She was sorry she couldn't draw the pictures he wanted, though. But he didn't seem to mind.

Humming to herself, Jenny skipped into the kitchen where her mother was making dinner.

Lydia smiled at her. "Will you set the table for me, honey?"

"Yes," she said and pulled the kitchen stool up to the cabinet where her mother kept the white Melmac dishes—the ones with the blue design around the edges. Her mother said they were flowers, but they didn't look like flowers to her.

"How 'bout some fresh lettuce from the garden?" Lydia asked, turning from where she was slicing tomatoes into wedges, then in thirds, just the way Jenny liked them.

"Yes! Yes! Please!" Jenny said, and clapped her hands. She loved the soft-leaved stuff her mother grew.

It was much better than the hard-ball kind that came wrapped in plastic from the supermarket.

"And basil?" Lydia asked.

Jenny made a face and Lydia laughed. "Okay, I'll leave it off yours."

The kitchen door swung shut behind Lydia, and Jenny carefully placed the plates on the table, then ran to dig knives, forks, and spoons out of the silverware drawer.

Something smelled delicious.

She held the silverware in both hands and pushed the drawer shut with her chest. On the kitchen counter right in front of her were the raw flounder filets that her mother was going to fry up for dinner. To the left of the fish, Lydia had put a paper plate full of seasoned flour; a bowl of buttermilk with a beaten egg in it, and another paper plate filled with dry bread crumbs. She knew how to do it. She'd watched her mother plenty of times. She'd help.

Jenny put the silverware on the kitchen counter and picked up one of the flounder strips. "First the flour," she said out loud, and plopped the fish into the first plate. Flour puffed into the air and she stepped back for a second. Then she reached for it again with one hand and put the fingers of her other hand unconsciously in her mouth to suck off the flour residue.

The raw fish taste slid down her throat with the flour, and saliva suddenly filled her mouth. She picked up the filet and bit into it. Chewed. Swallowed. It was the best thing she'd ever tasted.

She was reaching for the second piece when her mother came through the kitchen door with a handful of greens.

* * *

122

Jenny wiggled around in the chair while she listened to her mother tell Dr. Tremayne about the fish. Why was she so upset? It wasn't like she ate ants or anything, like she did when she was little. Her mother had been upset about that too. She liked the chairs in Dr. Tremayne's office. They were big and soft, and they made crackling noises when you moved around in them. Like now. And if you bounced a little, they made a *whooshing*—

"Jenny, sit still!"

Startled, Jenny stopped bouncing and sank back into the chair, her eyes on her mother. Her mother yelled a lot lately.

"Jenny."

Dr. Tremayne was talking to her and she turned her attention to him.

"Why did you eat raw fish?" he asked kindly.

She shrugged.

"Were you very hungry?"

"No, sir." Quick glance at her mother. "It smelled good."

Evan watched her for a moment. "Would you like to go play with Miss Alice again while I talk to your mother?" he finally asked.

"Okay."

Jenny watched Dr. Tremayne push a button on a box on his desk and talk into it, and in a minute Miss Alice was there smiling at her. She slid off the chair and put her hand in Miss Alice's. They both skipped down the hall to the playroom.

Evan picked up a thick sheaf of papers and tapped the edges on the desk, evening them out, then looked up at Lydia. "These are Jenny's test results. Her psychological evaluation, Wechsler, and medical tests are normal.

No, I take that back . . . a lot of this," he held up the papers, "shows that she's well above normal in many respects. She's a remarkably intelligent and well-adjusted little girl. And there's nothing in her or your family medical histories that would explain any of her recent problems, either."

"What are you saying?" Lydia asked. A cold feeling began creeping up her arms and she shivered. How could such positive words sound so ominous?

"I'm saying that we can't find anything psychologically or physiologically wrong with Jenny."

"Then what's happening to her?"

Evan got up and walked around to the front of the desk. He perched on the edge and looked down at her. "Dr. Burnham, our director, has a theory."

"Dr. Burnham?"

"Yes. He's a neuroscientist. An expert in the field of biochemistry. And genetics."

"Genetics?" *Oh, God. It was worse than she'd thought!*

"Yes. And he has a theory that Jenny's problems might have something to do with a genetic malfunction."

"Is it curable?" *Just say yes. All I want to hear is a simple yes.*

"I can't tell you if something is curable or not when I don't know exactly what the problem is yet," Evan answered. "But I can assure you that if Jenny's problem is genetic, there's nobody in the country who's more qualified to help her than Dr. Burnham. Do I have your permission to turn Jenny's case over to him?"

Lydia started to cry softly, but kept her eyes on Evan. "Yes," she said. It was an effort to get the word out.

Evan reacted on impulse; he knelt next to her chair

124

and put an arm around her shoulders. She twisted toward him and wrapped her arms around his neck. He held her for a long time while she cried.

Lydia liked Dr. Burnham too. He reminded her of everybody's grandfather, and Jenny obviously shared her opinion; she was happily sitting on his lap while she "read" a book.

Evan sat in a corner and watched them. Lydia had insisted that he remain in a consulting capacity even though Jenny was now officially Burnham's patient. He'd been more than happy to agree. And not only for professional reasons, if he wanted to admit it to himself. Both of them, Jenny and Lydia, had struck a deep chord in him, and he didn't want to let it go.

"So you see, Lydia," Harold was saying in his mellow, fluid voice, "I believe that we all, each and every one of us, has buried deep within our brains the vestiges of learning and memory handed down to us by our remote ancestors. And not so remote ancestors, too. For instance, you say Jenny's father was a renowned artist?"

"Yes."

Lydia was relaxed now. The easygoing, friendly attitude Harold Burnham displayed to his patients often did that to people, and Evan envied his technique. He watched her lean forward in her chair, fascinated by the old man.

"And Jenny shows remarkable ability along those lines, yes?" He didn't wait for confirmation, but kept talking. "Could it be her environment, her early exposure to the artistic creativity of her father? Many diligent parents expose their children to fine classical music even while the babes are still in the womb, and do we get Mozarts? Young Beethovens by the drove? No. No, we don't."

"Then it's heredity, right?" Lydia asked.

Jenny, bored now, wiggled off the scientists's lap and ran over to Evan. Flattered, he let the little girl climb in his lap. She cuddled in and let her eyes droop sleepily, then fought to keep them open. Evan wondered at her apparent ease with Dr. Burnham and himself. Were there any men in her life that she could relate to, or was she looking for a father substitute in them?

"I think heredity plays a large part in people's natural abilities, yes," Burnham was saying. "Just as they inherit brown eyes, skin color, or a propensity for certain diseases."

Lydia looked confused. "But not all children inherit their parents' talents," she said. "If they did, wouldn't we have a lot more great minds and great artists in the world than we do?"

Burnham smiled at her, pleased with her apparent interest in his favorite subject. "Ah, but here's where my theories come in. They do have the talents, I think. But they lack the ability of genetic recall for reasons as yet unknown to us. And some people, like Jenny, do have the ability . . . witness her father's artistic creativity . . . obviously within her recall . . . not latent as it is in most people."

He got up and began to pace, obviously excited by the concept he was trying to explain. "And here's the thrilling part! Jenny has proved her ability not only for recent genetic recall, but she seems to have tapped into a deeper part of the brain, which I believe is based in the hippocampus, that is pulling up ancient memories passed on to her from her distant ancestors!"

"My God," Lydia said, fascinated.

"Yes, yes! Witness her cave-type drawings! Obviously a talent passed on through generations of artists! Her father had the ability to draw on primitive genetic memory too! And I believe he passed the gene responsible for this ability on to his daughter . . . and the gene seems to have strengthened in her . . . perhaps evolved into a dominant gene!"

"Why Jenny?" Lydia asked. "Why can't everybody do this?"

"This is what my research is all about," Burnham answered. "This type of thing seems to be more prevalent in lower orders of animals . . . for instance a chicken. As soon as a chick hatches, it will run in terror from the shadow of a hawk on the ground. The shadow of any other bird will have little effect on it. It's drawing on genetic memory, brought about by years of ancestral awareness that a hawk represents danger. It doesn't have to be taught.

"People, however, seem to have for the most part lost this ability. Perhaps prehistoric members of our species had it, but centuries of civilization and the day-to-day pressures it has put on our brains have sublimated the ability. But it's there! People like Jenny prove it!"

Lydia glanced over at her daughter. Jenny was sound asleep on Evan's lap. And the obvious look of contentment on the doctor's face as he looked down at the little girl surprised her. She turned back to the scientist. "This is all fascinating, Dr. Burnham, but it's disrupting Jenny's life. What can you do about it?"

"First we have to make sure that this is really what's happening. As Dr. Tremayne told you, I'd like to do some genetic testing on Jenny . . . simple, noninvasive tests for the most part . . . except for a small blood and skin sample. Dr. Frankel, my coresearcher in genetic re-

127

search, will do the actual electrophoretic and immunological analyses ... he's head of a very advanced genetic testing and research laboratory in La Citrona.

"And we'll do an antigen-antibody test ... microcomplementation can detect the differences in a single amino acid ... and she'll have to go to La Citrona for some of that, and for the Magnetic Resonance test; our machine is undergoing repairs. And perhaps I can persuade Dr. Tremayne to accompany you as an observer ... and for moral support." He smiled over at Evan.

"I don't understand most of what you've said, Dr. Burnham," Lydia said. "But I feel better knowing that there seems to be so much you can do ... I was afraid that it was hopeless. . . ."

"Not at all! Not at all! Your daughter has a wonderful gift! When we know more, it may be simply a matter of a slight genetic alteration ..." Evan looked at him sharply, but Burnham ignored him. ". . . or medication ... or simple megavitamin therapy coupled with medication, to bring her back to normal. Not that I'm making any guarantees though, you understand."

"I think so. But I have one more question."

"Ask away." Burnham was beaming.

"What do you think caused this in Jenny?"

Burnham sighed. "Hard to say. According to the questionnaire you filled out, there was no birth trauma, no lack of oxygen during labor ... she wasn't premature or underweight ... has never had an illness that subjected her to high fever ... no known viral infections ..." He paused and seemed to consider the problem. "The only thing left that I can think of," he finally said, "is some sort of gene-altering exposure to radiation. A dose that wouldn't affect most people, but

128

because of her particular inherited genetic makeup, would have caused a slight genetic malfunction."

"Like cancer?"

Smart, Evan thought. Let's see you get out of this one, Harold.

Burnham looked uncomfortable. "In a sense, yes," he answered honestly. "And like a lot of cancer, treatable. I don't believe that this particular type of malfunction is fatal. Disruptive, yes . . . but the diseases are really unrelated, I believe."

Lydia looked relieved. "If it isn't a cancer, what do you call what Jenny has?"

Burnham put on a serious face, but his excitement glittered in his eyes. "I think Jenny is evidencing signs of what my colleague Dr. Frankel and I call the *Genesis Gene*."

"*Alter* her *genes,* Harold? *Megavitamins?* What the hell—" Evan was furious.

"Now, now, Evan." Burnham sat furiously filling in notes on the edges of Jenny's charts as Evan leaned over the desk trying to get his full attention. "We have to keep Lydia calm . . . have to keep her confidence in us—"

"You were feeding her *crap!* You don't have any *idea* how to treat—"

"I beg your pardon." Burnham looked up from the charts, obviously offended. "I . . . and Dr. Frankel . . . have some very good ideas on how to treat Jenny. If she truly possesses the Genesis Gene."

Evan fought back his rage. "You mean *experiment* on her. That's what you mean by gene altering, isn't it, Harold? If I'd had any idea that that was your intention

I never would have let you have this case. As a matter of fact—"

"And what would you have done, Evan?" Burnham asked coldly. "Let her sink deeper into the past? Watched while the activated gene stole the present from her consciousness and reduced her to a permanent prehistoric state of mind? That's what's happening, Evan. That's how this gene works. Unfortunately. Once it's activated, it's progressive. If you'd read my thesis you'd know that."

"Hypothetical."

"No. We've isolated it in a gel matrix. A particular strain of Rhesus monkeys came to Dr. Frankel's attention several years ago. When the newborns were separated from their mothers at birth, for reasons that don't matter now, they showed remarkable evidence of normally learned behavior . . . behavior that in their case would have been absent, given their restricted environment. He abandoned the original study and did extensive genetic testing on them. Their genetic pattern was different from the rest of their species; one small mutation in the normal DNA sequence allowed them to behave as if they'd learned normal monkey behavior from their mothers . . . which of course they had not. But the behavior was deeply imprinted in this usually dormant gene, and they had the uncanny ability to utilize the knowledge. And I think the same thing has happened to Jenny."

Fascinated now, Evan leaned toward Burnham. "What made this group of monkeys different in the first place?" he asked. "What original experiment were they bred for?"

Burnham looked uncomfortable. "It doesn't matter. The variable, which I think is what you're really asking me about, was exposure to a rare, particular type of radiation recently discovered to be present during the thinning of the ozone layer. Frankel was testing the hazardous effects of this type of radiation on newborn monkeys ... with government approval, of course. It could become a problem in the future, you realize, if this type—"

"Yes, of course," Evan interrupted, not wanting to get into a long discussion on environmental issues. "The Genesis Gene ... did it have any adverse, long-term effects?"

"It grows, Evan. Like cancer ... in spite of what I told Mrs. Matthews. And don't forget it's been several years since my initial observations were published. Dr. Frankel and I have made great strides since then." Burnham stopped writing in margins and looked up at Evan. His face radiated disappointment. "Those monkeys all died, Evan. If they died because of the Genesis Gene, and not because of the radiation exposure, we're that little girl's only hope," he said softly.

Evan stared at him, chilled. A core part of him, on a deep, instinctive level, screamed a warning.

Chapter Twenty-one

A whole free weekend to catch up on his reports. Without interruption. Nirvana. Evan tossed the stuffed briefcase on the glass-topped coffee table in his den and stretched the tension out of his muscles. First a cool shower . . . no . . . first a swim, then a warm shower . . . then a drink, a quick dinner . . . maybe just a steak and salad. Then the reports.

He wished he'd had the nerve to ask Lydia out for dinner. She and Jenny weren't his patients anymore, so he wouldn't be breaking any cardinal doctor-patient rules.

Maybe she already had a boyfriend. Stupid designation for males in our age group, he thought. Must be a better word. He couldn't think of one.

The phone rang and Evan groaned. Not an emergency, please, he begged silently. It was Jake.

"Where are you?" Evan asked, suddenly wanting company and hoping Jake was on his way in. Screw the reports . . . he needed to talk to somebody who wasn't steeped in problems for a change. All work and no play, etc., etc . . .

"I'm on Route 41." Jake's voice boomed over the

phone. "About forty minutes away ... had to stop and call ... make sure you didn't take off for the evening with some hot-for-your-body gorgeous female that you've been hiding from me before I got there.

"Pour me a drink and boil a pot of water. I'm bringing in a couple dozen live blue crabs and they're the biggest, most beautiful bunch of Jimmies you ever saw ... and wait till you hear what I've got to tell you ... never mind, I'll save it. Gotta see your face when I lay it on you!" He hung up.

Evan grinned at the dial tone. Jake's enthusiasm was infectious—just what he needed right now. Somebody to drag his mind away from psychiatry, illness, dull reports ... and Burnham. Good old Jake.

He dragged his crab pot out from under the recess of a little-used bottom kitchen cabinet, half filled it with water, and put it on a cold stove burner. Then he took a plastic bag of coleslaw out of the refrigerator and stirred in a few tablespoons of premixed dressing. Whistling, he stuck it back in the refrigerator to chill. Ready for you, Jake, he thought happily and headed for his pool.

Evan took long, easy strokes up and down the length of the pool, half his brain counting laps and letting the other half wander through unrelated thoughts as the exercise drained the tension from his muscles. He kept drifting back to Lydia and Jenny ... and Burnham, but there was something else he felt he should be remembering ... just out of reach. It nagged at him.

On the fourth lap he got it. Bett Wilson. Bett Wilson's problems were remarkably similar to Jenny's ... sleepwalking, vivid dreams of a prehistoric life, strange, primitive food cravings. Bett didn't have the aggression, but so what? The rest of it seemed to be more than coincidence. He stopped swimming. Two people in the same town, the same hospital at the same time for Christ's sake, with the same rare, progressive genetic malfunction? Why? How? And why now? Why these two people, and what had happened to trigger it off?

Both case histories were in his briefcase and he dripped water all over his rugs in his rush to get at it.

Jake found his friend sitting at a round glass table on the lanai, poring over stacks of paper that spilled out of an open briefcase.

"Whatever it is, it isn't as interesting as what—"

Startled, Evan jumped to his feet. He hadn't even heard the doorbell, and was glad he'd left the front door unlocked. The two men shook hands warmly and Jake ambled over to the outdoor bar.

"Take you up on that bet," Evan said seriously. "No names of course, but it has to do with evolution and I think you'll find this fascinating . . . right up your alley."

Jake turned around and looked at Evan with a curious expression. "No kidding. Me too."

"Me too, what?"

"Evolution. What I've got for you is about evolution too."

"Interesting coincidence."

"Yeah. Fix you something?" Jake asked. He waved a bottle of Chivas Regal at Evan.

"Martini. You first."

Jake mixed a martini for Evan and told him about sighting the thecodont. Evan listened carefully, his naturally logical mind fighting with his innate trust in the mental competence of his friend, and the memory of a certain drawing that lent added credence to the tale.

"And it gets better," Jake said eventually. "Let's boil that water and clean the crabs while I tell you the rest."

"There's more?" Evan asked, surprised.

Jake laughed. "More? You're going to think your old friend is bonkers by the time he's finished!" He turned in the doorway and put a hand on Evan's shoulder, his expression changed to serious. "This is the craziest, most exciting thing that's ever happened to me and it's not over yet. My name is going in the books, Evan."

Evan went into the bedroom and changed out of his bathing trunks while Jake started on the crabs, and he forgot about Jenny and Bett as he mulled over the implications of Jake's "find." A prehistoric animal truly living in the Everglades? Well, why not? Didn't they find a living prehistoric fish a while back? He'd ask Jake.

Jake was slamming through the kitchen cabinets when Evan came back in. "Got any Old Bay seasoning?"

Evan got it for him and went around the kitchen closing cabinet doors. "What was that prehistoric fish—"

"Coelacanth. Yeah ... I've already thought of that. Sets a reasonable precedent, doesn't it?" Jake dumped half a box of the seasoning into the boiling water and Evan winced. That stuff was hot. He was glad he had plenty of cold beer to douse the fire.

"We thought the coelacanth was extinct about sixty million years ago. Then they found one off the southern coast of Africa. Pretty exciting stuff until we found out that the people of the Comoro Islands had been catching and eating the damned things for years."

"That doesn't make it any less exciting in my book,"

Evan said. "It just points out the possibility that other seemingly extinct animals could still be alive today. Was the fish exactly the same as its ancestors?"

"Nope." Jake pulled two beers from the refrigerator and handed one to Evan. "Today's guys are bigger."

"And the thecodont . . . ?"

"Hard to tell, but my guess would be normal . . . for a thecodont. Some later descendants were a lot bigger than today's gators or crocs. For instance one croc, a descendant of the thecodonts called Deinosuchus could hit fifty feet. Thecondonts were smaller. No more than fifteen feet. Put the crabs in."

Evan dumped the crabs into the boiling water while Jake went outside to spread newspapers on the lanai table. "You haven't heard the best yet!" Jake yelled in at Evan.

Evan carried the coleslaw and two forks outside. "You really love building suspense, don't you?" he asked, grinning. "I'd say it's a latent form of sadism that creeps out of you every once in a while."

"Spoken like a true shrink." Jake grabbed a fork and dug it into the coleslaw. "Mmmm. Good. You ever hear of Diatryma?"

"Nope."

"It's a bird."

"Like Archaeopteryx?"

"Hardly. This thing was about ten feet tall. Flightless. Had a massive head and a beak like a parrot. Strong legs. Could be vaguely related to today's sandhill crane."

"You're kidding."

"Nope. Order Gruiformes. But Diatryma lived about fifty-four million years ago."

"You saw one of these too?" This was getting too incredible to believe. Evan was starting to feel a little bit skeptical.

"Saw it? It attacked us."

"What!"

"And then there was the herd of Coelophysis. Dinosaurs, to you. That was another close call. Damnedest couple of days I've ever had in my life."

"Jake . . ."

"No. I know what you're thinking. This is no joke, Evan." His voice and expression were serious enough to stop Evan from arguing.

Jake told him the whole story while they cracked crab claws with the bottoms of their beer bottles.

"My God," Evan said when Jake was finally finished. "Have these things been in the Everglades all along? Why hasn't anybody—?"

"I sincerely doubt it. Maybe something like this could happen in the Amazon jungle or some other huge, remote place, but as big as the Glades is, it isn't *that* big. Nope. My guess is that somehow, something . . . some commonplace, indigenous animal gave birth to these things. God knows why. Or how. Or when it started. Or what triggered it. But evolution seems to be running backward here. At a mind-blowing pace."

"Mutants?"

"Maybe. But not the way you mean . . . like Godzilla or an occasional two-headed sheep. These things actually existed once . . . were commonplace. And they ruled the earth for millions of years. Anyway, a mutant is something new that evolves from something that already exists, basically. I guess in that respect, everything alive is a mutation of something in one form or another . . . even us. Except here we have something ancient mutating out of something that exists today . . . like a kind of . . . I don't know . . . de-evolution."

"So fast? If I remember my Darwin, evolution takes millions of years."

"Yeah. That's what's so weird here. It would be like a human giving birth to a monkey . . . it just doesn't happen.

"And there's a molecular clock, you know," Jake added. "I think it's something like one amino acid substitution every five or six million years to get from a rhesus monkey to Homo sapiens . . . us. So it would take us about twenty-five million years to revert . . . if we want to follow this scenario. Less for other species, but for the numbers we're talking about—" Jake shrugged.

Evan picked absently at a crab, thinking. "Maybe they're wrong," he finally said.

"Who?"

"The Darwinists. Darwin's Theory of Evolution *is* only a theory, isn't it? Maybe it *can* happen faster, given the right circumstances. Atmosphere, climate, food . . . maybe radiation, polar shifts. Polar shifts . . . there's something that would let radiation bombard the atmosphere, right? We know radiation can cause mutations. Didn't man appear on earth right after the last great polar shift?"

"That's a theory too . . . about man," Jake answered. "And yes, Darwin could be wrong . . . there are some very smart scientists out there who call themselves punctuationists, who think Darwin was all wet. But let me get back to the polar stuff first. I was thinking about that on the way up here, trying to get a handle on how all this could have started. It was the only halfway reasonable theory I could come up with, and I want to talk to Ralph Jenner about it soon."

Evan frowned, trying to remember what he'd read about polar shifts. "There was an article a while back about it in *Scientific American,* but I can't remember all the details."

Jake nodded. "I read it. And polar wandering is a more accurate term than shift, by the way. And it's a hypothesis with some flaws too. But we do know that geomagnetic field reversals occur about every two hundred and thirty thousand years . . . from normal to reverse."

"So?"

"So that could have some bearing here. Maybe. Maybe there was a slight shift, to use your word. Just little enough to go unnoticed, but enough to let in enough localized radiation to sneak through the weak or thinning spots in our ozone layer and cause random genetic mutations in susceptible species."

Evan felt a chill stand the hair up on his arms. "Or individuals?"

"What?"

"In a minute. Let me get back to Darwin first. What I meant by evolution happening faster than Darwin thought is based on something I read a while back. It was about the punctuationists you mentioned a minute ago. Tell me more about that theory. What I read didn't tell me as much as I wanted to know."

Jake grinned. He loved playing teacher to his old friend. "Sure. I was getting to that. And I like their theory. I think those scientists are really on to something. They say that new species formed quickly . . . and from only a few representatives of the old species. That's why fossil records show a new species of animal that's obviously evolved from an older species sometimes

139

lived during the same time period. If Darwin had been right, that would have been impossible. The old, original species would have died out long before it gradually evolved into the new one."

Evan nodded. "And the article said that once a new species is formed, it shows very little change. That knocks out the idea of gradual, continuous evolvement."

"Right. Even modern man . . . and we can trace our modern ancestors back to a hundred and forty to two hundred thousand years ago . . . coexisted with an older and more primitive race of man that dated back five hundred thousand to a million years ago. See . . . we didn't slowly evolve . . . we sprang up as a separate species . . . mutated quickly, if you want to say it that way . . . from only a few individuals . . . probably the result of a sudden, rare, genetic mutation. The fossil records prove it, but a lot of scientists are screaming bloody hell over it." Jake grinned. "Bunch of old fossils in our field hate change . . . makes them look stupid when somebody says they've been wrong all their lives."

"But does this help, Jake? The punctuationists' theories? Does it prove there could be sudden mutations in the DNA that would explain the animals you saw in the Glades?"

"Who knows? There's so much we don't know . . . can't recreate accurately from fossil records. And don't forget, when we paleontologists say 'instantly,' we mean oh, maybe a thousand . . . or a million years, give or take a little."

"Uh huh." Evan drummed his fingers on the table. "This all fits . . . and it doesn't fit. There's a thread here someplace, but . . ."

"You want to let me in on your private ruminations or am I supposed to guess?"

Evan laughed. "Talking to myself is a danger sign, right?" He picked a lump of crab meat from a claw, but didn't eat it. "Do you think that whatever caused what seems to be the sudden genetic mutations in the Glades could also affect an existing individual, say a human, and manifest itself just within the brain? Could the same set of circumstances affect just behavior or other mental functions in that person, or would there have to be an obvious physical alteration . . . like in your animals . . . to correlate with the mental change?"

"You mean like when man took a leap forward in brain capacity, his physical attributes obviously changed too?"

"In a way, yes. But I don't mean over a long period of time. I mean immediately and within a single individual. A latent gene that could be triggered by something like your geomagnetic field reversals and cause both the physical mutations you've seen in the Glades and, uh . . . mental dysfunctions in humans . . . without there being any specific, immediate, external evidence of disorder or disease . . . like you see in the onset of Huntington's or Alzheimer's. Or suddenly growing hair on your back."

Jake squinted his eyes at the psychiatrist. "Uh huh. You mean a sudden onset of hidden DNA stuff like color blindness or hemophilia? Something not as visible as a thecodont running around the supermarket? No. Well, wait a minute. I don't know. Maybe. But the predisposition would have to be there I guess. Like an odd-ball gene ripe for change, and it wouldn't alter until a given set of circumstances triggered it. Yeah, I think you'd have to be born with it, already have it in the DNA. Then it would happen . . . an altered state of mind. What are you getting at? This isn't just off the top of your head, right?"

Evan told him about Burnham's Genesis Gene.

Chapter Twenty-two

What rotten timing, Bett thought. Here it's a weekend and Ray is home alone while I'm here having my body and mind poked.

She turned her face away while yet another nurse probed at the crook of her elbow for a blood sample. She didn't mind, but couldn't stand to watch. A few seconds' wait, and the nurse withdrew the needle and pressed a piece of gauze on the wounded spot. "Bend," she ordered, and Bett obediently bent her elbow to hold it in place.

The woman left without another word, and Bett sat alone, staring at a blank wall. There was no window in this room. Just a bed, a chair, and machines. Machines that would monitor her sleep, dig into her unconscious, and reveal her inner workings to the mad scientists . . . Now why was she thinking like that? She repressed an urge to cry. She wanted Ray. She was scared. Why had she fainted today? What was happening to her? Why wasn't Dr. Tremayne going to be here while she slept? *Stop it! Stop acting like a baby!* She threw herself on the bed and curled into a ball. The man has a private life. He can't be here twenty-four hours a day . . . but think of what a thrill he's missing! Bett Wilson . . . asleep.

"Mrs. Wilson?"

She hadn't heard the door, and she rolled over quickly. She recognized this one . . . should . . . she'd talked with him for hours today . . . first about the EEG she'd be hooked up to while she slept, and then about dreams and REM and NREM and other stages of sleep, and then about the dreams she'd been having. He'd been kind and attentive and she'd been comfortable with him. Almost as comfortable as she'd been with Evan Tremayne.

"Are you ready?" the man asked her with a smile.

"Guess so," she answered, and smiled back. She wished she could think of something clever to say, but couldn't, so she just waited patiently while he plastered wires to her scalp.

"Now remember what we said?" he asked. "These electrodes are attached to the electroencephalogram, and that's how we measure the five stages of sleep? And sometimes we're going to wake you up during the REM stage, and we want you to try and tell us what you're dreaming. Okay?"

"Yes."

"And we're also going to wake you up sometimes during deep slow-wave sleep. Remember what we said about the delta-wave stage?"

"Vaguely."

He laughed as if she'd said something terribly funny.

She'd thought it would be hard to get to sleep, knowing people were watching her and all, but she was so

bored now . . . and tired from being stressed out all day
. . . and night . . . Bett was asleep in ten minutes.

"It was . . . I don't know . . . a lake . . . but there was
a boardwalk and DeeDee Brightsway was there . . . I
knew her back in fourth grade. And I was trying to water some geraniums in a pot . . . but I couldn't reach the
water . . . and then my mother and DeeDee ran over to
a crowd of people who were getting ready for a dance,
and . . ."

"I was in a strange house with a bunch of people . . .
some of them are dead but I didn't remember that . . .
and there was danger upstairs . . . and then I was outside
in the snow . . . I wasn't afraid anymore . . . then I was
trying to fold a black sheet with somebody, but the ends
were dragging in the leaves and I was getting mad because I was afraid I'd have to wash it again . . ."

"I . . . I don't think . . . no. It's gone . . . can't remember . . ."

"I was trying to run . . . my legs would only go in
slow motion . . . don't know why I was running . . .
don't know where I was . . . couldn't see much . . . then
I was putting on boots . . . brown ones . . . I was in my
mother's house . . . she wasn't there . . . and then somebody brought in silver patterns for me to look at . . . and
they put this tray on a glass coffee table, but all the sil-

ver was wrapped up in different-colored pastel tissue papers and I couldn't see the patterns . . ."

Morning mouth. Bett ran her tongue over her teeth, then opened her mouth to breathe fresh air into it. Hospital! She remembered where she was and sat up quickly. Wires yanked at her scalp and she rolled off them, freeing them again.

Her scalp itched where the electrodes were attached, and she had to go to the bathroom. How was she going . . .

"Good morning!"

It was her "REM friend," as she'd been calling him to herself. "Were you here all night?" she asked, then said "Good morning" back. She straightened her nightgown, suddenly self-conscious.

"Yep. Night shift. I go home in ten minutes. How do you feel?"

"Fine. Umm . . . I need a ladies' room and these . . ." she plucked at the wires.

"Fear not! I'm here to unhook you . . . and Janice will be in here in a minute to give you fresh towels for your shower." He started peeling off the electrodes.

"How'd I do?"

"Looked like a nice, normal night of sleep to me . . . except for us waking you up and interrupting all your wonderful dreams all night."

"That's good. I guess."

He looked at her curiously. "Of course it is. But you'll probably feel a little tired today. All that interrupted REM, y'know? You can nap free of charge this afternoon. Not too long, though . . . you've got to be sleepy tonight."

Bett groaned. "How many—?"

"Just one more night if it's as normal as this last one was."

"And if it isn't?"

"Then you talk to Dr. Tremayne. He's the boss."

There was a soft knock at the door and a pretty young woman came in carrying towels and a washcloth. "Mrs. Wilson?"

Bett nodded and the woman smiled shyly. "Here's your things for the shower?" She had a soft southern accent—the kind that lilts up at the end of a sentence. "And your husband is in the waiting lounge?"

"Oh! I'll see him now." Free from the electrodes, she jumped off the bed and grabbed for her bathrobe. "Okay?" she asked Rem.

He shrugged. "Sure. Go have breakfast. Whatever. Just be back by ten. More tests."

Bett ran for the waiting lounge.

"He said normal, Ray."

Bett and Ray had opted for breakfast at Perkin's Pancake House instead of staying in and taking a chance on the hospital cafeteria food. Her spirits were up now, and she poured maple syrup over her silver-dollar pancakes.

"They do the rest of the tests today, and I sleep for them again tonight, and I guess I can go home Sunday morning and we can talk to Dr. Tremayne about all the results on Monday."

"You look good, hon," Ray said. He speared a sausage. "Maybe it's all over? You know, maybe it was just temporary and you're okay now. Maybe talking about your aunt freed you or something . . . you know what I mean? And it just took a couple of days to sink in?"

"Maybe."

They smiled at each other hopefully.

Saturday night. She'd have no trouble sleeping despite her afternoon nap. She'd had her CT scan. Then she'd been poked and prodded, had her temperature, blood pressure, respiration, and pulse rate checked; had eye tests, hearing tests, and olfactory tests. They'd tapped her with rubber hammers, stuck pins in her, and asked her to respond to dozens of seemingly ridiculous things like cotton dragged across her face, test tubes filled with hot and cold water, and holding keys and coins and identifying them, and . . . God, she couldn't remember what else.

She was asleep a few minutes after Rem left the room.

Rem, whose real name was Michael Dorset, sipped cold coffee from a Styrofoam cup. The polygraph showed stage 4, delta sleep, and slow, steady waves marched across the paper chart that snaked through the machine. He had about forty minutes before Mrs. Wilson would start reversing her sleep pattern—more before she went into REM. It was only the beginning of the night, and the first few REM stages would be short ones during the approximate ninety-minute sleep cycle. The longer, more interesting dreams would come later. He wanted a candy bar.

"Hey, Doug," he said to his assistant. "Keep an eye, okay? Be right back."

He took his time—chatted up a couple of the prettier nurses. Got more coffee. When he got back to the sleep lab, Mrs. Wilson was just going into REM, her second dream stage of the night—and she was sitting up.

"Hey!" He stared at the monitor screen, then back at the polygraph. "How'd you fuck up this machine, Doug!"

Doug looked frightened. "I didn't touch anything! I swear it, Michael!"

Rem pushed some buttons; tapped the machine a little; then looked up in horror as Mrs. Wilson opened her eyes and started yanking at her electrodes.

He sprinted for the door. Nobody . . . *nobody* could move during REM! During REM the large muscles were paralyzed—nature's way of preventing people from harming themselves by acting out the movements of a dream. And the polygraph definitely showed Mrs. Wilson was in the REM stage. She should be in stage 4—sleepwalking occurred during stage 4!

Tepi was terrified. Where was she? Where was Doga? Where was the tribe! She was closed in—a cage but not a cage—a thing with a smooth, solid roof and walls—like nothing she'd ever seen before.

Her heart hammered till she thought it must surely fly free! She took short, rapid breaths. Calm yourself, she scolded—this must be a sleep-story. Only a sleep-story.

Someone had attached vines to her head. She pulled them off. How real this all was! She looked down at herself—and at the thing she sat on. How wondrous! The little platform was the softest thing she'd ever felt. She ran her hands in admiration over the weave of the cloth that covered it. Never had she seen such work— and the garment that covered her body! Her mind struggled with the concept of such a thing.

Her fear was gone—after all, she would return to her people when the sleep-story was finished—and she slipped off the platform to explore the cage further. She must remember all she could and tell everyone everything she'd seen. It would certainly keep all their ears on her during the next circle-speak!

Her feet touched the floor. Another marvel of softness! She got down on her knees and ran her hands along the mat that stretched from one end of the cage to the other. It was almost as soft as the fur of the great long-toothed cats that her tribe feared.

A sound. Tepi looked up. A hole opened up in the cage and a man stood looking at her. No . . . not a man . . . she had never seen a man like this! He was taller . . . much taller . . . than the tallest tribe member, and his hair was the color of the sun!

A god. What god, she didn't know—but most surely a god! Tepi put her face on the mat and stretched her arms out in front of her in the proper form of worship. Now her heart beat with joy. A god had seen fit to reveal himself to her in a sleep-story! Oh how Zeb-Zeb would envy her!

He spoke. She didn't understand. Did he wish her to rise? He spoke again . . . his voice sounded anxious. Why? Curious, she turned her head slightly and peeked up at him. He knelt by her side and touched her arm.

"Mrs. Wilson? Mrs. Wilson?" Rem held Bett's pulse—it was strong, thank God—and turned his head over his shoulder to bark at Doug, who'd followed him into the lab. "Who's on duty . . . Dr. Paterson? *Get him!*"

Doug ran.

* * *

"Really. I'm fine. But I don't understand what happened. What happened, Rem?" Bett looked over at a solemn-faced Michael, who stood leaning against the wall while a tall, thin man with receding, sand-colored hair pressed a stethoscope to her chest.

"Cough," the man said.

Bett coughed. They'd taken her blood pressure, looked in her eyes and ears and down her throat, and taken another blood sample. Why did they always take blood? Did they expect it to switch from type A to type B while they weren't looking?

"You seem fine," the thin doctor said with an equally thin smile. "Call Dr. Tremayne in the morning," he said to Michael, and walked out.

Michael sat on the bed next to Bett. "What were you dreaming?"

"Nothing. All I remember is waking up on the floor with you kneeling next to me. What happened to me?"

"Umm . . . you started to sleepwalk." His eyes darted away from her, then back.

There's more to it, Bett thought. And he's not telling me. She plucked at the wires that lay in limp disarray on the bed. "Do we do this again?"

"Yes. Please."

Bett sat silently while he reattached the electrodes.

The rest of the night followed a normal pattern, but Michael didn't leave the sleep lab again.

Chapter Twenty-three

The phone dragged Evan up from several cozy layers of sleep. He rolled over, opened his eyes, and quickly reached for it.

"Tremayne," he said into the receiver. His eyes slid to the clock radio. Seven A.M. "Yes, Michael . . . What . . . ? She what . . . ?" He sat straight up in bed. "You're kidding. Maybe the machine . . ." He was completely awake now. "That's not possible. You must have read the . . . No, I'm not questioning your . . . Michael, nobody gets up and walks during REM, so it must have been . . . Never mind. How is Mrs. Wilson? . . . Good. I'll be in within the hour . . . No, let her sleep."

He sat on the bed for a minute and thought about what Michael had said. He should have asked if they'd called someone in to check out the EEG.

Coffee smell drifted in to him. Jake. He'd forgotten about Jake.

A short, cool shower put his mind back on full alert, and he went into the kitchen where Jake had the morning paper spread out over the kitchen table.

"Morning," the big man said pleasantly. "Some Java?

It's made." He pointed to the steaming Mr. Coffee on the counter.

"Thanks." Evan poured himself a cup. "What can I get you?"

"Already had toast . . . I start the day light, remember? Hey, maybe I should have answered the phone . . . let you sleep, but I wasn't sure . . ." He let his words drift off and lifted his coffee cup toward Evan. "That's a lie. I wanted you up. I'm anxious to get started."

Evan had promised to call Dr. Burnham at home and ask if he'd go over some genetics with Jake. If there was any connection between what was happening to Jenny and Bett and the prehistoric animals Jake had seen in the Glades, Evan was sure Burnham would be the best one to grapple with the possibilities.

"Yeah, listen, Jake. I have to make a stop at the hospital, but let me call Burnham now for you . . . see what we can set up." He dialed the phone.

"Hello. This is Dr. Tremayne . . . Oh . . . No, don't bother, I'm going over there anyway."

Jake raised an eyebrow as Evan hung up.

"That was his service. He's at the hospital already. We can catch him there."

"Don't you people ever take a day off?"

"We try," Evan said, grinning.

Evan left Jake with Dr. Burnham and hurried over to the sleep lab. The old scientist seemed to be delighted to have someone new to bounce his genetic theories around with, and they'd been deep in discussion when Evan left them.

"It's been checked out and there's nothing wrong with it," Michael said first thing when Evan walked in.

"Good morning to you too," Evan said and picked up the readout from Bett's EEG.

"Sorry. Good morning, Dr. Tremayne." Michael pointed to series of wavy lines on the paper. "Here's where she got out of bed."

Evan frowned. Not possible. "Is she awake yet?" he asked.

"Yes, sir."

"Good." He left Michael staring after him.

Bett, dressed but with her hair still damp from a shower, sat in the familiar chair in Evan's office. Ray sat next to her, and they listened to the psychiatrist with a growing sense of fear.

"Genetic?" Ray asked. "Is there a specific name for what you think she has? Is there a cure for it?"

"I'd prefer that you speak to Dr. Burnham about the details," Evan said evasively. "He's the one with experience in this field. The point is, I'd like him to do some simple genetic tests to either establish or rule out what I suspect the problem might be. If he rules out genetic causes, then, after all the neurological tests that you've had and passed, Bett, I'll continue searching for psychological problems. But I need to be sure that your problem isn't physical."

"What about my sleepwalking last night?" Bett asked. "I flunked that one, didn't I?"

Evan looked at her curiously. "Where did you get that idea?"

"From Rem . . . um, I mean Michael."

The flash of anger in the psychiatrist's face was obvious, and Bett hurried on.

"He didn't *say* anything! I mean, he just looked un-

154

comfortable . . . scared, sort of . . . when I asked him what all the fuss was about." Jesus. She didn't mean to get the poor guy in trouble.

Evan relaxed. "I have to assume a machine malfunction. Don't worry about it." Or maybe something out of whack with her melatonin—the hormone that influences sleep-wake patterns, he thought. Check that out too.

"So you want Bett to see this Dr. Burnham?" Ray asked.

"Yes. With your permission, I'll fill him in on your case history today."

Bett hesitated, glanced at Ray. He nodded at her.

"Yes," she said to Evan. "I guess I don't have much choice, do I?"

Evan smiled at her. "You always have a choice, but I think you made the right one." And this might shed some light on Jenny's case, he thought to himself.

Evan found Jake and Burnham right where he'd left them, deep in conversation.

"Marvelous! Marvelous!" Burnham shouted at him as he walked into the scientist's office. "If I didn't have so many pots bubbling here, I'd *beg* to go with him on his expedition!" He clapped his hands and beamed at Jake as if he were the prodigal son. Jake grinned back.

"I'm glad you two are getting along," Evan said mildly. "Harold, if you don't mind I'd like to talk to you for a minute."

"I'll wander around for a while," Jake said, and jumped to his feet. "Talk to you later, Harold."

Evan waited until the door shut behind his friend. "I have another patient . . . ," he said, and told him about Bett Wilson.

"This is most unusual," Burnham said after Evan was finished. "And disturbing. Unless they're related and they share the gene. Are they related?"

"No. And I think I know what you're thinking," Evan said. "It just occurred to me too."

"Viral? Bacteriological?" Burnham looked worried.

"Yes. A new disease. Contagious, perhaps. But how? I got so wrapped up in your theories of the Genesis Gene, that I overlooked that possibility till now. And am I right in thinking that the Genesis Gene is so rare that it's unlikely to show up in two people in the same place at the same time?"

"Yes, I'd say you're probably right . . . but I really don't know, Evan." Burnham sighed and rubbed his eyes. He'd been up most of the night reviewing his own data on genetics. "Well, let's not panic. I want to do the testing anyway . . . on Jenny and your Mrs. Wilson. Mrs. Matthews is bringing her daughter in today. Do you agree?"

Evan sat and stared sightlessly at the top of Burnham's desk, his mind racing.

"Evan?"

"What? Yes, sure, Harold . . . listen . . . how about this? Let me get Birdie Dugan on the computers and see if she can find any similar cases in the data banks of some of the other hospitals in Florida. We can't tap in to the private practices, but you have influence. Ring up some of your buddies and feel it out. Let's see what we're up against."

"Go do it, Evan. And I hope to God we don't have another Legionnaires' Disease type thing bubbling up on us here."

So do I, Evan thought grimly. *But at least nobody's died yet . . . I don't think.*

Suddenly a mere genetic malfunction didn't sound so bad anymore.

Birdie's plump fingers flew over the keyboard. "This is gonna take a while, Dr. Tremayne. If you wanna wait, I'll send Lorrie for some coffee for you."

He smiled at her. "Thanks, Birdie. But I'll check with you later." He walked out without a backward look, his mind already on his first appointment, and the long day he had ahead of him.

Jake wandered through the halls of the hospital, admiring the modern decor and apparent efficiency of the people who moved with purpose and decisiveness as they went about their tasks.

The place was huge—four stories of concrete and glass in the shape of a hexagon, and he was glad the corridors were well marked. Otherwise, visitors would have to drop breadcrumbs.

He wanted to ask questions—as usual—but hesitated to waylay anybody who looked busy. Instead, he walked through another set of swinging double doors and followed the blue arrows to the elevator. May as well go back to Harold's office, he thought. Evan might be finished with him. And nobody knows where to look for me.

The elevator let him off on the fourth floor and he ambled down the hall toward Burnham's suite. The receptionist smiled up at him when he peeked in the door. "Anybody looking for me yet?" he asked.

"I don't think so, Dr. Van Gower. Dr. Burnham is

with a patient and I have no idea where Dr. Tremayne is."

"Uh huh. Well . . ."

"Would you like to wait here? Dr. Burnham should be finished in a few minutes."

"Thanks. I'll do that." Jake threw himself into a chair and started picking through a stack of magazines that lay scattered on a low table in front of him. They were mostly outdated, like the magazines in every doctor's or dentist's office in the country. He picked up an old *National Geographic*.

He was halfway through a reasonably interesting article on the New Zealand tuatara when a woman and a very young child entered the waiting lounge. Nice, he thought, his eyes moving candidly over the woman. Very nice.

"Dr. Burnham will be with you in a minute, Mrs. Matthews," the receptionist said, and the woman murmured something back, then sat in a chair on the opposite side of the room. Her daughter glanced at Jake, then followed her mother.

Jake's eyes kept wandering from the printed page to Mrs. Matthews. She leaned forward to straighten her daughter's T-shirt; Minnie Mouse had crept up over the child's belly, exposing it, and the woman yanked it down. Her long, almost black hair fell forward over her shoulders, and she flipped it back with a toss of her head when she sat up straight again.

Her eyes caught Jake's, and she looked away quickly, shyly. Her eyes were a startling deep blue.

"My name is Jenny. What's yours?"

He hadn't even noticed the little girl sidling up to him; he'd been too intent on the mother. Now he looked down into the same deep blue eyes. They looked at him solemnly.

"My name is Jake, and I'm pleased to meet you, Jenny," he said and held out his hand. She shook it with a surprisingly firm grip for a little kid.

"Dr. Burnham is going to look at my jeans," she said, then giggled. "Not this kind!" She stuffed her hands in the pockets of her blue jeans and wiggled them for emphasis. "He's going to look at the jeans *inside* me. Is he going to look at your inside jeans too?"

The picture the child obviously had in her head made Jake burst out laughing, and she laughed along with him.

"Jenny, don't bother the man," the woman said from across the room, but she was smiling too.

"She isn't bothering me. Her concept is intriguing." Jake got up from his seat to cross the room. Jenny grabbed his hand and skipped alongside him. "I'm Dr. Jake Van Gower," he said, holding out the other hand.

"Lydia Matthews." She took his hand. "Are you a psychiatrist, Dr. Van Gower?"

"Jake, please. I'm a paleontologist and an old friend of Evan Tremayne's. He's a psychiatrist on staff here. And right now I seem to have misplaced him, but I figure he'll show up sooner or later."

"I know Dr. Tremayne," Jenny said. "He's my friend too."

It suddenly clicked in Jake's head. This was the child with the Genesis Gene, a patient of Evan's, waiting in Harold's office and talking about "jeans." He felt a moment of discomfort. This chance meeting, and his knowledge of the girl's case even though Evan had used no names, made him feel as if he were somehow breaching a doctor-patient confidentiality. He quickly brushed it aside as silly, then wondered if Evan had any personal interest in this woman. She was attractive, and a single parent, Evan had said.

"Jenny is here for genetic testing," Lydia said.

He smiled at the child. "Judging from her alertness and healthy looks, I'd say it can't be anything too serious."

Lydia seemed pleased by his remark. "Well, I don't think so either . . . not anymore, anyway. Dr. Burnham seems to think he can control the problem, and he's the best, isn't he?" She looked at him hopefully.

"He is," Jake said simply.

Harold Burnham suddenly opened his office door and ushered out a slight, gray-haired old man. "Thursday at two, Joseph," he said. The man nodded and scurried out the door.

"Lydia! Jenny!" Harold rushed over and picked Jenny up in his arms. She giggled and wrapped her arms around his neck.

"You've met?" he asked, smiling from Lydia to Jake. They nodded. "Good. We've had a slight change of plans, my dear," he said looking at Lydia. "Dr. Frankel can take Jenny now for the MRI, and since Dr. Tremayne is in the hospital today, I've taken the liberty of scheduling her. I'll page him and you can go over there with him right away. We'll do the other tests when you come back."

He turned to Jake. "I have some time if you want to continue our discussion, Jake."

"Thanks, Harold . . . but I think I'll tag along with Evan, if you don't mind. And if Mrs. Matthews doesn't mind," he added quickly. "It's been a while since I've seen Evan, you know, and we have a lot to catch up on."

"Of course, of course," Harold said, but he looked disappointed.

Lydia graciously said she'd be happy to have him come along, and the three of them walked back to Evan's office, talking easily about trivial things.

Lydia sat in the front seat with Evan while he drove his Mercedes to Dr. Frankel's genetic research center. Jake and Jenny sat in the back, Jake leading Jenny in several raucous renditions of "Row, Row, Row Your Boat" and "Frère Jaques." They were struggling with an hilarious attempt at "Itsy Bitsy Spider" when they arrived at the center.

Evan fought back a startling and guilty stab of jealousy over his good friend's natural casualness with Lydia's child.

Dr. Robert Frankel was a short, round, middle-aged man with a sunny smile and a disposition to match. And he was as enthusiastic about the possibility of a human Genesis Gene as Harold Burnham was.

He patiently explained magnetic resonance imaging to Jenny in simple terms, using the concept of a radio sending voices through the air and into her ears. To Lydia he explained brain tissue response brought on by measurable electrical signals as a result of high-frequency radio waves applied to the brain in a large, brief, magnetic pulse. "It's an invaluable tool," he said cheerfully. "Almost as good as direct visual inspection of the brain!"

Evan went to the test lab with Dr. Frankel and Jenny, and Frankel continued to educate Evan on the wonders of genetic research. He cleared up a lot of fine points that Harold had been vague about, and Evan listened carefully. Only occasionally did he think about Jake and Lydia together in the waiting room together, both surprising and despising himself for his silly paranoia. He began to think that something beyond his control had sneaked up on him and hit him in the head, knocking out his common sense. Just a strong physical attraction, he told himself. Get a hold of yourself. The pain of his divorce had dulled, but his head told him it wouldn't be wise to get involved in another relationship so soon. And yet . . .

"Someday we'll be able to cure all genetically transmitted diseases while the fetus is still in the womb, Evan!" Frankel rhapsodized. "What a wonderful world it will be, eh?"

They walked back toward the room where Jake and Lydia waited for them, and Jenny kept looking down at a large, yellow "smile" sticker that Frankel had stuck on her T-shirt after the test.

"And please understand my reticence in discussing this case with you in detail right now, Evan," Frankel added as he patted Jenny on the head. She looked up at him and smiled. "Harold is the physician of record after all, and though I appreciate your involvement in the case, I feel I should speak to him first, eh? And quite frankly, I'd like to review some of the details before I make any premature statements."

"Of course, but—"

Frankel waved a hand. "Now, now. Don't misunderstand me! I *can* assure you that the child is in no immediate danger . . . that is your concern, isn't it?" He twinkled his eyes at Evan. "Lovely child . . . and a lovely mother, eh?"

Evan felt a slight flush creep up his neck and turned his face away from the geneticist. Was he that transparent?

Evan and Jake left Lydia and Jenny in Dr. Burnham's waiting lounge. The director was busy with an emergency and had left word that he'd call Evan at home later.

Birdie Dugan had a folder ready for Evan. He picked it up without looking at it. Later, he thought. Right now he and Jake had a date with a pizza and a ball game. He was going to relax for a little while if it killed him.

Chapter Twenty-four

Phillies and Pirates. Evan and Jake sat sprawled across Evan's goosedown-stuffed, gray herringbone couch. Bottom of the ninth. Two outs. Pirates three runs ahead.

"Oh, hell," Evan mumbled through a mouthful of pizza. A Phillies fan from the days of skinned knees and training wheels on his bike, Evan tossed the crust edge into the box.

Jake was a Pirates fan—ever since he found out his best college friend was batty over the Phillies. He rubbed his hands together gleefully. "Not a chance in hell, ol' buddy! Get out your dime!" The standard standing bet from the old days.

"Again?" Evan pointed to Jake's empty beer mug.

"Uh-uh. Gotta keep a clear head. Want to run over to the mall after the slaughter"—he jerked his head toward the T.V.—"and pick up some supplies for the expedition. Personal stuff. You want to come along?"

Evan hated shopping. "Sure. What do you need?"

"Mainly, a couple of long-sleeved shirts . . . help keep off the mosquitos. All I brought was short sleeves. Extra canteen. More bug spray. Ralph is rounding up the major stuff."

Cheers and yells from the T.V. Evan tossed a dime on the coffee table. "When do you have to leave?"

"Whenever Ralph is ready. Couple of days, I guess. He'll call me here."

"What do you want to do tonight?" Evan asked. "I brought home work, but I don't feel like doing it, and I'm sure you don't want to sit here and watch me do it."

"I've been mulling that over," Jake said, elaborately casual. "What do you think . . . maybe we could give that attractive Lydia Matthews a call, and we could wine and dine her tonight? I'll bet she could use a little R and R. Get her worries off Jenny for a while. What do you say? Want me to call her?"

Evan hesitated only a fraction of a second. "If you like. Can't hurt to ask." He watched Jake's expression, and suddenly understood. Jake wasn't interested in Lydia for himself. He was playing matchmaker! Evan was amazed at the relief he felt.

Lydia was surprised—very surprised—at Jake's call. And pleased. She'd liked him. His friendliness and easy manner had made her feel very comfortable. And Jenny had liked him. But then Jenny seemed to like everybody.

She had a moment's doubt about leaving the child, but Jenny hadn't had any more "incidents," and her mother had been complaining about not seeing enough of her grandchild. (She had kept Jenny pretty close to home since all this started.) So she'd accepted. And Evan Tremayne was coming along with them. That made her nervous too. She'd thought about him a lot.

165

Too much. He was too good-looking, and she felt guilty for even noticing it. Was he bringing his wife? Jake hadn't said anything about that.

She tried to picture Evan's wife—came up with a picture of a cool, sophisticated natural blonde who wore expensive clothes as if she'd been born in them; a woman who discussed art, music, and the theater. She felt intimidated without even meeting her.

Lydia's mother was thrilled—her daughter going out with a scientist *and* a doctor! Jane Matthews practically gushed when Lydia made introductions. Lydia was embarrassed.

Jenny, her usual friendly self, kissed both men on the cheek when they left for the restaurant.

Lydia tried to peer into the car as they approached it. Was Mrs. Tremayne waiting for them out here? The car was empty. Surprised, she wondered what to do next— get in the front or the back? Who was driving? Evan solved the problem for her. He opened the front passenger door for her, and she climbed in the front with him.

The drive to the restaurant was peppered with a few awkward silences, but by the time the salad arrived, Lydia was over her initial shyness, and the conversation had turned lively. Jake, after swearing her to secrecy, told an animated and enthusiastic story about prehistoric animals in the Everglades, and she and Evan bombarded him with questions that he was more than happy to answer when he could. But she wasn't sure she believed all of it. It was too outlandish.

Evan talked about the Genesis Gene. Some of it she couldn't follow, but was fascinated anyway. Especially since it concerned Jenny. She was glad Evan—he'd in-

166

sisted she drop the "Dr. Tremayne"—seemed so confident in his knowledge. He made it sound as if curing Jenny's problem was only a matter of waiting for the test results. Not that he said it outright—but it was the impression she got from him.

She told them about her work as a naturalist photographer, and Jake seemed especially interested. He jokingly asked her if she wanted to come along on the expedition to photograph the dinosaurs. She was pretty sure he was joking, anyway.

And she found out Evan Tremayne was divorced.

Evan and Jake walked Lydia to her front door and said good night. She let herself into a semidark house. Her mother was asleep on the couch with the T.V. giving off the only light in the room. She'd sleep there all night, as was usual when she baby-sat Jenny. Lydia turned off Jay Leno and went in to check on her daughter.

Jenny lay curled in a little ball at the foot of her bed, Minnie Mouse clutched under one arm. Lydia tiptoed in and kissed her on the cheek. Little beads of sweat stood out on Jenny's nose, and the hair at the back of her neck was damp. Lydia brushed it up off the child's neck and smiled. Even with the air-conditioning on, Jenny always sweated in her sleep.

Quietly, she left the room and shut the door. Too keyed-up from the excitement of the evening, she went into the kitchen for a glass of milk. The calcium would help her sleep.

* * *

Evan had been quiet on the way home, and Jake had finally given up trying to make conversation. Now, back in Evan's living room, Jake stretched and yawned elaborately. "Guess I'll turn in," he said. "You mind?"

"No, you go ahead," Evan answered. "There's a report I want to look at anyway, so I wouldn't be much company."

Jake leaned against the doorjamb and folded his arms. Evan looked at him questioningly.

"I get the feeling there might be a few sparks between you and the lovely Lydia," Jake said with a grin.

"Don't be silly. I hardly know her." Evan busied himself with a stack of folders on the desk.

"Uh huh."

Evan couldn't help it. He returned the grin. "Thanks."

"For what?"

"Fixing me up."

Jake waved a hand, dismissing his good deed. "Anytime, old buddy." He went to bed whistling, leaving Evan alone with his reports.

Evan flipped open Birdie Dugan's folder and started to read. And couldn't believe what he was seeing. "Jesus Christ," he said softly.

Chapter Twenty-five

Evan didn't sleep much; at least he didn't feel as if he had. Everytime he opened his eyes to look at the clock radio on his nightstand, it seemed the digital numbers were crawling by in a maddeningly slow dance destined to keep him hostage to his bed forever.

Finally, at six-thirty, unable to keep his silence any longer, he got out of bed and dialed Burnham's home phone number.

Harold answered on the second ring. He sounded as if he'd been awake for hours. "I'm going fishing, Evan," he said cheerfully. "Just on my way out."

"I'm glad I caught you. First, did you have any luck getting information from any of your associates on cases similar to ours?"

There was a slight hesitation on the other end of the line. "Well, yes. Only two though, and they're rather inconclusive, I'm afraid. Why is this important right now, Evan? Can't it wait till tomorrow? I'll have all of Mrs. Wilson's and the girl's genetic test results by late morning, and we can put it all together then."

Evan told him about Birdie's report.

"There must be some mistake," Harold said.

"You want me to run it through again?"

Evan listened to a sigh on the other end of the line. "Yes, I guess that would be prudent," the old man answered. "I'll meet you at the hospital and see if I can round up some early test results while you get someone to run it for you.

"And I haven't heard from Dr. Frankel yet. I'll call him at home from my office. You say he was rather circumspect with you yesterday?"

"Yes. He said that you were the physician of record, and he wanted to talk to you first."

"I see. One more thing, Evan. The two cases I told you about? I didn't think much of it at the time . . . but they bear out your findings. I'll see you within the hour." He hung up.

The phone rang almost before Evan had taken his hand from the receiver, and he picked it up expecting Burnham had forgotten to tell him something important. But it was Dr. Ralph Jenner, asking for Jake.

Evan banged on Jake's door, and the paleontologist came out looking surprised and disheveled. He said "Yes . . . right," into the phone a few times, then listened through some long silences before hanging up.

"What's up?" Evan asked as he plugged in the Mr. Coffee.

Jake yawned and rubbed his eyes. "He wants me down there now. There's a tropical storm brewing in the Gulf and he wants to get in a couple of days out in the Glades before it hits . . . can't wait till it's all over, he says. Could take another week before the storm builds and passes through, and he's anxious. Says we can go out on a more extended stay after it's over."

"I didn't think he could prepare that fast," Evan said.

"Can't. We don't have the collapsible floating cages

170

yet . . . the Institute hasn't had time to ship them. Or the tranquilizer guns, either." Jake looked more alert now. He sniffed appreciatively at the brewing coffee and got two mugs out of Evan's cupboard. "He says we'll take a preliminary trip north, toward Okeechobee, and then swing back from the west . . . next time swing east . . . when we've got all the equipment. Unless we see some great stuff out there now. Then we'll just retrace our route."

Evan looked worried. "Jake, a storm in the Glades can get pretty rough, and pretty fast. Does Jenner know—"

"Yeah. The Park Service isn't thrilled, but Ralph got pretty hot under the collar . . . you know how he is. We have a radio, and he promised if they call us in, he'll obey their orders to cut off the trip immediately, no argument. So they okayed it. Reluctantly."

"I don't like it."

Jake started pouring coffee for them. He grinned up at Evan. "Mother hen."

"Sorry. Hey! Wait till you see this!" Evan hurried into the living room and came back with Birdie's folder. "I didn't want to bother you last night, but you've got to read this before you go." He handed the folder to Jake.

Jake scanned the pages, then looked up at Evan with an expression of disbelief. "Am I reading this right?"

"Yep. In the past five years, there have been twenty-seven reported cases of hospitalized patients with our Genesis Gene Syndrome . . . although they don't call it that. But all the symptoms are there; sleepwalking, blackouts, strange food cravings, some signs of aggression, and elaborate dreams of prehistoric life that they remembered in unnatural detail. And every single one of

171

them except Mrs. Wilson and Jenny are now on the missing persons' list."

Something shaking her—calling to her. What . . . ?

"Lydia! Lydia! Wake up! Jenny's gone!"

Lydia snapped awake. Her mother stood over her, tears streaming down her face.

"What?" Lydia threw off the thin sheet that covered her and swung her legs over the side of the bed in one motion. "What do you mean, *gone!* What time is it?"

"Seven o'clock." Jane was wringing her hands in helpless distress. "I went in to check on her and she wasn't in bed. And I went outside and called her and called her, and . . ."

Lydia pushed past her mother and ran for the kitchen door. Her nightgown dragged in the dew-wet grass as she raced for the oak tree in the backyard. No Jenny. Where? Where? She ran aimlessly around the fenced-in yard, screaming her daughter's name. Nobody answered her. Jane stood uncertainly in the kitchen doorway, watching her.

Through her panic, Lydia heard the phone, saw her mother turn back inside to answer it.

The police. They'd found Jenny wandering along a main road several miles south.

Birdie had weekends off, and it took a while for Evan and a young assistant programmer to access the files they needed, but when the printer finally started spitting out the information they'd managed to get on the screen, Evan sighed with relief. For a minute there, he

172

was afraid he'd have to call the woman at home; it was that important. And he'd have hated to bother her.

When he finally got back to Burnham's office, the old man was smiling over a disorderly pile of folders and papers spread over his desk.

"Good news, good news," he said as Evan walked in the door. "There's no problem of viral or bacterial contagion! These . . ."—he waved a handful of white paper at Evan—"bear it out. What we have here is definitely a genetic malfunction . . . not that I have all the results, you understand, but these preliminaries—"

"Great. I think." Evan stood in front of Burnham's desk, rocking on his heels with impatience. "What did Frankel say?"

"This is fascinating, Evan." Burnham was flushed with excitement. Bright pink spots stood out in blotches on his cheeks and his eyes glittered happily at the psychiatrist as he motioned him to a seat. Evan felt a little twinge of alarm at the man's obvious agitation, and he wondered idly if Burnham had any heart problems.

"I'll give you the bottom line first, then I'll explain it to you," Burnham said. "According to Frankel, there seems to be a web of some sort forming over Jenny's hippocampus."

Evan felt a chill crawl down his spine. Brain damage? In the hippocampus. His mind raced through the lectures and texts he'd memorized during his medical training, haphazardly recovering bits and pieces of information. Part of the limbic system—or the "animal brain," as it was called because its function and form seem to be alike in all mammals—the seat of emotion, learning, and memory. *Memory.* God. What else? What else? So much about the brain . . . !

"Are you listening, Evan?" Burnham sounded annoyed.

"Sorry. I was . . . never mind. Go ahead, Harold."

"Yes." Pacified. "Now. What I think is, the web is causing a strange sequence of synaptic transmissions in Jenny's brain, and the information transfer between the nerve cells is somehow altered and is now evidently causing pieces of her dormant, ancient genetic memory to be retrieved and remembered."

"Does Dr. Frankel concur?"

"Hypothetically, yes. We need more test results, of course. But by tomorrow—"

"Why is the retrieval so sporadic?" Evan interrupted, curious. "Most of the time she seems perfectly normal." This didn't seem too bad, judging from Harold's attitude. He seemed pretty sure of himself . . . at ease with his hypothesis. "Can you simply suppress the responsible neurons somehow . . . ?"

Burnham waved his hands at Evan, dismissing his suggestion. "No, no. Not that simple. And the reason I think she's having intermittent recall is because the web isn't completely formed yet. It seems to be stimulating the hippocampus in irregular spasms as it grows . . . like electrical stimulation of the brain can cause epileptic seizures."

As it grows. The implication of those words made Evan feel uneasy again. He slowly lowered himself into the chair opposite the scientist. Burnham was looking at him carefully. He felt more than uneasy now. He started to talk, cleared his throat, and tried again. "Project something for me, Harold."

Burnham nodded agreeably.

"When the web is finished growing, what will Jenny's state of mind be?"

174

"That's impossible to say, Evan." But the old man's eyes darted nervously away, and a slow flush appeared and died on his neck as he regained control.

He was lying. Evan waited, his eyes steady on the man. He remembered the rhesus monkeys and he was suddenly coldly certain that it wasn't radiation that had killed them.

Burnham tapped his fingers on the desk and looked from Evan to the ceiling and back again. "Well," he finally said. "My best guess is, unless she goes into a natural remission of some sort, it's possible that she'll remain in a permanent state of primitive recall." He looked at Evan nervously, wondering if he'd caught his intentions.

He had. "What do you mean, 'natural remission,' Harold?" Evan's voice was dangerously low. "I assume that you and Dr. Frankel intend to put forth every effort to reverse the process by any means available to you. I'm sure you didn't mean to make it sound as if you two intend to stand by and do nothing."

Burnham got up from his seat and walked quickly over to a large window that overlooked an adjacent park. He stared out at the winding paths that peeked in and out from between the trees and flowers that thrived under an army of gardeners' constant care. He avoided Evan's stare.

"Harold."

Evan sounded downright mean, and the scientist finally turned back to look at him, afraid not to. "Don't you realize the opportunity we have here!" Burnham shouted, his face and neck turning pink again. He paced around the room, moving his hands in spasmodic little jerks for emphasis. "The chance to study this phenomenon! I'll . . . we'll make medical history! Don't you

175

see, Evan? We have to let it follow its natural course—test and document it at all stages through its completion! We can't destroy this chance! Every other person who has manifested this rare syndrome has disappeared! How will we ever know the full extent of the—"

Evan slammed his hands down on Burnham's desk. "NO!" He leaped from his chair and grabbed Burnham by the arm, spinning him viciously around to face him. "You . . . will . . . not . . . use . . . these . . . people . . . as . . . guinea pigs," he said through clenched teeth, biting off every word in a clear threat.

"Let go of me, Evan," the scientist said quietly, but he was trembling.

Evan let go, fought for self control. The urge to hit the old man was overwhelming. What was he thinking! How could Harold even *entertain* the thought . . . ! He took several deep breaths, steadying himself. "Harold," he said finally. "I'll report this whole thing to the A.M.A. I'll take it right out of your hands. And this isn't the only country doing genetic research. I'll fly those people anywhere in the world at my own expense to get help for them if I have to. . . . But I'd prefer that *you* help them," he added.

The old man's shoulders sagged and he stared at the floor for a minute. "Yes. Of course," he finally said. "Of course you're right, Evan. I'm sorry." He threw himself back in his chair and looked at the man in front of him with sad eyes. "I . . . I don't know what I was thinking. Horrible . . . horrible." He shook his head in self-deprecation. "You're perfectly right. I let my scientific curiosity override my humanity for a moment. Of course Dr. Frankel and I will do everything in our power to help these unfortunate people."

Burnham's intercom buzzed suddenly and he reached out and punched the button.

"Mrs. Matthews and her daughter are here," a tinny voice said.

Burnham, in Evan's presence, explained their latest findings to Lydia after they listened to her story of Jenny's latest episode. And they decided that Jenny needed constant supervision. Burnham himself admitted her to the hospital.

Evan wondered where the child had been going. And where had Bett Wilson been going when she found herself in her nightgown at the shopping mall? And where had the rest of the people who had the Genesis Gene gone to? And why? There was one coincidence that kept running through his mind. Jenny and Bett had both been heading south. Toward the Everglades . . . and Jake's dinosaurs.

Chapter Twenty-six

At least the gray, overcast skies had knocked out a little of the stifling heat, Jake thought. He emptied a cardboard carton that Ralph had jam-packed with food into one of the built-in coolers on the patio boat. It would last for maybe five days. Then they'd fish and hunt, Charlie said—if they stayed out any longer than that. Jake doubted they would from the looks of the sky far to the west, but the guide had said the latest weather reports showed the tropical storm was moving northwest—toward Texas and Louisiana.

Jake hated hunting, and he watched out of the corner of his eye as Charlie stood on the bank and checked out a 300 Weatherby Magnum and a 30.3 Winchester carbine. Not a bad idea though, considering their last adventure. But he'd have preferred the tranq guns. They could bring down an elephant with no problem, and no permanent damage. Yeah ... Frank Buck ... bring 'em back alive. He wondered how many people remembered the big game hunter. He wondered if fifty years from now people would say, "Remember Jake Van Gower, the famous 'bring 'em back alive' dinosaur hunter?"

Now fishing was something else. He'd fished all his

life, ever since he was big enough to hold a pole, and the sense of peace and easy disassociation with the rest of the world it brought to him was something he relished. Not to mention the soul-satisfying taste of fresh-caught bass or trout or whatever.

Charlie had turned in the small pontoon boat for a bigger one. Life out in the little-traveled portions of the Everglades had none of the amenities available in the Park section, and the new twenty-nine-foot beauty that Charlie had shown up with this time had its own chemical toilet (in deference to Ralph), and mosquito nets tied in loose swags to the overhead awning bars. The seats at the front of the boat converted to a large sleeping platform. Not one of them cared to risk sleeping on shore at night, and they still planned to keep a rotating watch at night in any case.

By the time they putted out into the sea of grass, Jake's sense of adventure had switched on high again, and he stared out through the spiky sedge with a growing sense of anticipation. Today they'd be far from the regular tourist routes. Today they might see living things that no man had ever seen before. Today Jake's sense of drama was in full swing, and he was beginning to wonder if he'd ever be satisfied with the dry, lifeless disciplines of forensic biology again.

A steady ten-mile-an-hour wind blew gently, further cooling the air in the Glades. A perfect day, Jake thought happily, for dinosaur hunting.

He turned his back to the monotony of the landscape. It would be a while before they reached the jungle-like hammocks of land that jutted by the hundreds from the shallow waters—thick, concealing masses of vegetation that provided endless havens of refuge for anything that might choose to remain hidden. It would be impossible to explore them all. Even if they spent months out here. They'd have to get lucky.

Jake leaned back and propped his feet up on one of the metal-barred parrot cages. Would it soon hold an Archaeopteryx, he wondered? It sure as hell wouldn't hold a Diatryma or Coelophysis. Ralph had been irritated over the Paleontology Institute's foot-dragging on sending out the floating cages. Some snafu at the Institute shipping department, he'd said. Then he'd made the decision to take a run out into the Glades without them. Seemed like a damned waste of time and money to Jake. Couldn't the man wait a few days? And the fact that he hadn't been consulted, just preemptorily summoned, rankled a little. He watched Ralph and Charlie at the back of the boat, deep in conversation.

What the hell, he thought . . . not going to let it ruin my day. Putting his pique aside, he yanked a book from his backpack, *Everglades Wildguide,* by J. C. George. He leaned back on his bench with it, feet up, and pulled his safari hat down at an angle to protect his eyes from the sun. He'd thought the hat would get a few chuckles from his companions. He'd been wrong. He opened the book and started reading.

Eventually, tree islands appeared in the distance, their thick, verdant vegetation rising from the saw grass like isolated and mysterious primeval worlds. No one had ever counted them, much less explored them all, and it was that thought that excited Jake the most. *To boldly go where no one has gone before.*

They were all quiet now, the ancient beauty of the land gripping their attention and their imaginations as they glided toward the greatest concentration of the un-inhabited jungles.

"Let's try this one." Ralph waved a hand toward the riverbank, and Charlie nodded and turned in toward a moderately clear spot on the left.

A rush of wings exploded into the air, and a flock of egrets, startled by their arrival on shore, flew close overhead and headed south. Jake was first out of the boat.

The going was rough, and Charlie, in the lead, stopped more than once to hack away pieces of the undergrowth that barred their way. Eventually, the dense bottom growth thinned out. The thick canopy of leaves overhead blocked the sun from the jungle floor and limited growth to the hardy flora that could grow under dimmer light conditions.

Ralph and Jake followed close on Charlie's heels.

"How was your visit with your old friend?" Ralph asked now, looking back over his shoulder at Jake, who had taken the position of protecting their rear.

"Good. Fascinating." Jake had held back on telling his friend and colleague about Evan's patients, feeling that it would be a breach of confidence, besides the fact that there wasn't any real connective proof. Now he mulled it over, wanting to say something, and debating with himself if it would be all right or not if he told the story without using names. His gut feeling told him that there *was* a connection, and maybe together he and Ralph could come up with a scientific explanation that would fit all the pieces together and solve both mysteries . . . He dropped back a little, lost in his thoughts.

The two men ahead didn't notice his lag, and quickly widened the gap between them.

When Jake finally looked up, they were well ahead of him, almost out of sight. His first thought was that it would be a real bitch to get lost out here. He shrugged his shoulders to ease the position of his backpack and took a few steps. Stopped. What was that?

A heavy rustling in the undergrowth about a hundred yards to his right drew his attention, and he strained his eyes into the jungle, searching for any sign of movement. Nothing. He waited.

Now Ralph and Charlie were far ahead, their apparent concentration on getting through the underbrush and watching out for danger making them oblivious to his lingering behind. He hoped they weren't out of earshot, though it didn't seem likely. Anxious now, he gave a last look into the tangle of vegetation and began scrambling down the narrowly cleared path.

It crashed through right in front of him with a force and speed that broke medium-sized trees like twigs, and backlashed a large sapling into his chest, sending him sprawling into a clump of palmettos. He rolled, out of instinct, and it saved his life.

The animal thundered past him, squealing and snapping its short, furry jaws in warning. Thick claws dug the ground near Jake's head and sent dirt flying into his eyes.

He rolled again, frantically wiping at his eyes to clear them. On his back now, he squinted up at the monster that lumbered past him. A long tail flashed through the air, arced down, and narrowly missed his neck. The vicious spikes at the end of the tail slapped the ground, buried themselves in the dirt only inches from him, then ripped away and up into the air again. Then it ran, and Jake watched in mind-numbing shock as the nine-foot-long, heavily armored beast crashed away into the distance.

Glyptodont. My God. He sat there, stunned.

Ralph was beside himself with excitement. The commotion on the trail behind them had brought him and Charlie back at a run, and it had taken the combined efforts of Jake and Charlie to prevent the scientist from chasing off into the jungle after the Glyptondont. He'd asked Jake a dozen times to repeat the incident, grinning and nodding enthusiastically through each retelling, and now Ralph and Charlie stood on the patio boat, hunched over the map. A bright red circle marked the island they thought they were on, and Ralph wanted to explore it, and all the islands immediately around the mark. Now. He busied himself with his camera equipment, talking all the while.

Jake looked uneasily at the sky. Thick, dark clouds rolled and boiled in the distance, but he couldn't tell which way they were headed. The thought flashed through his mind that he'd originally come out here looking for a bird the size of a crow, and now he was up against prehistoric monsters the size of tanks.

The radio crackled to life. Charlie picked up the mike and pushed a button. Park Service. The tropical storm had changed direction. It was headed toward Florida. Come in. Now.

Jake could feel Ralph's disappointment, but the older man, surprisingly, said nothing.

Charlie started the engine and they backed slowly out into the channel.

They watched the shore as the boat glided past the dinosaur's refuge, each lost in his own thoughts.

Jake stepped over to Ralph, put a hand on his shoulder. Ralph didn't turn, but smiled in acknowledgment of Jake's presence. "This is the greatest thing that has ever ... *could* ever, happen to me, Jake," he said. "I can't describe the exhilaration I feel ... the extraordinary sense of discovery ... the sense of ... of ..." He finally tore his eyes from the shore; they glistened with emotion as he searched for appropriate words. "I'm fulfilled, Jake," he said softly.

Some of that emotion transferred to Jake, and he smiled his agreement down at the older paleontologist, but said nothing. Couldn't.

The radio crackled again, and Charlie leaped for it. A rumbling in the distance drowned out the Park Service message, but didn't hide the alarm in the tinny voice.

The storm was coming in unexpectedly fast, Charlie reported, then spoke into the microphone again. He gave their position, signed off, then grimly shifted into top speed. He eyed the rapidly advancing clouds warily. They were coming in from the west. He didn't need the Park Service to tell him to get the hell out of there, and it briefly occurred to him that he should probably up the ante to one fifty a day.

The sudden surge of speed rocked Jake and Ralph, and they sat down on the bench rather than fight for balance. As the first drops of rain pelted the canopy, Jake took one last look over his shoulder at the shoreline.

A face peered out at him from the bushes.

"CHARLIE!" He spun in his seat and gripped the railing, leaning out as far as he could. "STOP!"

Charlie cut the motor. "What? We gotta get outta here, man. I don't care if—"

"There's a man out there!" Jake yelled, pointing out at the shore.

Ralph and Charlie leaned over the side of the boat and stared in the direction of Jake's finger. Nothing. They looked at him.

"I tell you, I saw a face!" He cupped his hands to his mouth. "HELLO OUT THERE!"

"Jake." Ralph touched him on the arm and pointed to a spot about a hundred yards away from where Jake had seen the face. A figure crouched quickly and disappeared. A naked figure, or almost naked. It was hard to tell, it had moved so fast.

The wind picked up. The rain suddenly hit in blinding sheets, pounding off the canopy in a deafening drum of sound that almost eclipsed the steady roll of thunder that accompanied it.

Charlie left the rail, gunned the motor again, and the little boat flew forward, staggering the other two men.

Jake caught his balance and leaned forward. He grabbed Charlie's arm and spun him half around. "Are you crazy!" he yelled over the storm. "There are *people* out there! We have to . . ."

Charlie yanked his arm away. "You ever been in a tropical storm in the Glades, mister!"

"No, but we have to . . .!"

"No *way!*" Charlie's face screwed up in anger—or fear, Jake couldn't tell which. "What you see here"—Charlie pointed out toward the driving rain—"is nothing! This is drizzle! By tomorrow morning the wind'll snap this damn boat in half! And no way I'm gonna be out here!"

"Jake." Ralph plucked at Jake's sleeve. "Don't you think that people lost or in trouble out here would be desperately signaling to us from shore . . . not hiding in the bushes?"

"Then who—?"

"I don't know. But whoever they are, they don't seem to need us . . . and Charlie's right. We must go back before the brunt of the storm hits. We promised the Park Service, and if we don't comply with their wishes, they may not let us come out here again."

Outnumbered, Jake turned back to the railing and stared toward the shore. Sheets of rain blocked a clear view of the jungle and soaked him to the skin. He didn't notice. He was too upset. He would have felt a lot better about Ralph if self-preservation were his only motive for deserting the people on the hammock. But his motive for leaving them to their fate had been fear over being denied further exploration in the Glades.

Jake wondered how many human lives the paleontologist would be willing to sacrifice for the expedition.

Several pair of eyes watched the boat skim away over the choppy water.

Chapter Twenty-seven

There had to be a thread . . . somewhere. Evan rubbed his eyes and leaned back in his easy chair, stiff from hours of reading the anonymous charts and records. A gentle rain pattered on the windows, and the overcast sky made it look a lot later than it was. He switched on a lamp and turned back to the reports.

The patients had been male and female, old, young (seventeen was the youngest except for Jenny) and middle-aged. There was no common blood type or disease except for the symptoms surrounding the Genesis Gene, and they came from all over the state, so he doubted there had been any premeditated conspiracy among them to disappear. (The possibility of a newly formed cult of some kind had crossed his mind, remote as that possibility was.) They didn't seem to have anything in common that would give him a clue as to why they'd all disappeared, and why they carried the gene. Except that they were all white, with a few American Indians thrown in. But so what?

Try it from a different angle, Evan thought. Why *not* black or Oriental? What common denominator did those races have that precluded them from possessing the gene? Why *hadn't* any of them disappeared? He couldn't figure that one out either.

He flipped through the pages again, his eyes scanning "Race." Caucasian. Caucasian. Caucasian. Caucasian/Indian. American or India Indian? He'd missed that one before. Caucasian. Seminole. Caucasian. The rest were all white except for three more American ,Indians, no tribe specified.

Damn, he thought. What thread was he overlooking here? And what kind of American Indians, he wondered? Did it matter?

A picture of Lydia's thick black hair flashed in his mind. This is a wild hunch, Evan thought, and picked up the phone.

Lydia answered on the third ring.

"I have a question for you, if you don't mind," he said after the preliminaries were over. "What is Jenny's ancestry?"

"Well, her father's ancestors were English and French," Lydia said.

The cave drawings, Evan thought. Like the ones in France. My God, she really was dredging up ancient memories. He wondered why he was always so surprised when faced with new proof of the Genesis Gene.

"And I'm a real mix." Lydia laughed a little, as if apologizing for her mongrel heritage. "Italian, French, and Seminole, if you want to go back far enough."

"Seminole Indian?" Evan asked, his heart beating faster.

"Yes. My grandmother on my mother's side. She was a full-blooded Seminole. Claimed her heritage went all the way back to the old Calusas, but nobody paid much attention to that. Why, Evan?"

Evan glanced at the clock on his mantel. Almost four-thirty. "Can I take you to dinner?" he asked. "I'll explain then."

She hesitated only a moment. "I was just on my way to the hospital to see Jenny again. Can you pick me up there after visiting hours?"

Evan agreed, and hoped her acceptance of his dinner offer wasn't made just out of curiosity. *And you could have told her your reasons over the phone,* he thought. But he didn't want to.

He dialed Harold Burnham's number.

"Burnham," a tired voice said.

"Harold? This is Evan. Do something for me, will you," he asked. "Find out the nationalities of the two Genesis Gene patients you tracked down through your associates. I may be on to something, but I can't explain now."

"Why—?"

"What I'm looking for is common ancestry. If I can find it, it may give us a clue as to what's causing the gene to activate, and we may be able to predict who might have a propensity for the problem, and study them," he explained anyway. *And warn them,* he thought to himself.

"Wait," Burnham said. "I have it here."

Evan waited impatiently while the sound of rustling papers floated over the phone.

"Mixed ancestry," Burnham finally said.

Evan sighed with disappointment.

"Except for this."

Evan held his breath.

"They both list Seminole Indian blood in their backgrounds."

* * *

"So he said he'd try to get their names and addresses for me," Evan said as a waiter placed steaming platters of mixed seafood in front of them. "The psychiatrists who handled the cases can call the families and tell them what we're trying to do, and that we might be able to shed some light on what happened to their relatives. That should be enough incentive for them to talk to me."

Lydia poked at a broiled scallop. "I want to come with you."

"Why?" Surprised, Evan stopped eating and stared at her.

"Because it concerns Jenny. Those people *disappeared*, Evan. . . ."

"Jenny is safe in the hospital . . . safer than she would be at home. . . ."

Lydia gave him a sharp glance, and Evan backpedaled, furious with himself for such a tactless remark. "Wait! I'm not casting any aspersions on your ability as a mother, Lydia! Far from it . . . all I meant was that she has twenty-four-hour-a-day surveillance there, and at home . . . well, you have to sleep sometime," he finished lamely.

"You're right." Her face softened. "It's just that I feel I should be by her side, protecting her every minute. And right now I feel so helpless . . . and guilty."

"Why guilty?"

"Because I'm having fun." She didn't drop her eyes.

It took Evan a second to get her meaning, and he impulsively reached out and took her hand.

"Look, Evan . . ." She returned the pressure of his hand for a second, then pulled away. "I need to feel as if I'm doing something constructive to help Jenny . . . and the rest of those people too. And maybe the families

190

of those missing people will find it easier to talk to a woman—no aspersions on your ability as a psychiatrist," she added with a straight face. "But it can't hurt to have me along, and I won't feel so useless. It will—"

"All right."

"All right? I can come?"

"Yes."

Evan loved the way her sudden smile transformed her face. He wished he could make it stay there forever.

The patients' recreation lounge was almost empty now, and Bett sat staring at the T.V., not really seeing it. She was bored. Not one to mingle freely with strangers, she hadn't made any attempt at conversation with any of the other patients, and they'd left her alone too. Nobody on this floor seemed to act seriously ill, especially the children (and there were mostly children here, she'd noticed). She'd seen *One Flew Over The Cuckoo's Nest,* but it wasn't even remotely like that here. But, she supposed, that was different.

A nurse had come in with evening medication a while ago, and she'd asked about the patients. The nurse had smiled and said this floor was only for people with sleep disorders and mild behavior dysfunctions. Then she'd turned away before Bett could ask any more questions.

Feeling mildly rebuffed, Bett had retreated to an easy chair and flipped through several magazines, and tried her hand at a crossword puzzle, but they hadn't held her interest for long. She wondered what Ray was doing; hoped he'd cooked himself a good meal or gone out someplace to eat instead of popping a T.V. dinner in the microwave.

At one point, she'd noticed the woman and the little girl she'd seen in Dr. Tremayne's office laughing over a puzzle in the corner. She'd watched them for a while, then, when they left the room, she'd followed them down the hall on impulse. The child fascinated her, and she didn't know why. She wasn't especially beautiful, in fact was a little too plump, and her dark hair frizzed around her face, badly in need of taming, in Bett's opinion.

When the mother and daughter disappeared into room 306, she'd gone back to the lounge, vaguely disappointed that the girl was out of her sight.

She wondered how long she'd be here. Tomorrow they were taking her to some genetic testing lab for some test with magnets or something. Then she guessed she'd be back here until the results came in. Or longer, if she had any more "incidents," as Dr. Burnham called them.

She sighed. The laugh track from the sitcom was starting to annoy her, and she got up and walked over to the huge picture windows that overlooked the park. The view was pretty, calming, and she watched the steady stream of people going in and out of the building for a while.

She felt fine now. Had felt fine, in fact, all day. *I want to go home,* she thought. *I'm not really sick . . . I can live with this problem . . . all I need is some stronger pills to control my sleepwalking, right?*

A few drops of rain splashed against the windows and slid down in little rivulets. Within a few minutes, in typical Florida fashion, it was a downpour, complete with thunder and lightning, and Bett turned and went back to her room. It was almost time for dinner, and that would fill a little of her time.

Jenny waved good-bye to her mother and Dr. Tremayne. She liked Dr. Tremayne. He talked to her like she was grown up, not in that high, fake, smiley voice that a lot of people used when they talked to little kids. They were going out to eat, they'd said. She was hungry too. She pressed her nose against the window and looked down at the sidewalk to see if she could see them leaving. She couldn't.

"Dinnertime, girls!" Miss Mona came in wheeling a cart. She stopped in the middle of the room and clapped her hands just like Jenny's day-care teacher. But she was smiling just like Mrs. Oliveri smiled too, and Jenny clapped her hands back at her and laughed.

Ariadne and Joleene didn't laugh, but they smiled shyly at Miss Mona from their chairs at the small table in the corner.

Jenny shared the room with the two older girls, and both of them would wake up in the middle of the night, screaming. The first time it had happened, Jenny had been frightened. But after that first time, she stayed in her bed, out of the way. She knew somebody would rush in in a few seconds to sit with her new friends, and soon it would all be over. What she didn't understand was that neither of them seemed to remember that it had happened at all when morning came. She'd asked them about what she thought were their bad dreams—after all, she always remembered *all* of her dreams—but they just looked at her as if they didn't even know what she was talking about. Maybe, she thought, they didn't want to tell her because they thought she was only a baby and they didn't want to scare her. They were big kids. They were eight and nine.

Jenny lifted the dome off her plate and sniffed at the steam that drifted up toward her nose. Good! It was chicken, and she loved chicken. She wasn't that happy with the carrots, but she'd eat them anyway. She always ate everything on her plate.

Miss Mona left them alone, and they ate and laughed together, mostly Jenny and Joleene laughed—Ariadne was shy. And she was the oldest too, which surprised Jenny.

After dinner they had their choice of a bath or a shower. Jenny took showers like a big girl. And then they were permitted to watch T.V. or play quietly till bedtime. Tonight, bedtime for Ariadne was in the sleep lab, and when her mother came back to say good night, Ariadne hung on her neck and cried a little. Jenny watched her out of the corner of her eye. She wanted to tell her it was okay, it didn't hurt . . . but she didn't.

Later, Joleene went to sleep almost immediately, and Jenny stood by the window, staring out at the thunderstorm. The steady drum of the rain was soothing, and she half closed her eyes as she watched the occasional flashes of lightning crackle through the night. The drumrolls of thunder ran one into another, barely allowing any time for silence between their songs. The storm beat its violent sensory images into Jenny's brain. And the web that gently cradled her hippocampus grew a little, pulsed . . . and triggered a series of synaptic transmissions that had remained dormant and inhibited in the brains of Jenny and her ancestors for centuries. And Jenny ceased to exist.

Chapter Twenty-eight

One A.M. Bett put on her other shoe, then stared at it for a minute. It felt wrong, and she was agitated. If only the damn thunder would stop! It had given her a monster headache. Her clothes felt uncomfortable too, and she yanked and tugged at them, trying to make them feel more natural on her body.

A flash of lightning reflected from the mirror into her eyes, and she winced. That didn't help, either. She stood up and faced the door, then wondered where she was going. And why. She'd gotten dressed, so she must have been going someplace, right? She couldn't remember and sat down again.

Another clap of thunder made her jump, and she spun around on the bed to face the direction of the noise. Her heart thumped with fright, and beads of sweat popped out under her arms and across her nose. Stop! She screamed silently, and screwed her eyes shut against the power that lashed at her through the window.

Three spears of lightning forced their light through her closed eyelids and seared into her brain. She sobbed once, then forced her eyes open. Where was she? Panicked, she leaped to her feet and stared around the strange room. There was a vague familiarity in the furniture, but she couldn't quite place it. Oh. Hospital. Then she lost it again, and a new terror seized her. She had to get . . . get . . . who? There was someone she had to protect! Who . . .?

The overhead lights flickered. Went out. Confused, she sat in the dark and waited. The dark didn't bother her. She even felt slightly comforted by it. Slowly, her eyes adjusted to it while she struggled with her thoughts. She thought she knew where she was, but not why. And . . . she couldn't remember her name. It didn't seem important, though.

Suddenly she knew who she had to protect. Of course! Ja-nee! She jumped to her feet, a new sense of purpose washing away her fears and confusion.

Bett opened the door to a darkened corridor. Voices drifted around her in the dim light. Somebody said something about a generator in a sharp voice. Flashlight beams skittered around the floor. ". . . all asleep, anyway," somebody else said.

Bett walked down the corridor to room 306. Nobody stopped her.

She stood just inside the door and looked around, searching. One bed had a small lump in it. Not Ja-nee. A small sound from a corner caught her attention and she walked toward it. A shape hunched down against the wall moved slightly, and she smiled into the dark, hurried toward it, and knelt quickly. "Ja-nee," she said. "Abuna dom ista nakigi?"

The child lifted a frightened face and stared at her. Tears glistened on her cheeks and her lower lip trembled, but she didn't make a sound.

"Dom kinata su, Ja-nee." Bett held out her arms.

196

"Tota ma-da?" Some of the fright left the child's eyes.

Bett struggled to answer the little girl's question. Who was she? She wasn't sure, but the child seemed to think she was her mother. And she was, wasn't she? A name poised on the edge of her consciousness . . . Bee . . . no, Tep . . . Betep? What was the matter with her! Betepi! She had it! Betepi! "Betepi ma-da," she said softly, and Ja-nee wrapped her arms around Bett's neck and sighed.

They walked down the stairs in the dark. Bett held tightly to Jenny's hand, afraid of losing her in the unfamiliar territory. Nobody noticed them.

At the bottom of the stairs, a back door opened into the Emergency parking lot, and Bett half ran toward the shelter of a pair of live oaks, pulling Jenny along with her. The storm lashed at Bett's hair, whipping it around her face and blinding her for a second, and in less than a minute they were both soaked.

They stood huddled together for a while, uncertain what to do next. Suddenly the sound of squealing tires carried over the thunder, and Bett saw a car slide around the corner, expertly correct its direction, and careen toward them. Quickly, she and Jenny crouched down behind the sheltering trees and watched it speed into the deserted lot. It bounced dangerously over the speed bump and skidded to a stop in front of the Emergency room doors.

An obese, middle-aged man flung open the car door on the driver's side and heaved himself out, grunting with the exertion of it. With surprising agility, he rushed to the passenger side and gently eased a frail old woman to her feet. The woman clutched at her chest as the man half dragged, half carried her through the rain toward the darkened doors.

Bett watched the doors swing shut behind them, then looked at the green Ford that sat deserted and trembling in the storm. The wind? No. The thin sound of an idling engine hummed over the sound of the wind and rain, and Bett smiled.

"Ja-nee, tanto!" she yelled, and sprinted for the car. Jenny obeyed instantly, and in a few minutes they were driving down the highway. Bett turned the heat on for a few minutes to drive away the chill they both felt, and then reached over to pat Jenny's knee. The child patted her hand back and smiled.

They were going home.

Chapter Twenty-nine

Lydia knew. When the phone rang at six o'clock in the morning, she knew. Still, she kept telling herself how foolish she was being as she brought the receiver to her ear. And when the anonymous voice from the hospital asked her to come right away, she refused to agree and hang up until they told her why. She had to hear the words. Finally, the voice said them. Jenny was missing.

By the time she reached the hospital, a grim fury had eclipsed her initial anguish, and she mentally rehearsed the words of accusation and condemnation she fully intended to hurl at any and all responsible parties who had allowed her daughter to leave the grounds unattended. And in a storm! It hadn't let up at all since last night. What had ever possessed the child to go out in all this?

Her eyes had roamed ceaselessly from one side of the street to the other as she drove, a part of her fully expecting to see Jenny skipping along the street through the rain toward home. But it hadn't happened, and she reminded herself that Jenny didn't *know* the way home from the hospital. The drive was too complicated and too far for her to have memorized it during the few trips they'd taken.

Lightning cracked overhead as Lydia pulled into the hospital parking lot and raced for the front door. It fit her mood, and she slammed open the door, nearly colliding with Evan, who had been waiting impatiently for her.

"Lydia!" He grabbed her to steady her. "I tried to call you . . . there was no answer, so I figured that you were on your—"

"You said she'd be *safe* here!" she shouted. "You said . . ." and she started to cry, her rage instantly dissolving into fear and grief.

Evan held her while she cried.

Ray Wilson didn't understand. Bett wasn't in the hospital? He rested the phone receiver on the tabletop and looked through the house, then into the garage, then out the windows into the back and front yards. Surely she wouldn't be out there in the rain. But he looked anyway.

Puzzled, and only mildly alarmed, he picked up the phone again. "No," he said. "She isn't here. Did you look in the cafeteria? Well, maybe she got dressed and went out for breakfast. She gets up early, and . . . Well, look . . . I'm sure she'll show up, but I'll be right down anyway. I'd planned to . . . Yes. Right away. Yes."

He hung up and got dressed. She couldn't have gone far, he reasoned. He'd driven her to the hospital, so her car was still here in the garage. And besides, he didn't think she'd have left the hospital anyway. She was terrified of thunderstorms.

* * *

Lydia answered all the questions with forced calm, and the young police officer wrote everything down in a black notebook, occasionally asking her to repeat herself.

A team of police and hospital personnel continued their search through every room and corridor, but Lydia knew they wouldn't find them. Them. Jenny and a woman called Elizabeth Wilson. She'd lost all hope that Jenny would show up soon when she found out that the Wilson woman was missing too. A woman who had also been Evan's patient. A woman who also carried the Genesis Gene.

The police officer finally walked away after murmuring some encouraging words, and a short, slightly paunchy man hurried over to where Lydia and Evan sat.

"Dr. Tremayne," he said, and held out his hand to Evan. His eyes flicked over Lydia and he frowned. "Are you the little girl's mother?" he asked.

"Lydia, this is Ray Wilson," Evan said, rising and taking the man's hand. "Ray, this is Lydia Matthews, Jenny's mother."

"I'm sorry . . . I'm really sorry," Ray blurted, and his face crumpled along with his body as he dropped onto the sofa alongside Lydia. "She . . . my wife . . . wanted a child so much . . . she . . ."

"What?" Lydia looked quickly at Evan, startled by Ray Wilson's apparent assumption. Was he saying that he thought his wife had *kidnapped* Jenny?

"Don't . . . don't worry," Ray continued. He rubbed his face with his palms and sighed deeply. "She loves children . . . she won't harm her. Please, believe that. She—"

201

"Ray." Evan put a hand on the man's shoulder and shook it a little to get his attention. Ray looked up at him. "I don't think it's as simple as you think. We need to talk. Come on." Evan stood waiting while Lydia and Ray got up to follow him.

The three of them sat in Evan's office while he explained the pattern of disappearances that plagued the people who carried the gene, and how he thought he'd found the connecting link between them. "Did Bett have any Seminole blood, Ray?" he asked.

"No. I mean I don't know, Dr. Tremayne."

"Evan."

"Oh, yes . . . Evan. It wasn't something I can ever remember discussing with her . . . our ancestry, I mean. I guess it's possible."

Evan tapped his fingers on the desk, thinking.

Lydia watched him. "We have to do those interviews today," she said finally. "The families of those people might have some clues about where they've disappeared to . . . clues they may not even be aware of, not knowing everything we know."

"Do you think that's where my wife and your daughter are?" Ray asked hopefully. "With all the rest of the people who disappeared?" He jumped to his feet and walked back and forth in front of the couch, his head down, trying to puzzle it all out. "Why? Where? I don't get all this! It doesn't make any sense! Why would all these people leave their families and friends who love them and take off without a word? It's not . . . not . . . normal!"

"Ray," Evan said. "What Bett, Jenny, and the rest are going through *isn't* normal. The magnetic resonance imaging test your wife was supposed to take today?"

Ray stopped pacing and looked at Evan, waiting.

"I think," Evan continued, "that it would have shown the same thing Lydia's daughter's tests showed; that there's a web forming over the hippocampus, a part of her brain, that's triggering dormant racial memories. And that isn't normal."

"What happens to her . . . them . . . if we can't find them?" Ray asked bluntly.

Evan shifted uncomfortably in his seat and glanced quickly over at Lydia. She was staring at him too. "I don't know," he answered truthfully. "But my guess is, according to what Dr. Burnham believes, that they may revert to a permanent state of prehistoric mind. They'll lose their present identity until we can find them and treat them."

"They won't die?" Lydia asked. Her voice was firm and had no trace of imminent hysteria, Evan noticed with relief.

"No," Evan said to her. But he wasn't really sure.

"Okay . . . okay," Ray said. "So all these people are wandering around with some kind of amnesia. That makes sense. That explains why they could leave home without giving a damn about who they leave behind . . . but don't you think that one of them . . . someplace . . . would walk up to somebody and say, 'Hey. I don't know who I am or where I am. Can you help me?' "

"Normally, yes," Evan said. "But they may no longer have the ability to recall modern speech, if they've regressed to a primitive state." He didn't want to say this next, but he had to. They had a right to know. "It's likely that now they think and behave more like animals. They'd be afraid of modern man and his world. They'd search out unpopulated places to hide in because it would be more comfortable for them."

Ray and Lydia looked shocked.

"There are so many wild, unpopulated areas in Florida!" Lydia said as the meaning of Evan's words sank in. "They'll never find them! They can't possibly—"

"Please," Evan said, his eyes lingering on Lydia, willing her to keep calm. "Please believe me. I don't think they're in any immediate danger, because they can't have gone far in this storm. The police will—"

"What if you're wrong?" Ray asked. "What if all this has nothing to do with your Genesis Gene . . . except for the fact that the little girl has it. What if my wife, with all the stress of her sleepwalking problems, and her intense desire for a child, just suddenly crossed the line and kidnapped the girl . . . not even knowing or caring that the child was sick?" His face was twisted with pain at the thought, but he plunged on. "Don't you think, Evan, that that's more logical than all this primitive gene stuff?"

"No." Evan spoke firmly. Ray was losing it. "I'm her psychiatrist, Ray . . . and I can tell you that your wife's desire for a child was no stronger or more compelling than any other normal woman's desire for a child. When we find them—and we *will* find them—I don't think that under the circumstances, Mrs. Matthews has any intention of filing kidnapping charges against Bett. Do you, Lydia?" He turned back to her, a warning look on his face.

Lydia looked back at him in surprise. She hadn't had any intention of doing that. She believed Bett Wilson was suffering from the same problem Jenny had, and didn't blame her for her actions for one minute. As a matter of fact, she was glad that Jenny wasn't out there alone somewhere. And she told them so.

Ray's relief was evident, but he had something else to say . . . and it wasn't easy. "Look . . . I thank you for

204

that, Lydia. But if I may make a suggestion here . . ." He took a deep breath. "Let the police think my wife kidnapped the child."

"What?" Lydia and Evan said in unison.

"If you tell them about the Genesis Gene, and what you really think has happened here, they may not search as diligently for them." His voice shook. "Whereas kidnapping a child is a serious offense. You can be damned sure they'll look harder in that case . . . and I want them to look hard."

A knock at the door interrupted any reply that Evan or Lydia might have made, and a police officer stuck his head in the door. "Mr. Wilson?" he said. Does your wife drive?"

"Yes, certainly," Ray answered, puzzled. "Why?"

"Somebody stole a green Ford out of the Emergency Room parking lot last night."

Lydia suddenly felt sick.

"They were more than happy to comply," Harold Burnham said to Evan as he handed him a piece of paper with two names and addresses on it. "Anything or anybody who might be able to help, they said . . ." His voice trailed off and he looked up at Evan.

"Thanks." Evan took the paper and put it in his pocket without looking at it. "Did you get any more results back?"

"Yes, for all the good it does us now," Burnham said bitterly. He reached for a sheaf of papers, and Evan watched him riffle through them. "Here," he said, his finger marking a spot on one of the reports. "We've had some trouble reading the filler between genetic marks, but the new machine should sort it out before this afternoon. That part of the tests wasn't that important anyway, considering the rest."

He adjusted a pair of reading glasses and read, paraphrasing and adding his own remarks. "What we have so far is evidence of a damaged nucleic acid in an apparently mutated gene located in the mitochondria, the small part of the cell responsible for the cell's energy. And we were lucky it was there, where we had only thirty-seven genes to study instead of in the cell nucleus where we'd probably still be searching through about a hundred thousand of them. And microcomplementation and restriction enzyme tests corroborate the findings.

"And an interesting fact that you might already know—where genes in the nucleus are inherited from both parents, genes in the mitochondria are passed down only through the mother."

Evan raised his eyebrows at that one. "Interesting, but I'm not sure it means anything. How . . . why did it happen? The mutation, I mean."

"I don't know. My guess would be damage from a high dose of ultraviolet light. Where they would have encountered it, I have no idea. Or . . ." He looked thoughtful. "Exposure to a small dose of rarer light rays that wouldn't normally occur except under aberrant atmospheric conditions, and wouldn't affect the majority of people who don't have a propensity for this particular form of specific genetic damage . . . like in Frankel's rhesus monkeys."

Evan thought about that for a minute. Aberrant atmospheric conditions. The slight polar shift he and Jake had discussed. That was it. It was the only thing that made sense. So now he was reasonably sure of the "how." Now the problem was turning off the activated Genesis Gene. And maybe . . . "Okay. If that's the case, how about administering visible light? Photorecovery might trigger her enzyme systems and restore the damaged nucleic acid in the gene to their normal form, couldn't it?"

"You've been reading," Burnham said. He looked impressed. "Not normally your field, Evan."

"I'm concerned."

"Yes. Well." The scientist thumbed through a few more pages. "The mutated gene is disturbing the normal manufacture and catalytic function of its holoenzyme because the cofactor is broken. That's what I think we should concentrate on."

"What is the cofactor?"

"Magnesium. And it's preventing the migration of neurons somehow, and that just might be the cause of the web forming. A compensation of some sort . . . I don't know yet. Anyway, the result is a strange sequence of synapses in the brain that are apparently retrieving primitive, genetic memories. And because of the seizure type action of the web, there's massive neuronal activity that keeps firing after each retrieval. That's why, I think, the 'dreams' that Jenny and Mrs. Wilson have are so detailed, and why they remember them upon awakening."

Evan struggled to put it all together. "I still think photorecovery—"

"Yes, yes." Burnham waved his hand impatiently. "I fully intend to use it as an adjunct to whatever chemical therapies Dr. Frankel and I can come up with.

"The point is . . . repeated stimulation of the brain in this way can cause long-lasting changes in the synapses . . . structural changes." He looked at Evan carefully. Did he get the implication here? "Their brains are altering, Evan. And this is a memory function that we've never observed before. It could be that if we don't stop it soon, there won't be any way to reverse it."

Evan felt himself mentally recoil with denial from the thought. How could he ever tell Lydia that now? My God! "Wait, Harold, wait," he said desperately. "Ninety percent of the proteins in the brain are broken down and reformed within two weeks. So wouldn't we have repeated chances to alter its structure?"

"The proteins are reformed. The structure isn't," Burnham said bluntly. "We have to realter the structure, and if the changes go too far . . . become permanently imprinted . . ." He let his voice trail off and shrugged. "I just don't know enough yet, Evan. Dr. Frankel is using high-resolution fluorescent microscopy to locate the granular sites of cellular replication in the nucleus of Jenny's cells. Each granule contains DNA segments and enzymes needed for replication in the protein matrix. That protein matrix is *webbed* throughout the nucleus, which is normal, but that web is probably what has exploded out of normal bounds into the site of the hippocampus. That's what we're working on finding out now. We just need a little more time . . . this is all so new, and—"

"I have to find them," Evan said, his mind racing over the dire possibilities ahead for Jenny and Bett if he didn't.

"Yes," Burnham said softly. "Yes, you do."

Chapter Thirty

Jake watched the storm through the motel room window. Jesus! What a blow! And they were twenty miles inland, in a "safe" town just north of the Everglades. He couldn't even imagine what it might be like stuck in a little boat out in the middle of the Glades. The window rattled under the onslaught of another gust of screaming wind, and Jake backed away to the comparative safety of the center of the room. "Christ," he said under his breath.

Charlie grinned up at him from where he knelt fiddling with the T.V. set. "Only a drizzle, man. Should have seen it when Camille came through in '69. That was somethin'."

"You were a kid in '69," Jake said evenly. "Things always look bigger than real when you're a kid. It couldn't have been much worse than this." He sat on the bed and wished he were back in Montana.

"Wasn't a kid in '92, when Andrew came through." Charlie looked at him, completely serious now. "What's out there now is a sunshower compared to that monster. Homestead, a town south of here, looked like Hiroshima after the bomb when it was all over. Never seen anything like it." He sat for a moment, his eyes distant, remembering, then shrugged and went back to concentrating on the T.V. screen. The reception was lousy, mostly snow, and a series of hypnotic wavy lines that marched across the screen. The sound was sporadic too.

Jake watched him, marveling that they had any electricity at all. And he remembered Andrew. The television coverage of the hurricane and its aftermath had gone on forever, it seemed. Homestead hadn't looked like any place in the United States. It had reminded him of Mideastern war zones.

The screen dulled to a monotonous gray, and static crackled from the dying box. Charlie punched the "off" knob in disgust just as the lights went out.

Jake felt a curious sense of satisfaction, as if this storm were his, and it was now successfully competing against Charlie's Camille and Andrew for potential destructive power. But this is only a tropical storm, he reminded himself. It isn't even close.

"Shit," Charlie said, then stood up and frowned at the gale roaring outside the window. "Maybe I can get candles at the desk. I'll bring some over to Doc Jenner too."

"Ask him if he wants to come sit this out with us," Jake suggested. Jenner had opted for a private room. "I snore," he'd said. Jake and Charlie took a double.

Jake watched Charlie slip on a yellow rain slicker and start for the door. He thought of Maine sea captains and wondered how a nor'easter would compare with a Florida hurricane.

"Charlie."

"Yeah?"

"You were right about coming in when we did. I had

no idea . . ." He waved a hand toward the storm. "But I still worry about the people we left out there."

Charlie put his hand on the doorknob, then hesitated before turning it. "Look, Jake. If there was anybody out there, they're prob'ly used to it. There's rumors . . . always been rumors, far as I know. About lost tribes . . . descendants of the Calusa Indians, or some other tribe maybe. I don't know. Don't pay a whole lot of attention to that stuff. Anyway, they're supposed to be living out in the Glades. Could be what you saw, though you'd be the first one to ever really see 'em."

"Calusa?"

"Yeah. Ancient tribe. Wiped out centuries ago, they say. Don't say how. Nobody knows, I guess. Anyway, legend says some of 'em are still out there, and they never come near anybody. Wild people." He pulled open the door and ran out into the yellow twilight.

Interesting, Jake thought. Makes me feel a little better, anyway. Maybe there was something about the Calusas in the books he'd bought. He pulled them out of his suitcase and had just finished searching unproductively through the index of the third one when Charlie rushed back inside in a swirl of rain and wind.

"Doc was asleep," he said, putting a hand full of short, white candles in front of Jake. "Woke him up." He grinned as if it were an accomplishment. "He said thanks for the invite, but he wouldn't have any trouble getting back to sleep."

Jake couldn't imagine how anybody could sleep through all this. He lighted a candle and dripped some of the hot wax into an ashtray, then stood the candle in it, waiting until it held. The storm made it darker than it should have been for the early hour of the afternoon, and it was hard to read by the ambient light.

"Going to go play a few hands with Ollie at the desk," Charlie said. "Want to come?"

The invitation was polite, but Jake sensed Charlie's need to get away from eggheads for a while, so he shook his head. "No thanks. Think I'll catch up on my reading."

"Suit yourself," Charlie said. And he left, letting in another swirl of wind and water.

Jake struggled through a few pages in the flickering light for about twenty minutes before he gave up. He couldn't concentrate. His mind kept traveling back to the glyptodont that had nearly trampled him to death in the jungle. The towering, armadillolike creature had been a common sight during the Pleistocene Epoch— fairly recent times, if you want to call from between two million to fifteen thousand years ago recent.

And the Diatryma—looking like a huge ostrich with a parrot's head. Extinct for sixteen million years. And the herd of Coelophysis—from the late Triassic, about two hundred million years ago!

And the thecodont. My God, the thecodont. Ancestor to all the dinosaurs. Its primitive crocodilian form had disappeared from the earth over two hundred and twenty-five million years ago.

The search for Archaeopteryx seemed almost boring by comparison.

He itched to get his hands on a live specimen.

Leaning back in the green plastic chair, he put his hands behind his head and smiled. A book. Of course he'd write a book. And there'd be lecture tours. Grants. T.V. shows. He'd be famous! The whole world . . .

Jesus. He shook his head with disgust at himself. He was beginning to think like Ralph. But there was a problem here. News of their discovery would bring peo-

212

ple pouring into the Glades; scientists, reporters, hunters, and adventurers. The delicate ecosystem would be devastated. But on the other hand, he mused, wouldn't the spread of these huge primitive creatures do the same thing? The scientific and environmental implications of what was happening out in the Glades was awesome.

And what if the huge animals decided to leave the Glades in search of food or territory? The ensuing danger and panic would be unlike anything ever experienced by humans before. His guess would be that the government would step in and destroy the creatures. The thought left him melancholy, and more than a little angry. His mind raced, trying to think of a way to save the animals without posing a threat to civilization. He couldn't think of a damned thing. The throwbacks to ancient times, the most incredible scientific discoveries of all time, were doomed to a second extinction.

Chapter Thirty-one

Evan and Lydia raced through the rain to Evan's car. They'd turned down Ray's offer to come with them on the interviews, thinking that too many people descending on the bereaved families at once might be an overkill. Ray had reluctantly agreed to being left out after making them promise to keep him up to date on any new developments.

Now Evan drove slowly down Route 19, straining to see the road through the rapid flap of the windshield wipers, and the almost blinding sheets of water that showed no signs of letting up.

"Everts Drive should be coming up soon," Lydia said, checking for the dozenth time the slip of paper she held. The Hafferlings, the first address on the list, had been surprised that Evan had wanted to come out in the middle of a storm to see them, but had given him directions nevertheless, and Evan was glad that they lived only a few miles from the hospital.

The second address was miles away—near an Indian reservation close to the Everglades—and they'd made an appointment to see the Birdsongs the next day, when they assumed the weather would be better for driving.

"Here," Lydia said suddenly, and Evan slowed and turned right. A thick canopy of trees over the road blocked some of the rain, and driving the last few miles to the Hafferlings' house was a little easier than it had been on the open road.

A blast of wind rocked the car and bent the tops of trees as Evan and Lydia pulled into the driveway and ran for the front door. It was opened for them before they reached it, and a tall, angular woman in her midthirties ushered them inside, clucking over their bravery in daring the elements.

"I'm Joan Hafferling," she said as she took their raincoats and draped them over a wooden banister. "And I can't tell you how grateful I am that you'd come out in all this to help me find my mother."

Evan introduced himself and Lydia, and then followed Joan into the kitchen where she had a pot of freshly brewed coffee waiting for them. They accepted the steaming cups gratefully, and Evan filled her in on the bare bones of what they were trying to do. She kept nodding through his explanation, and listened attentively.

"The main reason we're here instead of talking to you on the phone," Evan said, "is to get a picture of your mother for positive identification when we find her and the others, and to try to help you remember anything that might help us to trace her. Things that you might not have felt were important enough to tell the police, but that might give us a clue in light of these new developments. Things about her background. Her knowledge of Indian lore, for instance. Was there a particular place that seemed to hold any unusual interest for her that might be related to her ancestors?"

215

Joan stiffened slightly and began stirring her coffee, lips pressed together.

Lydia glanced quickly at Evan. *What had they said wrong?* She rushed to break the silence. "We'd also like to borrow something that belonged to your mother. Something that she'd recognize immediately."

"We think . . . hope . . . that a familiar possession might trigger vestiges of her memory and make it easier to reach her if . . . when we find her," Evan broke in.

"Of course," Joan said shortly. "Wait here. I'll get what you need." She left them sitting, bewildered, at the table.

In a few minutes she reappeared with a framed photo and a silk paisley scarf.

Evan and Lydia studied the picture. Donna Whitcomb was tall, like her daughter—but there the resemblance stopped. Where her daughter was fair, Donna was dark-eyed and dark-haired, and her Indian heritage showed in her chiseled, high-cheekboned face.

"I have to apologize for my abrupt manners," Joan said now, interrupted their study of the picture. "You see, my mother's obsession with her ancestors has always irritated me." She rubbed her hands together as if to wipe out a chill, and sat down at the table again.

"I consider myself an American, but not with the all-consuming passion that she did. She thought that if you didn't have Indian blood, that you weren't an American and you didn't really belong in this country. Stupid. And her attitude got worse as she got older. Her husband, my father, was only one-quarter Indian, and after twenty-seven years of marriage, she decided it wasn't enough. She ridiculed him about his mixed ancestry and his blond hair and light skin until he finally walked out on her. And my husband doesn't have any Indian blood in him at all, so things could get pretty hot around here sometimes when they'd get going on it. So . . ." she finished with an apologetic glance, "I kind of tense up when I have to talk about it."

"Was your mother a Seminole?" Evan asked gently. He didn't want to make the woman uncomfortable because he needed her cooperation. But he wasn't about to drop the subject, either.

Joan nodded, seemingly resigned to the questioning. "Part Seminole. Her grandfather was full-blooded."

"Did she ever say anything about the Calusas?" Lydia put in, remembering her own grandmother.

"Who? No. Is it important?"

"I don't know," Lydia answered truthfully. "We're still trying to make connections."

They stayed for another hour, taking notes as Joan talked. Donna Whitcomb could hunt, liked to fish, and could ride a horse. The first two skills would help her survive in the wilderness if necessary, Evan thought, but nothing was said that gave them any clue as to where the woman would be likely to go to practice them.

The drive back was easier. The rain came down in a steady, soaking patter instead of in sheets, and breaks in the clouds hovered far to the west, hinting at the possibility of a little sun later in the day.

Lydia was quiet, and Evan glanced over at her serious face. "So what do you think? Any clues?" he asked.

She draped an arm over the back of the seat and rested her chin in her hand, thinking for a minute. "What I don't understand," she finally said, "is why Joan's mother was affected by the Genesis Gene and she wasn't. If this is all connected to people with Seminole

217

Indian blood, why haven't they all come down with symptoms and disappeared? Maybe we're on the wrong track."

Evan nodded. "I've been thinking about that too. But you know you can carry a gene and not be affected by it. Like color blindness or sickle-cell anemia. You can be free of any outward signs, but you can pass the trait on to your kids and they might be affected."

"Okay, that makes sense," Lydia said. "But I have another question. Why didn't Jenny show any signs of this before, and why did all those other people become infected . . . is that the right word? . . . at different times . . . over the past few years and at different stages in their lives? I mean, Donna Whitcomb has to be in her fifties and Jenny is only six! And Donna has been missing for almost two years and Jenny . . ." She stopped and suddenly twisted around in her seat to face the side window.

They'd reached the hospital, and Evan pulled into his parking space. "Lydia," he said, shutting off the engine and turning her back around to face him. "We'll find Jenny. I promise I'll never stop looking until I do. Right now I have some vacation coming . . . I'm going in now to tell Burnham I'm pushing it up a few days so we can keep on looking together. He can cover for me."

Lydia's face relaxed and Evan smiled at her. "My kids were supposed to come down and spend a few weeks with me, but I'm going to call my ex-wife and tell her I can't take them right now, that—"

"Evan! No! I can't ask you to give up—!"

"You didn't. It's my idea. And I'm not backing down on this." Evan cupped her face in his hands and forced her to look at him; she was trying to duck her head to hide tears. "Please don't cry," he said softly.

She cried harder.

"God, you're the cryingest woman," Evan sighed, trying to get a light note back. "If you stop, I'll try to answer the one question that turned into three that you asked me." He wiped tears from her cheeks with his thumbs and then sat back, smiling at her.

She looked at the silly expression on Evan's face; worried eyed glowering over a hopeful, off-kilter smile, and she couldn't help it. She giggled. Why did this man always make her feel better—give her hope when she almost felt there wasn't any? It was more than his professional training, she finally admitted to herself. A lot more.

"Okay," she said, shaking her head and smiling back. "I stopped. Explain."

"Right." He looked immensely relieved at her smile. "Well, I think that whatever caused the latent gene in these people to activate happened about five years ago. Remember what Jake and I said to you about polar shifts and atmospheric disturbances and the possibility of sporadic radiation leaks through the ozone layer? All theory, but since there were no mass disappearances before five years ago to add any other variables, those were the only possibilities we could figure out."

"I remember," Lydia said. "But Jake lost me somewhere in the middle with his scientific jargon." She grinned at the memory. "Remember how excited he was? Is he always that enthusiastic about everything?"

"That's two more questions," Evan answered.

Lydia opened her mouth to say something else, but Evan hurried on. "Anyway, whatever happened, when it happened, all the people who carried the inactive gene were different ages, so when the gene was triggered, it started to work on them at that point in their lives.

219

"And I think it grew in different people at different rates of speed, depending on variables like diet, proximity to the exposure of the activator, weight, and other factors in their genetic makeup that we don't understand."

Lydia looked thoughtful. "Do you mean that some of the relatives, because of other things in their genes, were affected more slowly . . . or not at all?"

Evan stared at her for a minute, his mind flying over what she'd just said. "My God . . . you might have something there," he finally answered. "I just meant that those factors might be responsible for the erratic development of the Genesis Gene, but you've given me an idea. Maybe you're right. Maybe some of you who carry the gene are naturally resistant! Maybe you carry an antibody that prevents you from being affected!"

"Did I say that?"

Evan leaned over and hugged her. "You sure did! Lydia, come on in and give us some blood samples!"

"Sure," she said agreeably. "Why?"

He gripped her shoulders and held her at arms' length, grinning into her eyes. "If we can find the factor in your blood that makes you immune to the activation of the gene, we may be able to create an antidote from it that will reverse the effects."

"You mean like an antivenin for snakebite?"

Evan burst out laughing. "That's close enough."

They ran toward the hospital holding hands, and Lydia couldn't help wondering what good a cure would do if they couldn't find Jenny.

Chapter Thirty-two

The driving rain had forced them to pull over to the side of the road and wait several times, and with each passing hour, she'd become more and more unsure of her ability to handle the machine that carried them closer and closer to home.

Images of a green and peaceful island filled with strange birds and insects flitted with disturbing regularity through her brain, and she frequently found herself hurtling recklessly down the almost deserted road with no recollection of how far or how long she'd been driving without paying attention to what she was doing. And as the day lengthened, it became less and less important. Now she welcomed the mind-drift and gave herself eagerly to it. It was someone else who expertly commanded the vehicle that sped through the pounding rain. Someone else who drove with an unerring instinct toward that beloved green island.

The child slept peacefully beside her, and many times when she was aware of her surroundings, she reached out a hand to stroke a chubby arm or leg, or to brush a frizzy wisp of hair from the girl's face. A tiny smile would form on Ja-nee's mouth at her touch, and she might shift her position or sigh contentedly, and Betepi's eyes would water with joy. She had saved her child from the strange, enormous cave that had imprisoned them.

Eventually, the "other" in her turned off the main road onto a packed-dirt road, and she negotiated a twisted, slowly narrowing path through a steadily thickening jungle. Only an occasional deserted, crumbling house marred the primitive landscape now, and Betepi's heart beat with excitement. Finally, she pulled off the dirt path and stopped the car at the edge of a sandbank.

"Ja-nee. Oktali, Ja-nee," she said, shaking the child awake.

Ja-nee opened her eyes and smiled. "Oombah," she whispered as she stretched the stiffness from her muscles.

Yes. Betepi was hungry too. *Soon, my child. Soon we will be fed.*

They didn't mind the rain. It was warm and familiar, and they lifted their faces to it as they walked slowly through the jungle.

But they were still far from home, and she began to worry. How were they to cross the sea of grass? She had no dugout. And she hadn't the skills to build one by herself. Suddenly she stopped, confused. How had she arrived in this place? Why were she and Ja-nee so far from their people? Her head ached, and she rubbed her forehead with one hand. The other hand had a firm grip on her child.

She vaguely remembered a white cave, but other images were blurred. And she remembered flying like the wind through strange places for a long time. Then even those images suddenly faded, and she stood staring around herself in bewilderment.

"Oombah, Betepi ma-da," Ja-nee said, and tugged impatiently at her hand. The voice was a whine now, filled with the demand to be fed.

"Ada," she answered distractedly. *Soon.* She tugged at the child's hand and led the way through the dripping trees. She could sense water nearby, and at least then they could drink. They trudged through the tangled underbrush toward the east.

After a while, the ground changed from dry to soggy, and Betepi knew they were close to her goal. A huge clump of cabbage palms blocked their path, and they skirted around it with some difficulty, their feet making sucking sounds as they pulled them from the muck as they walked.

But their efforts were rewarded. On the far side of the palms, a thin stream bubbled in a long, silver ribbon through the thick vegetation, and they both dropped to their knees and drank.

"Empa na," Betepi warned the child. *Not too much.* Too much after a long thirst would anger the girl's belly, and she couldn't handle that right now. She hadn't the yellow berries for the cure.

Ja-nee obeyed reluctantly. She knew her Betepi ma-da was right, but her mouth wanted more.

They followed the stream for a long time, stopping occasionally for another sip of water whenever Betepi thought it was safe to put more in their bellies. And eventually Ja-nee stopped complaining.

Far ahead, Betepi could see the stream widen and twist back to the right, and she frowned with disappointment. Her instincts told her they should be going east, and she hated to leave the comfort and safety of the life-giving waters. But as she reached the bend and peered to the west, she cried out with joy and fell to her knees

223

to thank the gods who had guided her steps. There, neatly tethered upside down on the banks of the stream, sat a long string of dugouts.

Only one chikee stood near the dugouts, and Betepi had never seen one like it before. It was raised above the water on stout poles, as was proper, but the owners had covered the sides as well as the top of it! How did they expect the cooling winds to flow through it and ease the heat of midday? But this was not her concern, she reminded herself as she crept up to the string of little boats. She motioned Ja-nee to wait, and she glanced back once to see if the child had obeyed. She had. Ja-nee stood as still as the great blue heron waiting for his prey, her eyes trustingly on her mother.

Why was there only one chikee, Betepi wondered? Was that all there was left to the tribe? And if there was only one family left in the tribe, why did they need so many dugouts? She thought about this as she struggled the nearest dugout from its moorings.

Stealing was against her nature, but it was most likely that the strange tribe was warlike, and she couldn't bear the thought of Ja-nee being slave to them or worse. And if they were not warlike, she would have no way of making trade with them anyway.

But no sound of life came from the strange chikee, and soon she became convinced that it was deserted. So the dugouts were sitting here uselessly, she reasoned. There was no one left to paddle them. And waste was worse than theft.

Finally the craft was free, and she motioned for Ja-nee to come. The child ran forward and clambered in next to her. Such a strange dugout, Betepi thought as she paddled away. It was nothing like the hollowed logs her people used. It wasn't even a log—the material it was built from was smooth, gray, and cool, and she marveled at its uniformity. The paddle was perfect too; not rough like the ones they used. How could people with such skill cease to exist?

She pondered these things, and all the strange things that seemed to be happening to her lately, as RAFFERTY'S CANOE RENTALS faded into the distance behind them.

The pounding in her head was gone. And the rain had slowed to a fine drizzle. Betepi was thankful for both things. She wasn't sure she could have negotiated the dugout through the wind and rough waters she was certain had slammed through the river of grass earlier in the day . . . when she was . . . what had she been doing? She couldn't remember anything anymore, and that troubled her. What would she say to the tribe when they asked her where she had been? Had she lived for such a long time that the age of forgetfulness was upon her? Surely not! But what other explanation was there?

They had passed many tree islands thick with familiar trees and birds, and now the land masses came closer together, almost touching at their edges. And they left the open, saw grass-jammed ocean behind them.

Betepi looked nervously around her. This was Calusa land, and she feared the vicious, warlike tribe more than she did the great long-tooth cat that stalked the nights. There weren't many Calusa left, but those who had survived still practiced the depraved rituals that demanded human sacrifices to their gods. And if they couldn't find a solitary, unprotected member of another tribe to sacrifice, they would use one of their own. They worshipped demanding, evil gods.

Ja-nee lay bellydown in the canoe, dragging her hand

through the water and watching the ripples she made swirl around her fingers. She knew they were almost home and wondered why she felt the sudden tenseness that flowed toward her from her mother. She turned around to look in the woman's face and caught a flash of movement near the bank they were passing on their right. Startled, and suddenly wary, she sat up and pointed.

Betepi instantly swung the canoe to the left and paddled for the opposite shore. A shriek of rage and frustration cut through the air and she glanced quickly over her shoulder in terror. She couldn't believe what she saw.

Her fear of the Calusa vanished in the face of this new threat—whatever it was.

A huge bird, its black and bright green feathers flashing in the weak light, stood over seven feet high, stamping its taloned feet and glaring at them from the opposite riverbank. It raked one massive foot through the ground, tearing up and flinging mud in every direction. Tiny wings flapped up and down uselessly as it jumped and screeched, its enormous hooked beak snapping like thunderclaps in anger at losing its intended prey.

Betepi's hands shook so hard that she was forced to pull the paddle into the dugout for fear of losing it. She held her breath and watched the monster stamp around at the edge of the water and then retreat with a series of ear-shattering shrieks.

It is afraid of water, she thought, relief flowing through her. Thank the gods it is afraid of water. She stopped the canoe and stared at the impossible creature. It took great leaps along the bank, honking and screaming in their direction and ducking its head in challenge.

Ja-nee was screaming too, her hands over her ears in

226

an effort to block the thing's shrieks. Her eyes were screwed tightly shut. Betepi reached out and shook her. Panic might tip the canoe, and seeing them floundering in the water might be enough to urge the thing after them in spite of its obvious fear of it.

Ja-nee yanked away from Betepi's hand, and the canoe rocked dangerously. Betepi yelled her name and the child's eyes flew open. They flicked from the woman she thought was her mother to the giant bird on the bank. Her cries dwindled down to frightened gasps, but she forced herself to stay still under Betepi's warning eyes.

They sat in their small craft, staring at the angry creature, and eventually it stood quietly staring back. Then with an angry clack of its beak, it turned and bounded off through the jungle.

Something bumped under the dugout, and the small craft again rocked precariously. And again Ja-nee screamed.

Betepi hushed her and steadied the boat by shifting her weight back and forth for balance.

Another bump, harder this time, and Betepi used the oar to steady the craft.

The water suddenly whirled around them, pulling them along in the wake of whatever swam beneath them in the shallows.

"DUN-DA, JA-NEE!" Betepi screamed, and the child obediently dropped to the comparative safety of the bottom of the boat, too frightened to question her mother's order.

The boat spun, and Betepi saw the glint of fins and tails flipping above the surface before disappearing again into the murky water. And then they leaped, their huge bodies clearing the shallows as they raced for their unknown destination.

Betepi gasped. Never had she seen such fish before! Twice the size of a grown man, with the teeth of a great bear snapping in vicious rhythm, they sped around and past her, dozens of them leaping and tearing the calm water into foam and mud.

And then they were gone, as fast as they had come.

Betepi sat quietly now, willing away her fear, her mind trying to make sense of the things she had just seen. What was happening to her world? For the first time, she wondered if they would ever reach home safely. Her body trembled as she dipped the paddle into the water again.

The rain had stopped, and she paddled on through the dark, guided by the light from the half-moon and the stars that had thankfully seen fit to shine tonight. Otherwise she would have been hopelessly lost, and the thought of spending the night in a land where strange and vicious creatures prowled, terrified her. She had no weapon, and who knew what other terrible things might now be living and hunting in this strange new world?

She was exhausted, and only her fear and determination to protect her daughter forced her to keep going. Ja-nee slept peacefully in the bottom of the canoe, and she was grateful that the child at least was getting some rest.

They were both past hunger now, but she wished she had one of her nets to catch a fish for Ja-nee. A small fish. Her belly tightened at the memory of the monsters that had nearly capsized them earlier in the day. Again, she thanked the gods for answering her silent pleas to keep them away. But she didn't think her strength would last much longer without food, either. She'd thought of stopping a few times. She was sure she could find succulent roots and berries with a quick search, but fear of the giant bird and the Calusa had made her hesitate and she finally give up the idea.

If she didn't find her people soon, there were many ways to perish.

Chapter Thirty-three

"No. And stop pushing me, Evan. That could take weeks . . . months," Burnham said. "And even then, in all likelihood a blood serum would probably only prevent activation in susceptible people, not reverse it in the people who are already undergoing alteration."

"Why are you fighting me on this?" Evan yelled. "You don't *know* it won't work! Why are you so resistant to even trying?"

"Trying it on whom?" Burnham asked mildly. "Mrs. Wilson and the Matthews girl are missing now, so it won't do them any good, and do you really think the FDA is going to let us shoot a vaccine into the people of the Seminole Nation for a disease that we can't prove exists and that we can't prove has any connection with them anyway?"

"Harold," Evan said, his voice dangerously low, "we're going to find those people, and if you don't have any better idea—"

"Ah, but I do." Burnham smiled smugly and reached into a desk drawer. The Genetic Institute logo was discreetly set into the top right corner of the blue folder cover. "Dr. Frankel and I think we might have the solution . . . if you or the police ever find those poor, unfortunate people."

He sat holding the closed folder, staring at it for a minute, and his face gradually lost the smug look. Now he looked almost as angry as Evan felt. "I can't tell you how disappointed I am that the staff let them slip away, Evan." He slapped the folder and looked up, and Evan was surprised to see how barely controlled the man's anger was now. Not a trace of real sorrow or compassion softened the look of frustrated rage.

"Do you realize the opportunity we've let slip through our fingers?" he said, his voice rising. "We may *never* find another subject to study! The loss to science is *incalculable!* We . . ."

"Do Dr. Frankel's and your findings include prevention, Dr. Burnham?" Evan interrupted with a slight derisive emphasis on the man's formal title. He pointed to the folder. "Or does your possible cure only work on people who evidence definite and progressive symptoms of the disease?"

Burnham glared at Evan. "What are you suggesting?"

Evan put his hands flat on the scientist's desk and leaned forward into his face. "Maybe you don't want to find a preventative measure for the Genesis Gene. Maybe you're hoping for some more human guinea pigs to waltz in here so you and Frankel can watch them deteriorate into primitive, savage remnants of the functioning people they used to be . . . all in the name of science, of course."

"That's ridiculous," Burnham said, but his voice came out in a whisper, and he dropped his eyes to the Institute report. "Would you like to hear what we've come up with, Evan? Or would you prefer to hurl a few more unfounded and insulting accusations at me?"

Evan sighed and threw himself into a chair opposite the old man. This wasn't the way to go. Fighting Burnham was stupid and he needed his cooperation. "Sorry, Harold," he said, forcing a tone of amiability into his voice. He rubbed at his forehead, feigning a headache in an attempt to elicit some sympathy and forgiveness for his outburst. "I guess I'm letting stress get to me over this. I . . . care about these people."

Burnham looked at him skeptically, then gave a little "hmmph" that sounded like appeasement and opened the folder. "First, Frankel agrees with your idea for applying photorecovery methods, but he plans to use it in conjunction with algeny. He—"

"Genetic surgery?" Evan was shocked. "That's experimental, Harold! There's been no *human* research done!"

"True." Burnham looked strangely pleased with himself. "But Dr. Frankel and I have been quite successful with dogs and rhesus monkeys . . . not the group that originally showed evidence of the Genesis Gene, unfortunately, but with later specimens. And the algeny has of course been unrelated to the Genesis Gene. Now this is under wraps, Evan . . . very hush hush, you understand. We're not quite ready to reveal our findings, and bad publicity could affect our funding. You know how upset the public can get over experiments in genetic engineering."

"How safe is it if we use your new procedures on people who carry the Genesis Gene?"

"Well," Burnham answered reluctantly. "There are always risks, but the alternative seems to be an inevitable state of regression. The people affected by the gene will deteriorate at a steady and permanent rate *without* treatment." He raised a quizzical eyebrow at the psychiatrist.

"Would it be worth the risk to you if you were affected?"

"So you're going to try to modify the faulty structure in the DNA molecule of the Genesis Gene," Evan said, avoiding Burnham's question.

"Yes. Dr. Frankel's lab has the necessary equipment for euphenic betterment, and we think we can correct the defective gene locus by altering the messenger RNA through antisense or reverse genetics. He's attempting to create a synthesized DNA that will correct the broken coenzyme now. The problem is, we can target the damaged DNA, but we're still not sure that we can permanently affect it. The synthetic DNA may not get into the target cell, it may not bind or disperse properly, or degrading enzymes could attack it before it does its work. We just don't know, and computer analyzation of the projected outcome isn't really satisfactory. I wish we had a means of animal experimentation ... like Frankel's monkeys. My mind would rest easier with that."

Evan watched the lightning flash outside the window for a few minutes, thinking. *Algeny. Drastic. Something he'd read about brain surgery lately—what?* Another flash. *That was it! Laser! A Swedish report.* "Harold. What about the gamma knife?" He leaned forward with sudden excitement. "They've been using it in Sweden for twenty years! No incision—they shoot gamma rays into the brain through a specially constructed metal helmet. It works wonders on brain tumors. Only destroys the abnormal tissue, and I think there are four hospitals in the States that have been doing it for about two years. Use it to destroy the web! Wouldn't that be a lot safer than algeny?"

"Yes. If it applied here," Burnham said. "But it

233

doesn't. In the first place, we don't know that the web is abnormal tissue, in spite of its rapid growth into abnormal areas. It could be as normal in these people as an extra toe is in other people. The result of a mutant gene, yes. But abnormal, like cancer cells? I don't know anymore. We have our doubts.

"Secondly, even if we could destroy the web, it wouldn't deactivate the gene. The mutated gene would simply keep reforming the web, and the patient would have to undergo periodic treatments under the Gamma knife. And that much repeated radiation applied to the brain would be unthinkable.

"More important," he added quickly before Evan could object to his hypothesis, "if, as Dr. Frankel and I suspect, the sudden activation of the Genesis Gene was *caused* by a chance exposure to gamma rays, the application of the Gamma knife might only exacerbate the problem. In my opinion, it could prove fatal."

Evan's disappointment was evident on his face. *Okay, Harold. One more time.* "All right. But what about the possible immunological properties in the blood of the carriers without symptoms?" Evan persisted. "I don't want to let that one go."

Burnham sighed. "Yes, yes. By all means, Evan. If you insist. Have some blood samples drawn from your lady friend and have them sent to Dr. Frankel's Institute. I'll call him and tell him what we want." He waved a hand, dismissing the psychiatrist.

Evan explained Burnham's intentions to Lydia, and she nodded. "I don't see that there's much choice. When we find her she might already be . . . changed drastically . . . and I can't allow her to stay that way."

234

Surprised, Evan asked if she had fully understood the risks involved. Her attitude seemed almost cavalier, out of character with her usual reaction to anything that threatened the safety of her daughter.

She looked at him sadly, but there was a hint of a curious mixture of strength and resignation behind the look that Evan hadn't seen there before. "The algeny could damage her irreparably. Or kill her. Is that what you want me to understand?" she asked bluntly.

Evan nodded slowly and started to speak, but she held up a hand to silence him.

"You haven't given me any proof that the activated Genesis Gene won't kill her eventually anyway, have you? Can you assure me that it won't, Evan? And how do you know that all those people who disappeared aren't dead by now . . . killed by the web that grew in their brains? Maybe death is the final outcome of this thing if it's left untreated."

It had occurred to him.

Lydia waited in Evan's living room while he went into the bedroom to call his ex-wife. Harold Burnham had agreed to cover for the four days Evan had pushed up his vacation.

She still felt vaguely guilty about his putting off his kids for her and Jenny, but, grateful for his help, she hadn't made any more objections.

I'm being selfish and I don't care, she thought as she looked around the tastefully and expensively furnished room. *I wonder if he had a decorator?* She walked over to the triple glass sliding doors and looked out at the pool without really seeing it. *I have to call my mother and tell her Jenny is missing. Oh God.* She turned around at the sound of Evan coming back. *Later. I'll call her later. I can't take any more stress right now.*

"The kids didn't seem too upset," Evan said wryly. "As a matter of fact, if I want to be brutally honest with myself, they sounded relieved." *First time I've ever shirked a responsibility,* he thought. *Or am I just trading one set of responsibilities for another?* He crossed over to a teak and chrome bar and took out two glasses. "Rye and ginger, if I remember correctly?"

Lydia smiled and nodded. She felt better with him just being in the room with her.

"I have some frozen steaks and frozen vegetables," he said while he mixed the drinks. "Will you stay?"

"Yes," she said as she reached for her drink. And her hands started to shake. A wave of dizziness blurred her vision, and she dropped the drink and clutched at the bar for support. "Oh," was all she could manage.

Evan raced around the bar and caught her before she fell. She felt herself lifted and carried through a haze of light-headed awareness, and a shrill ringing sounded in her ears. The rough feel of couch cushions seemed to be lumped out of proportion under her back, and she tried to twist away from them.

"Lie still."

Evan's command came from far away, and she frowned. He was right next to her, she could see him in a fuzzy, disoriented sort of way. Why did he sound like that?

Evan raced to the kitchen and soaked a dish towel with cold water. *Delayed shock . . . too much prolonged stress . . . should have expected it. Damn!*

He wrung the towel out and ran back to Lydia. Pushing her hips toward the back of the couch, he sat next to her and gently put the damp towel on her forehead.

236

"Take deep breaths . . . that's it. Try to relax . . . don't panic, that'll only make it worse. You'll be okay in a minute." He rubbed her hands and kept talking, reassuring her, then checked her pulse. *She's okay. She's okay.*

She was. It had passed. She looked up at Evan's worried face, then pulled the dish towel off her forehead and dropped it on the floor.

"Don't—," Evan said.

She put her hand, still cold from the damp towel, on the back of Evan's neck and pulled his face down to hers. He stiffened with surprise, and when she met his lips, he was unresponsive. But her sudden driving need for him, and the overwhelming urge to be held and loved—and to forget for a while the long days of mental agony over her child—drove back her normal instincts to retreat gracefully from his apparent resistance.

She ran her tongue lightly over his bottom lip and dragged her nails down his back.

Evan's few seconds of surprise dissolved in his sudden rush of desire. He forced his arm under her body, yanked her up into a half-sitting position and smothered her little cry of assent by burying his other hand in her hair and pulling her face toward his until their lips met in a deep, searching kiss.

Neither of them could wait to walk the short distance to the bedroom.

Chapter Thirty-four

The calm after the storm, Jake thought. He walked toward the small diner across the street from the motel and took a few deep breaths of the fresh, clean air. The only signs that a storm had passed through were a few downed branches in the middle of the road and dozens of puddles that glittered in the morning sunlight. He'd expected more damage.

A blast of air-conditioning hit him as he walked in the door, and he rubbed his arms as he looked around. It was clean, thank God. Two bearded men in jeans and blue workshirts sat at the counter. They looked up at him from their steaming cups of coffee, then away again. The only other person there was a paunchy man in an apron who ambled up to the table. He held a note pad and a stub of a pencil. "What can I gettcha?"

"Just coffee," Jake said.

"Jake! There you are!" Ralph hurried into the diner with Charlie close on his heels.

Jake smiled at the incoming pair.

Charlie leaned against the counter and motioned to the short-order cook for coffee. Jake thought Charlie looked distinctly hung-over.

"By some miracle the phone lines were open. I talked to the Institute," Ralph said excitedly. "And the cages and tranquilizer guns will be here in two days. That's as fast as they can do it. They can't believe what we've discovered! They want living specimens, and they're going to make arrangements with the Park Service to enlist the aid of Tropical Treasures for holding pens and tanks for us!"

"Tropical Treasures?" Jake asked. "What and where is that?"

"It's a small tourist attraction on the western edge of the Big Cypress Swamp . . . on Anhinga Bay. It's something like Sea World, but much smaller. We can pay them enough to close it off to the public for a while, and not worry about publicity until we're ready. And besides, when we finally reveal to the world what we've found, it will put them on the map! A great opportunity for them! And it has an access canal. We can float the tranquilized animals right in there!" Ralph was babbling with excitement, and his mood began to inch out and affect Jake.

"Are we supposed to go after these specimens by ourselves?" Jake asked, doubtful that even with the help of powerful tranq guns, he'd want to tackle the project with just the three of them.

"No, no . . . Charlie knows three men we can trust. And we'll aim for the younger, smaller specimens. Six of us can handle one or two heavily sedated youngsters."

"The Institute. Are they sending some of their own people down here too?" Jake asked.

"Yes. Of course. Some of the best biologists and zoologists in the country will be joining us the moment we notify the Institute of our success in acquiring the spec-

imens. All sworn to secrecy, of course. We don't want
to be inundated with the press just yet."

The two scientists sat grinning at each other, adrenaline elevated and humming through them because of the
enormity of the discoveries they were about to make
available to the world of science.

Evan rolled over in bed and got the phone on the second ring. Jake. Rambling on about thecodonts. Diatryma. Glyptodonts. Holding pens. Two days. He was
coming up.

"Jake. Wait. Hold it." Evan rubbed his eyes and tried
to concentrate on what was happening. "We'll be gone
all morning . . . have an interview with some people. I'll
leave a key for you with the neighbor . . . number 203,
in case you get here before we're back."

He said good-bye and hung up, then rolled over again
and kissed Lydia gently on the back of the neck.

Victor Birdsong and his wife lived in a small, neat
stucco house on the outskirts of the Everglades. A few
miles before the house, Jake and Lydia had passed
"Birdsong Bingo," a sprawling building big enough to
hold several hundred people. Evan had heard that bingo
was a big business with the Florida Indians, and he
wondered how much revenue it brought in. Whatever, it
hadn't been enough to save Daniel Birdsong. Victor's
son, an only child, had been missing for two years.

"My son will be twenty-four next week," Victor said
as he led Evan and Lydia into the living room. His wife,
a dark, tiny woman, hovered in the arched doorway, but
said nothing.

Evan asked for a personal belonging and a photograph of the young man.

"Get it," Victor said to his wife, and she scurried away.

Lydia stared at Victor Birdsong. All he needs are braids and a few feathers, she thought. Black-eyed, black-haired, with sharp features and a rigid posture, he looked every inch her stereotyped image of an Indian chief.

"Why do you think you can find my son when the police have failed?" Victor asked Evan.

Evan told about the new information they had connecting the man's son with the other disappearances and the Genesis Gene. "And there seems to be evidence that the people involved all carry Seminole Indian blood," he explained. "We think that some of you are naturally resistant to the gene. It's something we're investigating for a possible immunization program. Or possibly there's a connection that goes even farther back . . . to the Calusa or other primitive tribes . . . and that may be why so few of you have been affected. We're not sure. Not all Seminoles are descended from the Calusa, are they?"

"No," Victor said. "I still don't understand."

Evan smiled at Mrs. Birdsong as she hurried in with a photograph and a leather belt. She handed them to her husband, but he made no move to give them to Evan.

"Was there some place, perhaps just before, or during the first stages of your son's illness that he seemed to have an affinity for?" Evan asked. "Some place that might have a connection with his ancestors, and that he might be drawn to as his mind triggered more primitive images?"

"The Calusa lived in the Everglades," Victor said.

"We know that," Lydia broke in. "But can you be more specific? The history books aren't too clear on where they settled, or why or how they disappeared. And the Everglades is a big area to search. We know some of them were on the west coast, but that still doesn't narrow it down much. We thought you might have some legends among your people that aren't common knowledge. . . ." She looked at him hopefully, willing him to say that the old Calusa settlements were now filled with condos and tourist traps. If the Calusa had lived deep in the Everglades, her worst, unspoken fear would be realized. Jenny could be heading into the jungle swamps . . . right toward Jake's dinosaurs.

Victor sat silently for a few minutes. When he finally spoke, there was a mixture of pride and sadness in his voice. "The Calusa were a fierce and brave tribe. My son and I know through tales passed down from generation to generation that their blood runs through our veins."

He jerked his head toward his wife. "Her ancestors are the Mayaimi. Soft people. When the ancient blood of the Calusa warriors began to speak through my son, it was she who insisted he be taken to a psychiatrist. A white man who knew nothing of his heritage, and did not understand that my son's ancestors are powerful enough to speak to him through his dreams. Lydia glanced quickly over at Mrs. Birdsong. She remained sitting impassively across the room, not even seeming to pay attention to the conversation. Lydia couldn't imagine her insisting on anything.

"Can you help us locate them, Mr. Birdsong?" Evan said gently. "Tell us your legends."

Victor sat silently again, but his wife got up and walked over to a rolltop desk and rummaged through a stack of papers. She found what she wanted and walked with a straight back right up to Evan. Her husband frowned at her, but she ignored him. She opened a map of Florida and put it on the coffee table in front of them.

"His legends are just that," she said in a soft, lilting voice. "Legends. They will not help you." She ran a finger down the west coast. "My husband's people were here. They are all gone.

"My people . . . the gentle ones . . ." She pointed to a section southeast of Lake Okeechobee, a vast, largely unexplored area. "Began here. And a few remain there to this day. They survived."

Victor made a snorting sound of derision, but said nothing.

Lydia felt a chill of dread.

"Today they are the hidden people," Mrs. Birdsong continued, still addressing Evan. "They are as invisible to those who seek them out as is the wind. They speak the ancient language and hold to the ancient ways, uncorrupted by the outside world. They live in the depths of the Everglades as they have for centuries, and few have ever seen them."

Victor jumped to his feet and grabbed at his wife's arm. "You tell them that my legends are of no value, and then you fill their heads with your nonsense!"

She snatched her arm away and stepped back, then turned to Evan again. "My son was not alone with his illness. Four others of our immediate tribe shared his misery, and they also disappeared—within six months of each other. They did not seek the professional help that we did. I do not know if this is important to you, but I wish to tell you everything I know." She pointed to the spot on the map again. "Search there, Dr. Tremayne," she said firmly. "Search to the southeast of the lake . . . where my people live in secrecy. My son is there. I know this in my heart."

"I believe her, Evan," Lydia said when they got back in the car. "You might call her feeling a hunch or a psychic instinct or whatever, but what she said just felt right to me!"

"Whatever," Evan said. "But it's just the kind of lead I was hoping for. It narrows the search down from the Atlantic Ocean to Lake Superior." He grinned at her. "And we have our own personal expert on the Everglades coming to dinner tonight."

"Jake." Lydia smiled a little, then sat quietly for a while. She wasn't ready to think about his dinosaurs. She had to remain calm. And she still had more questions. "I'm a little confused," she said after a few miles. "Is all this connecting back to a genetic trait carried by the Seminole or Calusa or Mayaimi or what? I'm not sure how all this is connecting." *Because if it doesn't connect, Jenny isn't out in the Everglades with only a strange woman to protect her. And my hunch, and Mrs. Birdsong's hunch, are wrong.*

"I think," Evan answered, "that you can go back even further than that. According to my reading, the Florida tribes all go back to an even more ancient race of people, and maybe the connection is rooted in prehistoric times."

"Okay. But even if that's true, and it's that ancient race that carries the Genesis Gene, why did Jenny draw pictures that are similar to the ones found in caves in France? If I'm the connecting link because of my ancestry, that doesn't fit."

Evan drove slowly through a deep puddle that covered the road. "I've thought about that. I think the Genesis Gene can trigger across genetic lines. I think you have it, even though it's inherited from one parent, and it's probably through the mother because as I told you, Burnham found the gene in the mitochondria. It can draw memories from all your ancestors. Simple."

Lydia nodded and felt the fear for Jenny's life sneak back into her. If it was inherited from the mother, Mrs. Birdsong was probably right about where her son was. With her people.

"Evan."

He caught the tremor in her voice and glanced sharply at her.

"How many of those reptiles do you think are out there?"

Evan reached out and put a hand on her knee. "She's going to be all right. We're going to find her. I promise you." He hoped he sounded more convinced than he felt.

She had no more questions, and they drove on in silence.

Chapter Thirty-five

A thick mist floated heavily through the jungle, twisting through the trees and filtering the dawn light to a gray-white luminescence that spread an eerie, primordial glow over everything in her sight.

Ja-nee struggled to dip the heavy paddle in the water again, then pushed against the current, sending the canoe forward and a little to the right. Her arms were getting tired.

The woman who said she was her mother—at first Ja-nee had thought that she was, but now she wasn't sure—sat slumped in a heap between the seats, exhaustion having finally forced her into a deep, unmoving sleep.

Hours earlier, the erratic drift of the canoe had awakened Ja-nee, and she'd opened her eyes to a dark and threatening place filled with black shadows and the cries of night animals on the hunt. Fear of drifting onto land and the possibility of another attack by one of the strange, giant birds had made her grab the paddle from the hands of the sleeping woman and maneuver them back to the center of the stream. She tried not to think of the huge fish that had leaped past them earlier. She wasn't sure what had frightened her more, the bird or the fish, and finally decided on the bird. The bird had looked at them. The fish hadn't seemed to care about them at all. Half reassured by her own decision, she held the boat to the center of the river.

She'd found it easy at first, and had kept paddling in the general direction they'd been headed, but by the time the shadows had lifted, giving way to the concealing fog and mist, she was exhausted too. She wished the woman would wake up.

Why did the woman want her to call her Betepi ma-da? She wasn't her mother, was she? As she studied the sleeping face, she was suddenly sure. She wasn't. But she couldn't remember her own ma-da, try as she might. No face came into her head. And she wasn't even sure her own name was Ja-nee. But she couldn't remember that for sure either.

Sighing, the child pulled the paddle into the canoe and let it rest across her knees. Her arms burned and shook with the long effort of paddling upstream, and she had to rest.

The morning was noisy with birds and insects, and she'd long ago stopped the useless slapping at the buzzing, whining things that constantly deviled her. Now she scratched idly at one of the many bumps that covered her body. If the woman who called herself her Betepi ma-da (the Be in front of the woman's tribe name signified respect, Ja-nee suddenly realized) wanted to take care of her, she guessed that was all right. Besides, she didn't know what she'd do out here all by herself. That was too frightening to even think about.

The canoe started to drift sideways. Ja-nee reached out and shook Betepi's leg. "Betepi ma-da. Anag pada." *Wake up.*

Tepi woke with a start, almost upsetting the canoe. Instantly alert, she grabbed the paddle and quickly looked in every direction, searching for danger. But the morning jungle was peaceful except for the sounds of birds greeting the day, and she relaxed and smiled at Ja-nee. "You paddled," she said to the child in their language. "Well done."

"I'm hungry," Ja-nee said.

Tepi nodded and reluctantly headed the boat toward shore. They had to eat. There was no way around it.

The canoe bumped against a small bare spot along the bank. They sat there for a while, their eyes probing through the Spanish-moss-laden trees and tangled underbrush for any sign of the giant bird—or worse.

They jumped at the sound of a splash to their left, and watched a long-nosed reptile with bony plates covering its back slip into the water. Its nostrils flared just below its eyes, and Betepi saw the two holes fold shut before the strange creature sank silently below the surface of the water. Which way was it headed? Toward them or away? The question was enough to make them scramble from the canoe and onto the now comparative safety of land.

They walked around ancient live oaks, crushing fern and bracken under their feet, and edged past the tangled vines of the strangler fig, staring in awe at the great, twisted columns of branch and root that wove intricate patterns around the parent trunk. But they soon lost interest in favor of a more immediate need; a need now easily satisfied.

Cabbage palm grew in clumps everywhere, their prickly fans glittering in the dappled light, and Tepi and Ja-nee kicked and tore at them until they exposed the succulent hearts.

Their hunger slightly appeased, they wandered a little farther inland. Several birds' nests built low enough for them to reach held eggs, and they eagerly sucked them dry. Not as good as fish or game, Tepi thought, but it would do for a while. If only she had a net. . . .

By the time the mist disappeared from the forest, the heat had risen to an uncomfortable level and they were happy to get back to the canoe and the slight breeze that rippled the surface of the water.

And they began the second day of their journey.

Twilight brought new swarms of mosquitoes out in full force, and Tepi wished she had fish oil to rub on their bodies. And the ache in her head had come back. Another spasm shot through her brain, making her eyes water, and she stopped paddling for a minute and rested her head in her arms.

"Betepi ma-da?" came a soft voice through the haze of pain. "Shall I paddle for you?" it asked in the ancient language.

The pain abruptly disappeared, and she looked up at the child who sat staring at her with a worried frown. Confusion and a sudden stab of fear raced through her. *Who is this child? This is not my Ja-nee! And why does she call me Betepi ma-da?* "Who are you?" she asked softly, and reached out a hand to touch the child on the knee.

"I don't remember," the girl answered truthfully. "But you call me Ja-nee and you say you are my Betepi ma-da."

Surprised and uneasy at the child's reply, the woman chose her next words carefully. "Yes, I am Tepi, but not your ma-da. But I will take care of you until we get home." The age of forgetfulness was surely upon her! Why was she on the river with a strange child? She longed for the sight of her husband, Doga. He would explain.

"I will call you Ja-nee for now," Tepi said, "since that is what I have been calling you." The tribe will tell me her name, she thought . . . or gift her with a new one if she is not of our tribe and does not remember where she came from any better than who she is. And if that is the case, it occurred to her with sudden elation, perhaps Doga will let me keep her!

Tepi smiled and dipped the paddle in the water again. Another young one to teach!

Suddenly Ja-nee pointed to the shore. "Be . . . Tepi! See there!" The woman had indicated that she wished the *Be* dropped, and she remembered to obey.

A human shape ducked behind a clump of cabbage palms at the child's shout, but Tepi had seen it too.

Someone of their tribe? But why would they hide themselves? But who else could it be? They were far from Calusa land, so she had no fear in her heart over that possibility.

She pulled the paddle over her knees, cupped her hands over her mouth and cried out the ancient form of greeting. "We are the peaceful ones! Grant us food or safe passage!"

The riverbank was suddenly filled with people.

Chapter Thirty-six

"Jesus, Evan!" Jake shouted. "I saw them! I'll bet you anything that's who I saw!" He paced along the edge of Evan's pool, sloshing his scotch and water over the rim of his glass as he gestured with it.

Lydia could hardly breathe. Thank God. Jake had found them! And if those people could live out there safe from the dinosaurs, so could Jenny. She *would* believe that! She *must* believe that! She squeezed Evan's hand and barely repressed a desire to throw her arms around Jake.

"Do you know exactly where you were?" Evan asked.

"Yes," Jake answered. "Charlie marked the nautical charts, and I brought them with me to show you where the hell in the middle of nowhere we were . . . didn't think they'd come in this handy at the time." He grinned at Lydia and Evan, then his smile dimmed a little. "But even if this is the 'lost tribe' that your Mrs. Birdsong was talking about, how can you be so sure that that's where Jenny is?" he asked gently, not wanting to destroy Lydia's hopes, but needing to put things in perspective.

"It fits," Evan said shortly, fighting back his own doubts. "And it's the best shot we've got."

He pulled his hand from Lydia's and crossed the room toward the phone. "Jake? Will you get your chart, please? I'm calling the police. It's time to explain everything about the Genesis Gene. We need their help to search, now that we have something definite to go on."

When Jake came back inside with the nautical chart, Evan was still on the phone, and he watched Lydia watching Evan. The new intimacy between them was hard to miss, and Jake smiled to himself.

The floating cages had been delivered to Tropical Treasures—two of them—and the two scientists, Charlie, and the three taciturn, well-muscled men Charlie had hired, worked in the blazing heat to put them together. The eight-foot square fiberglass bases bolted into sidesaddle pontoons, and sturdy hinges held the four interlocking panels of six-foot-high steel bars in place, five on each side for extra strength. The roof was a steel web. Escape through the roof was a favorite egress of most untranquilized animals—their natural instinct was to leap for freedom. Jake had no intention of bringing back untranquilized dinosaurs, but he checked the latches on the roof for the third time anyway.

The cages would be a tough squeeze for holding a full-grown Diatryma, Coelophysis, or glyptodont, tranquilized or not, and he hoped they'd find some younger, smaller specimens. They'd have no trouble transporting a thecodont. They were flexible.

One of the men carried a small, gasoline-powered air compressor aboard one of the big pontoon boats. It would be used to regulate the ballast they needed. The

252

fiberglass floor of the cage would be raised above the waterline with inflated ballast bags for transporting the giant bird, Diatryma, or the huge armadillo-like glyptodont, or the light-boned Coelophysis. Deflated, the bags would allow the floor to sink several inches below the water for transporting the thecodont. The four parrot cages for Archaeopteryx remained on the second boat.

A floating cage would be hooked behind each pontoon boat, and the extra weight would make the going slow, not to mention the added problem of reduced maneuverability, but Jake figured he could use the extra time to start writing his preliminary report.

He watched Ralph push a campstove under a seat— but he thought of Lydia. Lydia had been torn between waiting at home for the police search teams to report in on what they'd found in the Glades, and renting another boat and following the expedition into the wilderness. Evan had convinced her to wait. Jake chuckled to himself. Ralph would have had fits, but there wouldn't have been much they could do about it, not if Evan and Lydia had paid for the boat themselves.

Jake had told the others in the expedition about the Genesis Gene while they put the cages together. They'd shown more than a casual interest, and Ralph was positive that it had a connection with the unusual, sudden appearance of prehistoric animals in the Everglades.

When they were finished, the crew divided themselves between the two boats and shoved off. The waterway trail through the cypress swamp was well marked, but difficult to maneuver with the big boats and the cages dragging behind, and Jake and Ralph were silent while Jake carefully threaded his way along the shallow path after Charlie. When they finally reached the more

253

easily navigable sea of grass, Jake relaxed and let Ralph take over for a while.

"I've been thinking about everything you've said," the older man said now as he backed off a little to give himself more space between their boat and Charlie's. He drove a car the same way, Jake thought with amusement; very carefully, allowing the requisite one car-length for every ten miles an hour between himself and the vehicle in front of him.

"I've been trying to figure out, if there is a connection between our prehistoric animals and your Genesis Gene, why the animals have reverted physically and the people have reverted only mentally. Or are you aware of any unusual births?" He looked hopefully at Jake.

"Nope." Jake grinned. "No newborn Australopithicus or Neaderthalensis that I'm aware of. Not even in the *National Enquirer.*"

"Oh, I see," Ralph said, disappointed. He'd missed the joke. "Well then, the only thing I can think of is that the lower orders of animals that are susceptible to the gene have been affected differently because of their radically different genetic makeup in all other respects. My hypothesis in that case would be that in Homo sapiens the Genesis Gene affects memory over a long term, and in the lower orders of animals it must instantly affect their reproductive cycles, because I haven't seen any evidence of a gradual evolutionary process out here. It seems to be an instantaneous and complete change, a radical reverse mutation, do you agree?"

"Yes," Jake said. "The punctuationists are going to leap all over this."

"I dare say," Ralph agreed. "it would be interesting to put one of the thecodonts through magnetic resonance to see if its archipallium had formed a web, though." His eyes took on a dreamy, thoughtful look.

"Archipallium . . . the reptilian equivalent to the human hippocampus," Jake said, equally thoughtful. "Good idea. But my guess would be the web is forming on the gonads in all these lower vertebrates, not in the brain."

A great blue heron glided in front of the boat with a large, flapping fish dangling from its beak, and they watched it descend and disappear into the saw grass a hundred yards or so from the water trail.

Ralph broke the appreciative silence. "Did you say it was a broken magnesium coenzyme responsible for the change in the DNA? . . . yes, yes . . . the coding . . . of course." He seemed to be talking to himself, so Jake kept quiet. "And the homeobox . . . ," he mumbled on. "Master genes . . . yes . . . of course!" He turned to Jake, grinning. "The genes that contain the homeobox, a short sequence of DNA, produce proteins that specifically bind them to the DNA of other genes and control them, and these genes are the master genes of development! They control the positioning of cells in the embryo! Your Genesis Gene could easily have taken hold there if the gonads of one or both parents had been affected by the same set of circumstances that affected the DNA of the little girl and the others.

"Whatever happened years ago simply affected humans differently than it affected the lower orders of animals. The same way rats and dogs in a laboratory will be affected differently by an experimental drug, than a monkey or a human." He looked pleased with himself.

"When did you learn so much about genetics?" Jake asked, impressed.

"I'm a well-rounded man," Ralph answered with a trace of smugness in his voice.

Suddenly a low-flying helicopter, the *whup whup whup* of its blades bending the tall saw grass flat, whizzed over their heads and flew toward the northeast. Then another one. Jake and Ralph watched them recede into tiny dots. Part of the search party, Jake thought. He silently wished them good luck.

Chapter Thirty-seven

Small brown hands pulled the canoe out of the water and helped Tepi and Ja-nee to dry ground. The dark-eyed people smiled and chattered at them, asking so many questions at once that Tepi barely had time to answer any of them. They crowded around, stroking and petting the two newcomers, and trying to identify themselves in a high-pitched babble of words that rambled and flowed into a barely decipherable competition for attention.

Tepi laughed and put her hands over her ears to signify her confusion. At once, they dropped into a respectful silence and waited for her to speak. She put one hand on Ja-nee's shoulder and looked around at the friendly faces. They spoke her language, but try as she might, she could not recognize even one of them. Had her forgetfulness extended this far, that she failed to put one name to one face in her tribe? No. She remembered the most important name.

"Doga?" she asked. "Where is my husband, Doga?"

Happy smiles faded and Tepi's heart beat faster in alarm. Had something terrible happened to him?

The dark-skinned people looked at each other and put

their palms up, questioning each other. Could anyone think of a face that belonged to that name? Then they all looked at the ground in denial and sorrow that they could not give the newcomer her request.

How could they not know Doga, Tepi wondered? But at least they had not signaled that he was dead, and that gave her new hope. Perhaps she had been gone for a long time and the tribe had split—some moving off to new fishing grounds. Still . . . Doga was a name to be known among her people.

A man gently pushed his way through the ring of people and stood looking down at Tepi. He was taller than the rest by more than a head, and his features were sharp and fierce, but the black eyes that moved from Ja-nee to Tepi were filled with warmth. "We are sad that we cannot bring forward the one you seek," he said. "But we make you welcome and will now feed you. And if you wish to remain with us, it is nothing to build another sleeping platform."

"You are generous," Tepi said. "But I will seek my own tribe after a few days with you. They must worry about me."

The people listened to her words and once again put their palms up and dropped their heads.

The tall man spoke. "Your words are strange to us. We are The Tribe. There are no others besides us." But he looked uneasily away as he spoke, as if he disbelieved his own words.

"This cannot be!" Tepi cried. "You are all strange to me! This one," she pointed to Ja-nee, "is even strange to me! There must be others! And there are the Calusa! They are others!"

A low murmur rippled through the crowd. The people flashed their eyes at each other. They did not understand this woman's words. There were no others, in spite of what a few had once believed. But they were too polite to argue.

Tepi looked from one to the other. She did not understand anything that was happening to her, and she was afraid.

Ja-nee tugged at her arm. "I am hungry."

Tepi stroked the child's hair and forced a smile. There was no helping it. They must stay here. Perhaps in days ahead, the mysteries would come clear. Until then, they would make their lives with this kind and peaceful tribe.

She looked up at the tall man. "I am a first weaver of nets," she said with a touch of pride in her voice. "This child and I will be no burden to your tribe. My skills are now your skills, and this one"—she patted Ja-nee—"if no one here has a name that they remember for her face, I accept her as my responsibility." She looked around at them, but no one spoke a name for the child. So. She did not belong to them either. Had she sprung from air? Another mystery.

Tepi sighed. There was no use in wondering. Answers to her many questions would not march across her path no matter how hard she willed it. And she had never been one to puzzle out problems before, anyway. Doga had always told her how everything was before. Doga . . . the ache in her belly at the thought of his face was not from hunger, she knew.

Four of the small people lifted the strange dugout above their heads and trotted ahead, and the rest smiled and pulled at the newcomers' hands, leading them into the tangled depths of the jungle.

* * *

259

The cookfires had long been doused, and the last notes of the evening songs had died when the tall man, who was named Akuda to his tribe, crouched beside Tepi. "Ja-nee can go to sleep with Mabeeka and her family now," he said. He motioned to a smiling woman who stood behind him. "You may join them when you are ready tonight, and tomorrow we begin your sleeping platform there." He indicated a spot near the northern edge of the camp. Small fires burned beyond the sleeping platforms, fires that ringed the entire camp, and Tepi squinted against their lights to see where he was pointing. The fires must be kept burning at night to keep away the great animals, Akuda had told her. During the day, the noise of the tribe's activities seemed to be enough to hold them at bay.

Ja-nee had been leaning, half asleep, against Tepi's side with her thumb in her mouth, but at Akuda's words she jumped up and ran to Mabeeka. Mabeeka had a girl child about Ja-nee's age, and the two children had giggled together all through the night meal. Ja-nee had in fact charmed everyone in the few hours they'd been with the tribe, and Tepi's heart was proud as she watched her trot off with the smiling woman.

"I must speak," Akuda said softly, drawing Tepi's attention back to himself.

Tepi nodded and they walked a short distance from the center of the clearing, away from other ears. When they stopped in the shadows, Tepi had to bend her neck far back to look up at him. Akuda is a handsome man, she thought suddenly, surprising herself with the unbidden and disloyal thought. She quickly dropped her eyes. He is much too tall, his arms and chest are too muscled, and besides, he probably belongs to another . . . as I do, she scolded herself.

260

"We said to you that there are no others," he began. "This is not so." He looked toward the center of the clearing where several families sat storytelling to the older children who had not yet gone to their sleeping platforms. They glanced curiously at Tepi and Akuda, then politely away. It was clear that he desired private time with the newcomer.

"My thinking tells me that what the tribe believes, that they are the only tribe, is not true. Otherwise you and Ja-nee would have already been here, and not come from someplace else." He watched her carefully to see if she understood him. When she made no comment, he plunged on. "And we sometimes see others . . . with pink skin and hair the color of sunlight . . . like yours . . . pass by in great, fast-moving dugouts. The people of my tribe believe they are not people, but gods. And had you not spoken to us in our language, they would have thought you were simply a river goddess and her child inspecting their domain. So they keep the idea that they are the only ones."

Tepi stared at him in shock. She had not looked at herself in the water even once, not in the entire two days and nights they had paddled. Could her hair have turned to the color of the mists as it always did in the great-aged people of her tribe? But Akuda had said sunlight, not mist—and she reached back and yanked at the bindings that held her hair away from her face. He watched her curiously.

The thong pulled at her hair as she tried to remove it, and when it finally came free, she stared at it. It made a perfect circle, and stretched more easily than a piece of wet leather. And when she released the tension on it, it immediately returned to its original shape. What was this thing? And now that she thought of it, where did

261

she and Ja-nee get the strange garments they wore? They were not like the adornments of this tribe, but neither were they of her tribe. More mystery. Her brain was becoming very tired of mystery.

Akuda reached behind her and took a handful of her hair. He drew it slowly across her shoulder and let it fall down on her breast. His fingers stroked the length of the long strands and lingered on the ends, rubbing them between his fingers before letting his hand drop to his side.

Tepi looked down at her hair. She had never seen such a color. It was ugly, and she swallowed a cry of distress. *I am in a sleep-story. I must be in a sleep-story. Or I am dead. Was not death a sleep-story without end?*

"I have one more thing to say, if you will listen," Akuda said, unaware of her self-absorbed thoughts. "It is, I think, the most important thing."

Tepi nodded and returned her attention to the tall man. I must resign myself, she thought. There are lessons to be learned in the second life, and I cannot waste time regretting the loss of the first one.

"I too have come from someplace else," Akuda whispered, then glanced quickly around to make sure he was not overheard. "And I, like you, do not remember my life before this one.

"And there were others, also. Some came in strange dugouts such as the one you and Ja-nee arrived in. Others spent many days and nights on end walking through the swamps and tall grass, swimming once in a while when the water was deep enough, until they reached the only tribe. So the legends go."

"Are we dead?" Tepi asked. "Is this the way we struggle on our journey to the second life?"

Akuda threw back his head and laughed, his teeth

howing white against his dark face in the dim moonlight. "I think not! In my long walk across the great wilderness I bled and hungered and thirsted and slapped at hungry insects as would any living man! The second life promises freedom from such earthly things, does it not?"

Tepi considered this. What Akuda said was the truth. So she was not dead either. "What drove us to this place?" she asked. "Why would we leave our tribes to come here, and why would we not remember the beginnings of our journeys?"

"I have no answer for you, Tepi. Not for you and Ja-nee, and not for myself. My memory is also lost to me. It is a sadness we will share." He lifted her chin with one finger and looked straight into her eyes.

Tepi felt heat color her face at his touch, and she backed away. Akuda did not press her.

"Who are the others that you spoke of?" she asked quickly to cover her nervousness. "I would speak with them too. Perhaps they have answers for me."

Akuda shrugged. "As I said, they are legend. Until you and Ja-nee, I was the last traveler to arrive here, and the tribe does not like to speak of the others often. It disturbs their belief that they are the only ones. That is why I speak to you now in privacy. I do not wish to upset these kind people. It is difficult enough for them to accept my existence at all, and they like to pretend I began my life within their fold."

"I do not understand," Tepi said. "If these people you speak of were legend before you arrived, where did they go? Why did they not stay with the tribe?"

"It was once whispered to me in confidence and sadness by the chief fisherman, then never spoken of again," Akuda answered. "A sickness came upon them one by one; a beast that chewed inside their heads for many days and nights, never giving them peace. And the sickness attacked others of the tribe too . . . but only a few."

Tepi put one hand over her breast in alarm. "And then?" she whispered.

"They are all dead," Akuda said. "Every one of the lost ones . . . except me. And now you and Ja-nee."

Chapter Thirty-eight

It was the first time Jake had ever heard Ralph curse. The string of helicopters that crisscrossed the Everglades at regular intervals, swinging low over the tall grass and almost touching the tops of the trees in the bayheads and hammocks, had driven Ralph into a permanent state of agitation.

"This will never do!" he shouted over the latest roar of whirling blades. "Those damned things will drive every creature in the Glades into hiding! The expedition is ruined!"

Jake had to admit that he was probably right, and wondered if it would drive the lost tribe into hiding too.

By nightfall of the second day out, they hadn't seen anything but flocks of fleeing birds and an occasional disgruntled alligator, and nobody was in a good mood.

After a quiet meal of Charlie's fresh-caught bass, canned beans, and fresh fruit, Jake stretched out on the boat deck, his bedroll under his head, and stared up at the sky. The Park Service was breaking all the rules in their search for the missing people, he thought with appreciation. They were allowing the Glades to be disturbed by the 'copters, and had approved the use of noisy, forbidden airboats in the search if that failed. He hoped it wouldn't come to that—for the sake of the lost people, the birds, and animals in the Glades . . . and the expedition.

Now the night was quiet except for the constant, primitive night sounds, and the drone of subdued voices from the other boat. The rustle of pages being turned drifted over to him; Ralph reading by the light of a Coleman lantern. He wondered what time the search would start again tomorrow.

The expedition was awake and underway by the time the first faraway sounds of the search helicopters disturbed the Glades. Jake and Charlie shared the first boat today, and the guide whistled through his teeth as they snaked along the narrow waterway.

A short distance ahead, several islands rose from the shallow water and formed a cluster of dense vegetation intersected by deeper, free-flowing channels overhung by sunlight-killing branches of tall trees and drooping vines. The temperature dropped a few degrees as the expedition boats glided slowly into the primordial scene.

An hour and a half later, Charlie cut the motor on the boat and spread the navigation chart over a bench. The twists and turns in the channels had been complicated and continuous, and several wide branches of the dark water that could have been main routes—but they had ignored—had added to the confusion. He bent over the chart and traced his finger around the marks on the paper.

"Don't match," Charlie finally said. He stood up and stared at the trees as if the answer to his problem would magically appear there in front of him.

"What's wrong?" Ralph shouted from the other boat.

"Gotta go back!" Charlie shouted back. "Can't trace our route by the map! We need to go around!"

"How can the map be wrong, Charlie?" Jake asked.

Charlie shrugged. "Old map. Island drift. Too many islands for the cartographers to bother with out here where nobody cares. A lot of guesswork. Getting all the little uninhabited islands right isn't important. They mainly care about only the ones in the Park area—and the big ones out here."

"So how do people get around out here?"

Charlie grinned at Jake. "They don't, man. Only crackpot scientists risk coming out here."

"And crazy Indian guides," Jake added, grinning back. "How are you going to turn these boats around with the cages hooked up?"

Charlie's grin faded. He looked around at the narrow channel, gauging the distance, and shook his head. "Yeah. See your point. And it's too far to back out ... take forever."

"So go forward," Jake said easily. "I'll draw a new map as we go." He grabbed a paper and pencil and began to rough out where they were and what he could remember of where they'd been.

Charlie shrugged again. "You're the boss ... we get lost out here a month, you still pay by the day." He amiably started the motor again and chugged forward.

Jake had three pages of maps drawn when Charlie pointed to a huge mound of rotting vegetation on the left bank.

"Gator nest," the guide said. "Biggest damned nest I've ever—"

An explosion of mud and water no more than twenty feet in front of the boat cut off his words. The peace of the afternoon was shattered by deep grunts of rage and the heavy thrashings of two great reptiles as they slapped water and snapped their jaws in a vicious battle over the nest.

They cut the motors and watched. It took Jake more than half a minute to see through the roiling water and rolling bodies to identify the creatures. And when what he had assumed to be a mother alligator protecting her young from a marauding bull raised her head and opened her huge jaws in a frantic attempt to fight off the larger animal, he leaped for the tranquilizer gun.

He shot the big bull first.

Charlie instantly followed his lead and grabbed for the other tranq gun. He fired a second, accurate shot into the smaller animal and then they waited.

Within minutes, the powerful tail-slaps diminished to feeble jerks of fading anger, and when the two giants began to roll over in the water, Jake leaped overboard with a wire noose and treaded through waist-deep water toward the drowning animals.

He slipped the noose over the bull's jaws and yanked it tight, lifting the massive head above water with every bit of strength he had. "Charlie!" he screamed. "Save the female!"

A splash behind him. He turned quickly, and another noose flashed by his face and landed neatly over the female's snout. "No sweat," the younger man said, smiling at Jake as he tightened his noose, then wrapped one arm around the animal's slowly sinking body and dragged it up above the waterline.

Then the three other guides and Ralph were in the water. They pulled the unconscious animals through the water and into the cages, laughing and splashing as they tried to maneuver the ungainly bodies into comfortable positions.

Finally it was over. They all crawled back into the second boat and stood smiling and dripping water while they stared triumphantly at the two thecodonts.

Jake slapped Charlie on the shoulder and held out his hand. Charlie grabbed the hand and shook hard, unable to keep a silly grin of success off his face as he kept looking from Jake to the animals.

Ralph hurried to the front of the boat and tugged a small Styrofoam cooler out from under a bench. When he turned around again, he held plastic glasses in one hand and a bottle of Dom Pérignon champagne in the other. His face was flushed with excitement as he held the bottle over his head and waved it in the air. "To our success!" he shouted, and they all cheered with him.

"Sorry it's warm," he apologized as he popped the cork and poured, "The ice didn't keep." But he was smiling . . . and nobody cared that the champagne was warm.

"Now what?" Charlie asked after they'd drained the bottle.

Ralph walked to the back of the boat and looked closely at the smaller thecodont. "She's hurt," he said. "I can't tell how bad it is, but I think it would be best to go back in and have her attended to."

"The stream seems to widen a little just past the nest," Jake said. "Can we turn around there, Charlie?"

Charlie turned and studied the spot he was pointing at. "Tight. Maybe." He reached for the ignition.

"Wait!" Jake yelled suddenly. He grabbed Ralph's empty cooler and jumped overboard again.

Puzzled, the others watched him wade toward the nest, then cheered when they saw what he was up to.

Jake lined the box with some of the rotting plants that made up the nest, then from the top, carefully wiggled his arm deep into the mess. He pulled out a dozen eggs, placed them gently in the box, then covered them with more nesting material.

He and the rest of the party were too intent on what he was doing to notice the half-dozen pair of eyes staring curiously at them through the underbrush.

Chapter Thirty-nine

Lydia felt sick with disappointment. Four days of searching the Everglades, and they'd come up with nothing. She put down the phone and stared unseeingly at it for a minute, then turned to Evan. "I'm going out there myself."

Evan closed the book he was reading on ancient Indian cultures. "What did they say?" he asked, surprised. "Have they given up?"

"They said they haven't found any sign of anybody with the helicopters, and they're starting to search with the airboats tomorrow."

Evan stood up and put his arms around Lydia, drawing her away from the phone and onto the couch. "Give them a chance, sweetheart." He stroked her hair. "I know asking you to be patient is tough, but there isn't anything we can do out there that they aren't already doing, and probably doing better."

She opened her mouth to protest, but Evan kissed her lightly, quickly, to silence her. "I promise," he said before she could try again, "if they haven't found her by the end of the three days they promised to search with the airboats, we'll charter a boat ourselves, hire a guide,

and go out there and look for Jenny until we find her."
He smiled down at her. "Okay?"

"Okay," she answered reluctantly. She put her arms
around him and buried her face in his shoulder. *Please,
Bett Wilson,* she begged silently . . . *please take good
care of my Jenny out there.*

Ray Wilson paced Burnham's office. He'd hounded
the police and the doctor for days, trying to assure himself that everything it was possible to do in the search
and research was being done. He didn't know what else
he could do, and he'd never felt so helpless and frustrated in his life.

Burnham had just assured him that the work on synthesizing the normal DNA sequences was going well
and would be tested for accuracy and safety by computer in the next day or so. There was nothing left to
say, but Ray still wasn't satisfied. "What if they find
them too late?" he asked, finally thinking of something
to say and glaring at Burnham. "Can it ever be too late,
or is this procedure you're working on effective at any
stage of the disease?"

Burnham sighed and scribbled something on a prescription pad, then held it out to Ray. "We're dealing
with a lot of unknowns here, Mr. Wilson. I can't give
you any definitive answers."

Ray looked at the paper but didn't move to take it.

Burnham waved it at him. "This is a prescription for
a mild tranquilizer. Take it. You aren't going to do your
wife any good when they bring her in if you're in this
state. And they will find her. Be patient."

Ray turned and walked out.

* * *

The sleeping platform was almost finished. Tepi's fingers flew, expertly weaving the palm fronds into a tight, waterproof roof. The tribe had marveled at her skill. Every once in a while one of them would shyly approach her and place their hands on hers in admiration. She accepted the compliments gracefully, and had offered to teach her methods to any woman who was interested. Every one of them had clapped their hands in grateful acceptance.

Now she looked down from the platform at Ja-nee. The child and Mabeeka's little girl, who had the name of Pa, were slapping in the mud at the edge of the clearing.

Ja-nee knelt in front of a small space she'd cleared of twigs and grass. Her pudgy hands smoothed the wet, sandy ground and she patted at the lumps and fissures with fierce concentration. Finally she had it the way she thought she wanted it and she jumped to her feet, eyeing it critically. "Now, Pa," she said, grabbing the smaller girl by the arm and pulling her forward. "This is how you do it. I'm going to show you one more time and then you do everything just like I did it."

Pa nodded and crouched beside the smooth spot. Her new friend was wonderful and she wanted very much to please her.

Ja-nee picked up a short, pointed stick and hunkered down. She stuck her tongue out of the side of her mouth in concentration. Carefully, she drew a graceful, arced line in the sand. Pa watched her. The stick flew, faster and faster, until Ja-nee grunted with satisfaction and stood up. A faithful image of the huge bird that she and Tepi had seen on the riverbank stared up at them.

Pa hopped up and down with delight. "Kuku!" she shouted. "You made Kuku!"

Tepi smiled as she watched Pa take the stick. After a few unsuccessful pokes at the ground, Ja-nee put her hand over Pa's and guided it into drawing a reasonable copy of the great bird.

A few members of the tribe stopped their chores to watch, and most placed their hands over Ja-nee's in admiration of her unusual talent. Two or three tried their own skill at the game, laughing at themselves when they failed to do as well as Ja-nee.

"Tepi!"

She brought her attention away from the children and looked down. Akuda stood beneath the sleeping platform, smiling up at her. "Will you fish with me?" he shouted, waving a net above his head.

She felt the heat come up in her face at the sight of him, and ducked her head to hide the color. But she came down from the platform and followed him into the jungle.

Chapter Forty

The wounds had been superficial. Within two days in a spacious pen at Tropical Treasures, the female thecodont was basking contentedly in the sun and eating what Jake swore was twice her weight in fish every day.

The male's appetite wasn't as good, and he spent a lot of time underwater, his long, narrow snout jammed into the far corner of his pen.

The zoologists and biologists sent down by the Paleontology Institute had swarmed all over the place within hours after Ralph notified them of their catch. Private planes had hurried the anxious scientists into the Tampa airport in the middle of the night, and limousines had sped them to Tropical Treasures. The general attitude was euphoric.

Jake took another peek into the incubator that one of the zoologists had brought with him. Nothing yet. If the thecodont had the same breeding cycle as an alligator, the oval, leathery eggs might not hatch for another two months. But if the cycle was different, which was entirely possible, they could hatch any minute. He laughed at his own impatience—a nerve-wracking and unsuitable trait in a paleontologist who might go on digs for years without finding anything important. Somehow this was different.

A sudden uproar outside near the larger holding pen distracted him from the eggs. Curious, he walked out of the building toward the commotion and turned the corner just in time to see several of the scientists leap over the concrete wall into the enclosure that held the large male. He sprinted toward the pen.

Half a dozen people were bent over the thecodont, shouting orders at each other. As Jake watched, one of the zoologists, a heavy man in his late forties, let go with a string of black curses and walked away from the great beast's side. He had tears in his eyes.

Jake vaulted over the concrete wall and pushed his way through the huddle of people. And he understood the fat man's sorrow. The thecodont was dead.

The biologists did an immediate autopsy on the animal while Jake and Charlie sat sipping warm Cokes at the refreshment stand, waiting for the results. There'd been no outward harm done to the thecodont, and even if an autopsy failed to reveal the cause of death, it would yield valuable information on the anatomy and physiology of the animal. Even so, they would have preferred that the thecodont had lived and bred in captivity.

The owner of Tropical Treasures, a white-haired old man with two missing front teeth, sat alone at the end of the refreshment counter muttering to himself. "Never seen nuthin' like it," he said several times into a can of beer. "Woulda made me famous, ya know?" he shouted over to Jake and Charlie. "And I bin takin' good care of 'em ... feedin' 'em real good! Ain't my fault!" He dropped his head and addressed the beer can again. "Ain't my fault."

Neither Jake nor Charlie felt up to taking the time to reassure him of his blamelessness, so they ignored him.

"A lot of animals can't be kept in captivity," Jake said and tossed his empty can into a waste bin. "They can't adjust, and—"

"The female is doing okay." Charlie said.

"Maybe it was just old age," Jake mumbled, hearing the rationalization in his voice. Then he sat quietly, staring at a spot over Charlie's shoulder.

"We can go back out there and get more, can't we?" Charlie asked. "Come on, cheer up. Besides, we still have the female."

Jake looked at Charlie strangely for a second, as if he hadn't been aware of his presence until now. "What if it's the Genesis Gene? What if that's what killed it?"

Suddenly Charlie understood. "Oh shit. All those people . . . the little girl." He was saved from further comment by Ralph and another scientist who came hurrying out of the large storage shed that had been cleared out and set up as a makeshift laboratory by the visiting scientists. Ralph put a hand on Jake's shoulder and said without preamble, "The gonads were greatly enlarged, but functioning. You guessed at that.

"The surprising thing though . . . the archipallium was also infected, but of course we had no way to test genetic memory retrieval in the animal, so we couldn't have anticipated that. And if it hadn't been for your information on the Genesis Gene, we wouldn't even have known what we were looking at."

Jake felt sick. "The archipallium . . . ?"

"Hard as a rock . . . looked like a little prune. The web seemed to be completely calcified."

The other scientist jumped in. "And at the time of death, the web was spreading. There were more than a dozen brittle tendrils that had invaded other parts of the brain. Never seen anything like it."

Jake's mind began to race. "How old was the thecodont? Was its age a factor in the terminal growth of the web? Would the web be less likely to calcify in a younger specimen?"

The scientist hopped up on a stool beside Jake. "We think it was about five years old. The rest . . ." He shrugged. "If we could get a look at the female's archipallium we might be able to tell more about the progression, but I'd hate to kill—"

"That's it!" Jake pounded a surprised Charlie on the back. He turned on Ralph. "We'll take the female to the genetic testing lab that Evan's been working with! They know everything about the Genesis Gene! They can give us answers we can't even guess at out here with this setup!"

Ralph frowned. "I don't know, Jake. These are good people here." He waved toward the shed where the scientists were still dissecting the thecodont. "They might not appreciate having the project pulled out from under them."

"Ralph." Jake grabbed the older man's shoulders and stared into his eyes. "Don't you think that those men of science in there would do anything to help along the research on this find? Don't you think they want to know not just the anatomy of the thecodont, but *how* these ancient creatures came to be?"

Ralph nodded slowly, thinking.

"Dr. Frankel and Dr. Burnham can tell them that, Ralph," he urged. "And more. Much more." He lowered his voice dramatically, and Charlie and the scientist leaned forward to listen. "Without their knowledge and cooperation, the female will eventually die in the same

ay that the male did. You know that now. But they're
working on a procedure that might keep her alive ...
and enable her to breed again. Think of it!"

"Well ..." Ralph was weakening.

Here comes the real point, Ralph. "And if they can
prove that their genetic surgery is effective on the theco-
ont, they can modify and utilize the information to
safely treat the people who have been affected by the
gene. A live specimen that responds favorably is a much
more reliable indication of success than a computer
readout for safety! Think of your medical contribution
to humanity, Ralph!" He was pushing it, but what the
hell, he was right.

"The DNA of a reptile is hardly compatible with human DNA, Jake," Ralph said, but Jake could see he was
intrigued.

"If it's a broken magnesium coenzyme causing genetic damage in both cases, it won't matter," Jake persisted, remembering Evan's detailed explanations.
"Come on, Ralph! It's your party! Go in and tell them
what you want to do!" He waved an arm at the shed.

"I say we go for it," the scientist said suddenly.

Jake grinned his thanks at him.

"Do I have a say in this?" Charlie asked. "If I do,"
he continued without waiting for an answer, "I say we
do anything that will help cure that little girl ... and the
rest of the people."

Jake slapped him on the back, then looked quickly at
Ralph.

Ralph nodded.

Dr. Frankel would be delighted to cooperate. That
was the message finally passed down to Jake after a

number of excited calls back and forth between Evan,
Dr. Burnham, Jake, and Dr. Frankel.

Burnham ordered the swimming pool, normally used
for hydrotherapy at the hospital, drained of its chlori-
nated water and partially refilled with fresh. It would
serve as a temporary home for the thecodont, now
named Millie, in between her short trips to the Genetic
Institute where the more sophisticated testing equipment
was housed.

The remains of the male, packed in ice, were also
sent to the Institute along with the incubator full of
eggs.

The team of scientists hadn't objected at all to the
new plans.

Millie was causing quite a commotion at the hospital.
A steady stream of people from the staff found conve-
nient excuses to troop into the room where she swam la-
zily around in the half-drained pool. Banks of
full-spectrum lights normally used for Seasonal Affec-
tive Disorders, mainly winter depressions in Florida,
had been set up at the shallow end, allowing Millie to
bask in the artificial "sun."

And it was a simple matter to grab a cod or halibut
from the refrigerator and toss the goodie to her as a gesture of friendship. Soon Millie recognized the vibrations
of approaching feet and voices, and she'd hurry to the
side of the pool and open her great jaws expectantly; a
remarkable sign of intelligence for a reptile. Everybody
loved her.

The DNA from Millie and the male thecodont proved
out to contain the expected defective magnesium coenzyme, and Drs. Burnham and Frankel worked long into

the night to adapt the new, synthetic DNA to Millie's physiology.

And on the morning of the third day of Millie's confinement in the hospital pool, they were ready.

Lydia, Evan, Jake, and Ray watched the thecodont glide to the far corner of the pool. Since the day before, she'd ignored all offers of fish, and now stubbornly turned her back on her new friends. She pushed her nose into a corner of the tank and stayed there.

"What's the matter with her?" Lydia asked anxiously.

Jake shook his head. "I don't know. My guess is she's pissed off about being bombarded with foreign DNA. Maybe she's just a little sick to her stomach."

"What if she's dying?" Ray asked. "What if the synthetic DNA doesn't work? What if it's killing her instead of curing her?"

Jake poked Ray in the ribs with his elbow and glanced quickly at Lydia.

Ray glowered at him. "Look, let's be realistic here. If Millie dies, are they going to know whether it was the what-do-they-call-it . . . antisense genetic therapy . . . or the Genesis Gene that killed her?"

Jake was saved from saying "I don't know" for the dozenth time by a trio of scientists coming in to do Millie's fourth scheduled blood test.

They watched the three men slip a noose over the reptile's snout, then crawl into the tank with her.

She didn't fight them at all when they drew her blood.

Chapter Forty-one

The giant, armadillo-like creature rubbed his head against the rough bark of the water oak and grumbled with rapidly escalating annoyance. The familiar ache had started again. But the rubbing eased it, and he soon lumbered off into the jungle, his thirteen-foot-long, seven-foot-high body crushing the undergrowth and bending and snapping the saplings that were unfortunate enough to be in his path.

The bird's enormous hooked beak flashed down, cracking the rabbit's spine in half. She ran with long, loping strides back to her nest, the dead animal bumping and dangling lifelessly against her chest as she tucked her head down for a better grip on her prey. Her chicks were hungry.

Two days ago, her mate had dropped to his knees, then with a great cry had crashed to the ground, his powerful legs kicking and flying out in a useless attempt to right himself. She'd watched, uncomprehending, until he was still. No amount of prodding or calling to him had brought him to his feet, and finally, she'd given up and hurried back to the nest with the kill he'd dropped when he fell.

Now the job of caring for the five chicks was hers alone. She had little time to rest.

Most of the parents lived only long enough to see their brightly colored, starling-sized chicks leave the nest. The youngsters would flap and glide from tree to tree, their long, bony tails whipping up and down for balance, until they made a mistake and landed in a frantic flurry of feathers on the ground. Then, screeching with excitement, they would clamber up the nearest tree to safety by digging the three curved, clawed fingers of their winged forelimbs into the soft bark.

Then they would sit for a while, snapping their sharp-toothed beaks with indecision, and daring each other to be the first to take off on the next adventure.

Self-sufficient by now, they hardly noticed that their parents no longer came to them with choice bits of lizard, frog, or insects.

The barely audible sounds came from the huge mound of rotting vegetation on the riverbank. It was enough to send the more common denizens of the Everglades fleeing in every direction. Instinct told them that when the baby reptiles began to hatch, a protective and vicious mother couldn't be far away.

The sounds grew louder, and soon the mound was covered with foot-long, squirming babies, their calls of "chee-ohw, chee-ohw" going unheard by the mother they cried for.

But they were basically self-sufficient too, and soon

they'd wriggled into the water on their own. They swam together in a loosely knit group, snapping happily at flashing schools of minnows with their long, narrow snouts.

They had no idea that a dozen of their siblings were missing.

Chapter Forty-two

Tepi sat cross-legged on the ground, her fingers quickly weaving and knotting the strong, supple grasses. This net was for Akuda.

She frowned a little as she worked. Her fingers were sore from the hours of work, as if they'd become soft from long disuse. How could this be? Had she been away for so long on her mysterious journey that they had lost the ability to withstand the pressure of a simple net thread?

She sighed and pushed the endless unresolved questions from her mind.

The net was finished. She had given it to Akuda, and the rest of the tribe had laughed behind their hands and pushed gently at each other when she had presented it to him at the circle meeting, and he had placed his lips on her cheek in gratitude.

It had been a bold thing for her to do, but since she'd found that Akuda had no mate, the gift had been an acceptable one, if a bit forward.

He'd then given his old net, a gift from a kind and

ancient widow of the tribe, to Ja-nee, and the old woman had smacked her gums together with approval at the gesture of favors exchanged. Most of the women of the tribe thought Akuda too big and light-skinned for their taste, and the crone was glad that the new woman, homely as she was, found him favorable—and that the attraction seemed to be mutual. To be of an age to reproduce in the tribe and not to have a mate with which to accomplish this necessity was frowned upon.

Ja-nee had spent the rest of the meeting wriggling around in Akuda's lap, anxious to be off and playing with Pa and the new-old net. But Tepi had cautioned her about playing too far from camp at the twilight hour, and the child had finally fallen asleep with her head on Akuda's chest, and the net tangled around her feet.

The next morning, Tepi left the two children in the care of the rest of the tribe while she and Akuda went to the deep stream to fish together again. She looked over her shoulder once as she left. Pa was proudly showing Ja-nee the fine points of casting the old net into a puddle.

"This is a fine gift, Tepi," Akuda said as he carefully pulled in his third batch of flopping fish. Tepi nodded her thanks but kept her head down as she tried to keep up with his skill. As he dumped the fish on the ground beside her, she would slit their bellies open with her sharp-edged stone, then remove the insides and toss them into the stream to draw the attention of more fish. She remembered the great fish that she and Ja-nee had seen during their journey, and had told Akuda about them, but he had never seen such fish. Sometimes she wondered if she had imagined it.

After Tepi had slit the bellies, she would pack the cleaned fish into a large woven-reed basket, layering them between wet bunches of the peppery-tasting green plant that grew in the stream to keep them cool.

Today, when the basket was almost full, a strange sound far downstream startled them into alertness.

"Come. Hurry," Akuda said and snatched the basket from the ground. Tepi quickly threw two live fish that were left on the bank back into the stream, grabbed the net, and followed him into the protective underbrush. They crouched behind a clump of palms and peered through the leaves, watching for the source of the rapidly building sound.

It was like nothing she'd ever heard before, and she covered her ears with her hands as the sound, louder than the rumblings of a thousand summer storms, drew closer.

Now she couldn't believe her eyes. The thing that rounded the bend in the stream moved faster than a great reptile on the hunt—and it was much bigger.

As it flew toward them she had an even bigger shock. Two men rode the yowling beast! One sat low down and to the front of it, and the other sat perched high in the air on a seat far above its back! The noise of the strange thing as it roared past them was deafening, and she wondered how they could stand it—and how they had managed to master it.

Then it was gone and she was left with the lingering impression of the fleeting glance she'd had of the man who sat on top of the great waterbeast—a man with the same strange-color hair as her own. Was it a sign of someone who'd made a long journey and was now trying to find his way back to his tribe? Somehow she thought not . . . and besides, Akuda was a lost one too. And his hair was black.

"Come," Akuda said when the angry roars of the beast had died away. "We have enough fish for the tribe." He swung the basket to his shoulder and started off through the jungle.

Tepi thought he looked strangely disturbed, and she hurried to catch up with him. And she had many questions too. Why did he suddenly seem cold and aloof? "Wait! Akuda!" she cried out. "Speak to me!"

He waited, and the face he turned back to her was both sad and puzzled. "I am sorry, Tepi," he said. "The sight of the noisy beasts of the air and water disturb me. It is sometimes almost as if they are known things to me, but that cannot be, for I really do not understand what they are at all."

She suddenly remembered the airbeasts that had flown close overhead for the past few days. The tribe had chanted "Chunga! Chunga!" and had pointed and laughed at them, for they never perched, but always flew harmlessly away. Nor did the waterbeast seem a particular threat . . . especially since it was obviously controlled by men. Or possibly, as the villagers said . . . gods. But they looked like men to her.

So why was Akuda disturbed by them? Had he perhaps once controlled one of the great beasts himself, and now had only the dimmest memory of it? Had the men who rode past them on the waterbeast been of his tribe? Were they perhaps looking for him? Or were they gods, and Akuda was a god too, and did not realize it?

You continually have too many questions, Tepi, she scolded herself yet again. You must learn to be content with what is today.

"Tepi?"

Akuda had been speaking to her, but she had been too preoccupied with her own thoughts to hear him. Embarrassed for her inattention, she apologized and asked him to please repeat himself.

Now it was Akuda who looked embarrassed. He put the basket down and clasped his hands behind his back. He looked at the ground as if it held something of great interest, then back up at her face. "I asked you," he said, then paused and cleared his throat before continuing in a louder voice than was necessary, "if you would honor me by sharing my sleeping platform."

Tepi stared at him.

"I will be a good father to your Ja-nee," he added unnecessarily—that he would be a good father was obvious to Tepi.

She had been expecting him to ask, but not so soon. "Yes," she said simply.

The joy in his face drove the last wisps of a lingering ghost named Doga from her heart.

Chapter Forty-three

The extended two-week search was over. The authorities concluded that the lead had been a blind one, and continued attempts at finding the missing people somewhere in the Glades was a waste of time. They were apologetic, but adamant. And since Lydia refused to formally declare her daughter kidnapped, well . . . they were limited in what they could do. But if anyone came up with more substantial proof concerning the whereabouts of all those people, or just Jenny, they added, they'd be happy to resume the search. But until then . . . the reporting officer shrugged helplessly and left Lydia's house to go about more immediate business. He didn't mention that he'd had little hope of finding anybody in the vast wilderness of the Glades anyway, even if there had been a platoon of people wandering around in there.

Two of the searchers, Brad Brown and Vilma Haggerty, while searching with binoculars from their 'copters, had caught just the barest glimpses of some mighty strange things. But Brad had been on a bender the night before, and was careful to keep his opinion of what he thought he'd seen ducking quickly down into the jungle to himself. Vilma was in the middle of a nasty custody battle for her two children, and wasn't about to open her mouth and risk being judged insane. And soon they'd both convinced themselves that they hadn't *really* seen impossible-looking, monstrous animals wandering the Glades.

Lydia sat silently at her kitchen table, her hands loose in her lap. She watched a mockingbird through the window. It hopped along the ground, diligently pecking up bits of edible things that were too small for her to see clearly. She thought it must be insects . . . or worms. She wondered if the bird was one of the babies that she'd photographed in its nest . . . how long ago? She wasn't sure. Ages.

She needed Evan. She fought off a desire to sleep . . . escape . . . and reached for her car keys and her purse. Evan was at the Institute with Jake. And Millie. Was Millie still alive? Had the Genesis Gene killed her yet? Or had the genetic surgery been too much for her system to bear, and had her life ended that way? Would it be too much for Jenny? Would they find Jenny?

The questions spun endlessly around in her head as she raced toward the hospital. But she knew what she had to do now.

Too calm. Evan watched Lydia watch Millie. She'd announced the end of the search to him in an even, rational voice, then asked to see the thecodont. None of the hysteria he'd expected was even remotely evident. He worried that she was sublimating her grief, losing touch with reality. And now he felt he was too emotionally tied to her to assess her competently. Maybe he could get her to talk to Burnham later. . . .

Now he put an arm around her shoulders and spoke

291

enthusiastically. "So it seems to be working. It took four sessions before they think it took hold properly, and daily applications of photorecovery therapy, but the broken magnesium coenzyme has finally disappeared from her DNA!"

She looked at him and smiled a little. "I saw Jake in the lobby. He told me it keeps recurring . . . whenever you think you have it licked, it starts showing up again. And you can't keep fooling around with her DNA forever, can you? It would eventually kill her, or at least maybe cause some other dangerous side effects, wouldn't it?"

"Burnham and Frankel are going to use an immunological serum they've developed from normal alligator blood to use in conjunction with the synthesized DNA and photorecovery," he answered evasively.

She looked at him curiously. "You mean like using my blood and the blood of other resistant carriers as a base?" she asked.

Evan nodded.

"But if the alligators they used aren't related to Millie, how is that going to work? If they don't carry the dormant gene in their DNA, it won't do any good, will it? You've already told me that before. You'd need to find her parents and one of them would have to be an alligator . . . obviously resistant . . . wouldn't it?"

Definitely not out of touch with reality, Evan thought with relief. But he didn't know how to answer her. He had the same doubts.

Lydia looked back at Millie. The thecodont still sat with her long, narrow nose stuffed in the corner of the pool. She still refused all offers of food.

"Go get Jake," she said to Evan, but her eyes were still on Millie. "Find out how to contact his guide.

want him to take us back to the place where they saw the people."

Evan didn't move.

She turned to face him. "You promised," she said evenly.

Evan went to find Jake.

Jake and Ralph sat over breakfast in the hospital cafeteria. They invited Evan to join them, but he stood while he explained what he wanted.

"Sure thing," Jake said, getting up. "I'll call Charlie right now . . . hope he hasn't picked up a new job. But even if he has," he added quickly at the sight of Evan's worried face, "I have the nautical map. All we'll have to do is hire a new guide and boat . . . I'm not all that sure about going out there by myself."

"I don't expect you to get involved here, Jake," Evan said, surprised at the implication in the paleontologist's words.

Now it was Jake's turn to look surprised. "Hey . . . no way I'm letting you two go out there alone. You know what's out there. And the Park Service wouldn't allow it anyway. They haven't rescinded the Back Country permits' suspension yet. Ralph and I have one that's in effect as long as we want it." He grinned at Evan. "There's not much for me to do here right now anyway. We haven't scheduled another hunting expedition till late next week . . . when we'll be sure of the results on Millie. And my reports can wait," he added, anticipating Evan's next objection.

"I'm going too."

They turned to look at Ralph.

"I want to help," he insisted. "I owe you, Evan. For

allowing the use of your hospital facilities. And besides, I'd never pass up an opportunity to further explore the Glades."

Evan smiled his thanks at him. "I'll take all the help I can get." Then he hurried out of the cafeteria to call Charlie.

Charlie was available—at his usual rate of a hundred dollars a day.

Lydia called Ray Wilson—they'd promised to include him if they had to search for themselves.

At six o'clock the next morning, the five of them stood waiting anxiously for Charlie and his boat at the entrance canal to Tropical Treasures.

A little after seven o'clock in the morning, Millie's eggs began to hatch.

Jake resisted the urge to ask about taking along the cages. They'd move much faster without them, but he couldn't help thinking of the opportunities they might miss.

As they packed the pontoon boats with supplies—the one Charlie had arrived in, and the one that had remained behind at Tropical Treasures, Charlie glowered at Jake, but said nothing. The six of them could easily have traveled in the one boat, but two would be needed to ferry back some or all of the people that Jake hoped they'd find. Charlie had wanted to travel light, and just bring back the little girl and the woman, if they found them. Disrupting the lives of the legendary ancient tribe, if they existed, was, to him, wrong. He was overruled.

By 8 A.M. they were under way—Charlie, Jake, Evan, and Lydia in the lead boat, and Ralph and Ray following closely behind in the second, smaller craft.

Chapter Forty-four

Tepi stood alone in the center of the clearing. She smoothed her hands appreciatively over the long, thick Spanish moss skirt she wore. It was nothing like the short, thin ones that the women of the tribe wore every day. This one fell in many graceful tiers right down to her ankles, and the cascading layers fluffed out at least six inches around her hips and legs.

Wooden beads hung in the six traditional lucky strands around her neck, and each one was intricately carved with a symbol for either long life, eternal happiness, good health, or fertility. Most were carved with the fertility symbols.

Tepi turned her head to look for Ja-nee in the crowd of people who stood or sat in an admiring circle around her. The shells woven into her hair clinked and rattled with the movement, and she shook her head a little harder—just to hear the pleasant sound of it.

The tribe laughed behind their hands and pointed her with happiness. They were all dressed in their finest too—but not as finely as Tepi, of course. After all, was her mating day.

When the sun hit its high point, the drumbeat

began—the soft thump of palms on stretched-taut animal skins—and the tribe made a space in the north point of the circle to let Akuda in. He strode quickly to Tepi's side and took her hands in his own. He smiled down at her.

Tepi no longer thought that Akuda was too tall and too muscled. In truth, she never had thought so, but had only made those excuses to herself in order to deny the true feelings that had seemed so inappropriate at the time of their first meeting. But in the many days that had passed since then, as her memories of her life with Doga had rapidly dimmed as quickly as if it had been someone else's life, she had admitted to herself the strong attraction she felt toward the tall man who had the name of Akuda.

Now he stood before her, his hair parted and braided on either side of his head, each braid tied with the lucky six white shells. Soft rabbit skins circled his waist and dangled to his knees, and loose rings of the carved wooden beads clicked around his ankles and wrists.

She stood there, her hands in his, and her heart filled with love for him.

The tribe began to chant the mating song and clap their hands softly. They sang in easy counterpoint to the drumbeats while the oldest man of the tribe stepped forward into the circle. He hobbled toward them with the help of a wooden stick, and his wispy, mist-colored hair waved and floated around his wrinkled face with each step. The wrinkles deepened as he stopped and smiled up at them.

The chanting and the drumbeats slowly faded until all were silent.

"Are your hearts prepared to say the important

things?" the old man asked. He nodded his head as if to encourage them in their answers.

"Our hearts are prepared, ancient one," Tepi and Akuda replied in unison.

The village women had spent most of the evening before, coaching Tepi in the proper responses. The mating ceremony in this tribe was much different from what she was used to, and they had giggled and pushed at her gently whenever she made a mistake. But now she was ready, if a little tired.

The old man spoke again. "By what gods do you swear the truth of the things you are about to say?"

Akuda answered first. "I swear by the god Mak who rules the light. I swear by the god Grotha who rules the hunt. I swear by the god Nadakata who makes the fish to swim to my net. And I swear in the name of Zokeeda, who is my own personal god." He stamped his feet four times to summon them as witnesses to his words.

The old man nodded and turned to Tepi. "By what gods do you swear the truth of the things you are about to say?" he asked, smiling and showing his nearly toothless gums to her.

Tepi took a deep breath. "I swear by the goddess Nat who rules the moon. I swear by the goddess Rena who rules the water. I swear by the goddess Afareta who guides my hands in their skills. And I swear in the name of Lomati who is my own personal goddess."

She had been granted the protection of Lomati only last night in a quick ceremony performed by the old woman who had given Akuda his first net. She hoped the goddess was not angered by the lack of adequate preparation, but the tribe had not remembered to give her the protection of a deity until she had suddenly announced her intention to share Akuda's sleeping platform. Then there had been a frantic hustle and many loud conferences between the elders to find the name of a proper protective goddess for her, for it was impossible to mate without a name god.

The old man coughed discreetly and poked at her with a bony finger.

She had almost forgotten! Quickly, she stamped her feet four times.

The old man smiled again. "The gods hear you and mark your words." He motioned to a couple who stood waiting at the edge of the circle. They ran toward Tepi and Akuda and stood behind them, laughing softly with the joy of the occasion. Each held an end of a mating blanket, a beautiful thing made of the most supple, scraped deerskins carefully stitched together and decorated along three sides with hundreds of feathers——pink and white from the flamingo, dusty blue-gray from the great blue heron, green and red from the tiny parakeet, and many lengths and textures of brown, black, and white from the hundreds of species of birds that made the Everglades their home.

This special couple stretched the blanket out behind Tepi and Akuda and held it high. The tribe sighed with admiration at the workmanship displayed in the tribal mating blanket. The women of a long forgotten generation had worked on it for many seasons until it was finished, and since that time it had been given to every newly mated couple of the tribe to use for one night, then carefully wrapped and put away again until the next couple came forward with their intentions. And the honor of holding the blanket at each mating ceremony went to the couple who had borne the most children for the tribe. The couple who now stood behind Tepi and

Akuda had four living children. One infant more was slung over the young mother's back, but it would not be counted as a true future member of the tribe until it had lived past the critical age of three summers.

The old man waited until the murmurs of appreciation had died down. "Say your words, Akuda," he commanded.

Akuda's hands shook slightly. He was not used to being the center of attention. "I, Akuda the fisherman," he began in a whisper.

"Louder!" the tribe shouted. They would not be denied the most important part of the ceremony because of shyness.

"I, Akuda the fisherman," he repeated in a louder voice. This time he looked into Tepi's amused eyes and his nervousness faded. Was he not the proudest man on earth to have won such a prize? He deserved the tribe's admiring attention! ". . . choose Tepi the weaver as my one life-mate. Her worries will from this day on be my worries. I am responsible. The gods have heard my words."

The old man nodded, satisfied, then turned to Tepi. "Say your words, Tepi."

Tepi's voice was clear and calm. "I, Tepi the weaver, choose Akuda the fisherman as my one life-mate. His worries will from this day on be my worries. I am responsible. The gods have heard my words."

The old man began circling slowly around them, stamping his feet and raising a good amount of dust. "The gods take your words and hold them as truth!" he shouted. When the circle was completed, he turned toward the silent, smiling tribe. "All see, hear, and remember! It is done!"

He raised his arms, and at the signal, the couple who

held the mating blanket draped it quickly around Akuda and Tepi's shoulders. The mating ceremony was over.

The tribe crowded around the new couple, touching them for luck and laughing behind their hands. "May you have as many children as there are feathers on the blanket," they each said before they stepped back to let another come forward.

Ja-nee pushed between legs and bodies to get to Tepi. She shouted for attention, and when Akuda finally heard her over the noisy well-wishing, he reached down and grabbed her, then swung her up over his shoulders. She twisted her plump fingers into his hair so she wouldn't fall, then leaned to whisper in his ear. "Are you my Akuda ma-da now?" she asked.

"Forever and ever," he answered.

Akuda had tried to keep his lovemaking gentle, but his passion for Tepi and her uninhibited response to his attentions had made it impossible. But she'd only laughed at his eventual apologies and had assured him over and over again that she was pleased with the intensity of his love for her.

Ja-nee was spending the night with Pa and her family, so they were alone. After this night they would share the sleeping platform with Ja-nee and any other children they had. And when they wished to make love, they would either make use of one of the two fertility huts on the edge of the camp, or go to a secluded spot in the jungle for privacy. It was not proper for a child to be instructed in the ways of mating until he or she was nine summers old. And anyone younger caught peeking into the fertility huts was severely reprimanded with a firm slap on the backside.

Now, much later, Akuda raised himself up on one elbow and looked down at his mate. She slept on her back with one leg bent and her arms crossed over her belly. Her yellow hair was spread out in a tangle around her face, and he gently brushed a few strands away from her mouth.

He could not sleep. A grave matter worried him. He sighed and stared out into the dark. Only a few hours ago he had promised the gods that he would share all his worries with her. And now he had his first worry and he was reluctant to keep his promise. He had not anticipated sharing would be so difficult a thing. But it was not a selfish reason that caused his desire for secrecy, he reasoned with himself and the gods that he was sure were frowning down upon him now. He simply wished to spare Tepi any unhappiness. Was it right to give her a worry when she had none? He didn't know, and the frightening headache that had troubled him on and off for the past few hours did not help him to think clearly. How could he tell her that he was afraid he had the sickness that was fatal to all the lost ones?

Chapter Forty-five

Evan had watched Lydia's initial confidence and determination slowly wane as the hours went past. By late afternoon she turned to him with a decidedly worried frown. "She can't be out here, Evan," she said, letting her gaze wander from his face to the endless wilderness spread out around them. "I had no idea how enormous the Everglades was. How could she possibly get all the way out here, even if she had Bett Wilson with her? The people Jake saw . . . maybe they are the lost tribe, but that doesn't mean Jenny is with them, does it?"

Before Evan could think of some sort of reassuring reply, Charlie glanced over his shoulder, taking his attention temporarily away from the narrow channel they were navigating, and answered for him. "That's easy, lady. A boat . . . just like us. No problem." He turned quickly back to his steering, but kept talking. "Could've rented a canoe . . . or stolen one. Happens all the time."

Lydia looked pleased by Charlie's remark. She stepped over a cooler and leaned on the railing next to him. "So you don't think this is a wild-goose chase? You think all the missing people could really be out here?"

Charlie shrugged. He didn't look at her.

Lydia made another effort to establish a friendly relationship. "I can handle one of these boats, you know. If you want a rest, I can—"

"No woman handles my boat," Charlie interrupted her. "Woman are bad luck on a boat." He stared straight ahead, dismissing her.

Evan looked at Charlie in surprise. "Is that a belief of your tribe or a personal opinion, Charlie?" he asked lightly, his professional curiosity prompting the question.

Charlie was silent for a minute. The boat glided into a more open patch of water, and he glanced quickly around at Evan, weighing whether or not he wanted to reveal anything personal to this stranger. Their eyes met for a second, and Charlies sensed that it wasn't just an idle question asked out of boredom or nosiness.

He motioned Evan to step closer, and Lydia, catching his need for privacy, sat down at the far end of the boat and turned her head away.

"I had a wife," he said when Evan stood beside him. "We knew we'd be married from the time we were both six years old . . . there was never anybody else for either of us." He paused, considering how to tell his story. Evan waited silently.

"Her father was a shrimper," Charlie finally continued. "Made lots of money. She wanted to do it too. Said I didn't earn enough. Everybody knows women on a boat are no good . . . bad luck. We were married eighteen months. I told her to forget it."

Evan could see Charlie struggling with his memories, and he wondered if he'd ever told his whole story to anybody else before. It not, he could understand how long-suppressed angry or helpless feelings over a person

304

or event could negatively affect a person emotionally. And if that was the case, maybe he could help. Not that one telling would get Charlie over it, but it would be a start. And he'd be more than happy to help the guide toward establishing a better relationship with women. *Psychiatrist to the end.*

"She was an only child," Charlie went on, his voice barely audible over the thrum of the motor. "Her father never said no to her. Even about going on the boat. She was too proud to just take his money so we could live better . . . insisted on earning her way on his boat. I begged her not to go out on that boat with him. She didn't listen. He didn't listen. They went too far out in the Gulf. Unexpected storm. The whole crew was lost. They never found the bodies." He stared out over the Glades. He was finished.

Evan watched Charlie's face. If the guide believed that his lack of control over his wife was the reason for her death, the emotionally debilitating self-blame could easily manifest itself in an intense dislike of all women on boats; an unconscious fear that an accident could happen again. And it would be his fault again . . . in his mind. It could be that simple.

"I'd like to talk to you some more about this," Evan said gently. "Privately, when we have more time. I think that I may be able to help you feel better about it, work out some of those hostile feelings. Will you do it?"

Charlie looked at him for a minute, uncertain. "I'll think about it," he finally said.

Evan nodded and walked back to where Lydia sat pretending not to listen. She gave him an easy smile. "We're going to find her. I feel it."

A sudden shout from Jake made them all turn to look. He was pointing to the shore—up in the trees.

305

Dozens of brightly colored birds, their green and red feathers flashing in the light, glided oddly through the air or clung to tree trunks.

Evan and Lydia leaned over the side of the boat for a better look. There was something strange about them. With a shock, Evan suddenly realized that the birds were crawling up the trees by using claws that protruded from the front of their wings. They moved like lizards!

"Damn!" Jake shouted, his voice high-pitched with excitement. "Archaeopteryx! Damn!"

They hadn't even brought a bird cage.

Jake wrestled with his mixed feelings of elation and disappointment as they glided past the colorful, noisy show.

Lydia impulsively slipped an arm around Jake's waist. "We'll help you come back for them after all this is over."

He returned the gesture and kissed her on the forehead, then looked back at the birds. "Damn right," he said.

Ray had guided his own boat as close to the shore as he'd dared so he and Ralph could get a better look at the Archaeopteryx. Now he glanced over at Evan and Lydia as he turned it back toward the middle of the water. Their obvious closeness made him ache for Bett.

Three more tiny, pointed snouts broke through the eggshells.

A group of grinning scientists crowded around the incubator.

Harold Burnham stood looking over their shoulders. He frowned at the wriggling reptiles.

Millie ignored the live trout that swam in ignorant circles around her. She kept her nose pushed into the corner of the pool.

Another egg cracked. Another snout pushed its way out of its leathery prison. This snout was broad and black, and curious nostrils sniffed at the warm air from its tip.

Dr. Harold Burnham smiled.

Chapter Forty-six

Akuda had been quiet all day. Tepi peeked over at him from where she sat teaching Ja-nee and Pa the basic steps of beginning a fishing net. He was crouched in a circle with four of the other men, playing a game of bones. His throws seemed to lack their usual enthusiasm, and more than once another player had to poke him on the shoulder to remind him of his turn.

Had she in some way disappointed him last night? She thought not. Not at the time, anyway. She wanted to speak with him, but it would be unseemly to interrupt the game between the men. She sighed and turned her attention back to the children.

Pa was almost as quick and clever as Ja-nee with the knots and weaving, and the two little girls had a spirited competition going between them. Tepi smiled at them as they repeatedly held their own piece of fishnet up against the other's for comparison.

When she looked up toward the game once again, she caught Akuda's eye, and he left the men to hurry to her side.

"I did not mean to interrupt your game," she said to

him as he knelt in front of her. But she was glad he had chosen to leave it for her.

"I did not wish to join the game in the first place," he assured her. "But I did not wish to hurt their feelings either, and you seemed busy with Ja-nee and Pa." He reached out and rubbed his hand affectionately over Ja-nee's tangled curls, and she looked up from her concentration on her net and grinned at him.

"Look, Akuda ma-da!" she cried. "Is mine not better than Pa's?" She held up her scrap of net.

"You both have great skill!" he answered with raised eyebrows, as if he were astonished by their competence. "You shall both soon make Tepi ma-da jealous!"

The two children giggled at his kind lie and went back to their work.

"Come," he said, taking Tepi's hand and pulling her to her feet. "I must speak."

Her heart beat faster as they walked hand-in-hand into the jungle. His tone of voice had been serious. There was no hint that he required privacy for lovemaking. His intention was different, and she was afraid. Had he tired of her in one night? Had her abandoned response to him been improper? Did he think her indecent?

They had walked nearly to the wide river that ran between the greatest islands before he turned to her and spoke. "I promised before the gods to share worries with you," he said softly, "and all day I have questioned the wisdom of that promise. But I finally came to think that if you had my secret and did not share it with me, I would be angry. So . . ."

He held up a hand for her silence when he saw she was about to speak. "I must say this all at once before

I lose the courage to say it at all." He told her about the growing ache in his head.

Tepi felt as if the short-lighted days of winter had suddenly wrapped their cold arms around her. It was much worse than she had expected to hear. Had he not told her that not even one of the lost ones had survived the beast that chewed inside their heads? She could not lose him! There must be something they could do! What she did for the moment was to allow unstoppable tears to run down her cheeks.

"Tepi! Stop!" Akuda stamped his foot in frustration. "I cannot stand this! Your tears are far worse for me than the ache in my head!"

She forced herself to stop.

Akuda grabbed her by the shoulders and made her look at his face. "Now you must tell me. Has the ache come to you and Ja-nee yet? And you must not lie . . . the gods listen to your words."

"No. I swear," Tepi whispered. "Not since the days we traveled on the river to get here. I speak the truth."

The relief was apparent in Akuda's face.

There was no such expression on Tepi's face.

Chapter Forty-seven

The rest of the day had been hot, dull, and uneventful. Even though they knew they were still far away from where Jake and the rest of the exploration party had seen the lost tribe, they repeatedly slowed the boats and searched every jungle island they passed. They'd sweep binoculars over the shore, pausing and concentrating on any movement in the brush they saw or imagined they saw. Occasionally they'd circle the larger islands, then stop the boats and wait, listening for any sound of human habitation. They had no way of knowing whether the tribe had a permanent location or were nomadic, wandering from place to place as the mood struck them. And they weren't taking any chances on missing them. At this rate the search could take weeks, but each one of them was committed to it for his own reasons.

In one way the monotony was welcome. Although the lost tribe had not appeared, neither had any of the dinosaurs. Every hour that passed without incident cheered Lydia a little more. Maybe Jake's prehistoric beasts were not as prevalent in the Glades as they had first thought. If not, Jenny and Bett's safety was more prob-

able, though she wondered if Jake and Ralph were se
cretly disappointed.

By the end of the third day they were deep into the
unexplored regions of the Glades, and the anticipation
of possible success at any moment had emotions run
ning high and hopeful during the daylight hours. Even
Ray's morose attitude had lifted, and he spent more time
talking with Ralph as they followed the lead boat
through the winding waterways. Mostly he talked about
all the cute, funny, or wonderful things his wife had
done.

Once they saw a school of half a dozen enormous
fish, but the creatures were gone almost as quickly as
they had appeared. Ralph and Jake had been excited
over the brief sighting, and Ralph had guessed that the
fish were Dunkleosteus, believed to be common during
the late Devonian period when sharks and eels first ap
peared.

At night they'd gather together on one of the boats
and cook over a campstove, then sit by the light of a
Coleman lantern and talk far into the night. Evan's skills
as a psychiatrist were taxed more than once when he
had to bolster the group morale during these sessions. In
spite of the high spirits during the daytime, doubts and
disillusionment tended to creep in with the dark when
they were tired from a long, uneventful day of searching.

Surprisingly, the only one who never lost a positive
attitude was Lydia. Ever since her announcement to him
earlier in the excursion that she'd "felt" they would find
Jenny, her mood had been unflaggingly confident

Sometimes Evan thought it was she more than he who kept everyone's spirits up during the low times.

Since they'd sighted the flock of Archaeopteryx, and the school of Dunkleosteus, nothing else of unusual interest had crossed their path, and Jake was looking forward to reaching the point where they'd captured Millie. He was anxious to check out her nest again to see if any of the baby reptiles had hatched. His conversation had centered around the de-evolution, as he chose to call it, of the Glade's inhabitants. It was a subject that fascinated all of them.

Day four. Shortly past noon. Jake, Ralph, and Charlie shared the first boat, and Evan, Lydia, and Ray trailed behind.

The early morning mists had given way by late morning to thick gray clouds that came whipping in off the Atlantic. Jake used the radio to call in for a weather update. Nothing to worry about, they'd said—just one of your typical Florida thunderstorms, and a welcome one this time. Except for the tropical storm that had hit during their second trip into the Glades, the weather had been exceptionally dry in south Florida this year.

By early afternoon the threatening clouds had whisked quickly across the sky toward the west, depositing only scattered bursts of rain, and creating very little of the usual thunder and lightning. And by the time they came close to the spot where Jake expected to see Millie's nest, the sun was out with a vengeance.

Jake, stripped to the waist for comfort, and liberally doused with insect repellent for protection, suddenly pointed to the left bank and shouted, "There! There,

313

Charlie!" He waved his hand at the other boat. Pull it over!"

They'd found Millie's nest.

Ray cut the motor on the second boat and let it drift in toward shore too. He and everybody else leaned over the sides to get a better look at the rotting mound of vegetation that rose like a monolith from the swampy shore.

The boats scraped the bottom of the shallow waterway about fifteen feet from shore, and Jake stripped down to bathing trunks and slipped over the side. Slowly, he waded in thigh-deep murky water toward the nest. It looked different—flatter and disheveled around the edges. He frowned. *Had a predator got at it since Millie wasn't around to protect it? Stupid! Should have taken* all *the eggs!*

No. As he reached the nest and clambered up on shore, he couldn't see any evidence of rampant destruction that would indicate a major attack on its inhabitants. There were no holes, broken shells, or partially devoured bodies. Hopefully, he started carefully digging his hands into the crown of the nest. Nothing. He dug in up to his elbows, then felt around for the smooth, leathery shapes that would indicate all was well.

The group on the boats watched him in silence.

Still nothing. Puzzled, he gently began removing the top layer of debris. In a few minutes he was covered with the slime of rotting leaves, and the smell of warm decay rose up around him. And then he saw the first empty shell. An inch below it, his hand broke through to the main hollow of the nest. All empty. He laughed, one happy bark of realization, and turned back to the group.

"They hatched!" he shouted cheerfully, and stepped back into the shallow water.

Their faces held frozen expressions of shock—not at all what he'd expected.

Lydia screamed.

But the screech that blasted out from behind him drowned out Lydia's warning, and he spun around in sudden, heart-stopping fright.

It stood on the far side of Millie's nest, flapping its useless wings, one predatory black eye cocked in his direction. Diatryma!

Jake ducked low in the water and backed slowly toward the boat. Then stopped. It was only a baby—maybe five feet tall. His mind raced with possibilities. Why hadn't he insisted on bringing a cage! Or the tranquilizer guns! Damn! Could they keep it tied up for the whole trip? On the boat with them? No. Impossible. Cruel. But just how tame was it? It didn't seem to be making any aggressive moves. Maybe . . .

"Jake! Get back in the boat!" Evan shouted.

He made a chopping move with his hand for silence. Maybe if he approached it slowly . . . He started wading back toward the nest.

A muffled curse and a splash behind him. He turned his head slightly, not wishing to make any sudden moves that might scare the dinosaur-bird off. Evan struggled through the water toward him.

When Evan caught up with him, Jake whispered, "You go around to the left and I'll circle to the right. Don't try to grab it . . . just see if it will let you pet it. If it does, maybe we can—"

"Pet it?" Evan asked incredulously. "Do you see that beak! Are you crazy!"

"Shhh! Don't scare it!" Jake hissed. "Go on!" He

gave Evan a light shove on the shoulder and then began moving slowly to the right of the great bird. This is insane, he told himself, but he kept going anyway. The lure of befriending the prehistoric chick was too strong to ignore. An opportunity like this might never happen again—

It shrieked at them again, but didn't move, its curiosity over the two strange creatures holding it in place.

The two men widened the gap between them. The bird swiveled its head from Evan to Jake, slightly confused by their tactics. Unsure of them now, it took a step back into the jungle. Evan and Jake stopped and waited.

Two minutes. Three.

Charlie stood with his arms draped casually over the railing, grinning. Did they really think that a wild animal was going to stand still long enough to let them grab it? He'd give the weird thing another ten seconds before it bolted into the jungle.

Ray leaned over the railing with his mouth open. "What the hell is it?" he whispered over to Ralph.

"Diatryma," Ralph answered shortly, not taking his eyes from the creature. "Prehistoric bird. Relative of the dinosaurs. A baby."

Ray stared at the creature and wondered uneasily where its mother was.

Lydia stood near Ray and silently watched the two men circle the great bird. What the hell were they trying to do? Did Jake expect to drag the thing on the boat with them? It sure didn't look very friendly to her. Especially that beak. She jumped a little when the thing leaned toward Jake and clacked its beak at him in an obvious warning not to come any closer.

Jake stopped again. They were both within six feet of

the bird now, but its actions had become less fearful, more aggressive with every step closer they took. It had obviously decided that they were no threat, but wasn't sure what to do next. Suddenly Jake wasn't so sure either.

The bird crouched low, stretched out its neck, and shivered its wings at them. One huge, taloned foot scraped angrily in the mud and it shrieked another warning—or challenge. Jake fervently hoped it was the former. He looked over at a grim-faced Evan. Evan had apparently had enough. He motioned for Jake to back up.

It exploded through the trees in a sudden and unexpected frenzy of protective rage, its maternal instincts driving it to a fury over the imagined threat to its chick. The terrorized screams of the onlookers were drowned out by the high, screeching challenge of the mother Diatryma. Its enormous beak clacking like gunshots, it headed straight for Jake.

And its mate was right behind it.

Jake, never a good swimmer, turned and threw himself flat out in the water. His nose and chest scraped the bottom of the riverbed as he dove out of the maddened creature's reach. He dug his hands into the mud and pulled himself forward underwater, trying to put as much distance between himself and it before he surfaced.

He felt, rather than heard, the churning of the water around him as his lungs burned for air. Something hard and sharp caught him in the back of the knee and it took every effort of will not to gasp in a lung full of water with an involuntary scream of pain. Instead he rolled, his head breaking the surface of the shallow water about five feet from the boat.

As the female Diatryma plunged recklessly into the water after Jake, Evan leaped—with his best racing dive—right after them. In a few short strokes he was in front of his friend. He flipped himself to his feet, grabbed Jake under the arms and lifted him clear of the slashing talons of the furious, eight-foot-high bird. Adrenaline poured through his system in a rush, and he almost threw Jake the last few feet toward the boat before throwing himself clear, and in the direction of the second boat.

A white-faced Charlie frantically hauled Jake over the railing. It had all happened too fast for him to reach for his rifle, and he cursed himself for getting careless about the possible dangers.

Jake gasped in a burning lungful of air and clutched at his leg as he rolled onto the desk.

Ray and Lydia's screams of "Look out!" cut through the air above the shrieks of the three birds.

The male had hesitated only a second, checking to see that the chick was unharmed. Now, with an earsplitting scream of his own, it stalked Evan from the left, kicking its powerful legs out in front of it and clawing at the air in a menacing gesture of challenge.

Adrenaline still pumping, Evan leaped for the second boat's railing only a few feet ahead of the female's snapping beak . . . and was almost deafened by the explosion that went off near his left ear. He somersaulted onto the deck, knocking into Lydia, and her second shot went wild.

Her first shot had grazed the male, and blood spurted from its inner thigh. It reached down and bit savagely at its own leg, as if it were capable of exorcising the pain with sheer rage.

The female hit the boat like a freight train. The boat

318

rocked crazily, and Lydia and Ray went down on their knees, grabbing at each other for support. Lydia's rifle flew overboard. It landed with a splash near the wounded male, and its head flashed out toward it in a blur of movement. They watched in horrified disbelief as the bird lifted it high in the air and increased the pressure of its beak on the wooden stock. The stock dissolved into splinters and it dropped the remains of the rifle into the bloody water that roiled around its feet.

Charlie crawled on the floor of the rocking boat toward his own rifle. The female Diatryma turned her attack to him and his boat, and Charlie screamed to a shocked, white-faced Ralph to hang on. It was an unnecessary order; Ralph had a stranglehold on the railing.

The great bird's head flashed down. The entire side gave way in a sickening crunch of destroyed timber and fiberglass under the enormous power of ripping talons and beak. The rifle slithered past Charlie and disappeared into the vortex of water created by the sinking ship. Charlie grabbed at the dangling edge of a bench that had been knocked almost free of its moorings and hauled himself away from the sloping floorboards that were being systematically destroyed by the heavy-headed attack of the raging bird.

Jake, his leg pouring blood, rolled toward the back of the sinking boat, his shock almost obliterating the pain he tried to ignore. The combined screams of the engraged birds and the terrified people hammered in his ears and disoriented him. Where the hell was Evan! Fear for his friend's safety forced him to his feet in spite of the agony that shot down his injured leg.

It saved his life. The great, horned beak of the male crashed into the floorboards inches away from where his head had been.

It raised its head, shrieking, for another strike. Jake dropped and rolled. The back of the boat disintegrated with a cracking sound like gunshots as the bird connected.

The wounded male Diatryma had his own prey to destroy. His powerful body slammed into the boat as he advanced on Lydia, smashing the two boats together with a force that sent all the humans tumbling and scrambling for balance.

A hand grabbed Lydia by the back of the blouse and hauled her up and away from the advancing bird. Evan dangled by one arm from the high side of the boat railing only several feet from where the male relentlessly tore at the floorboards. Lydia instinctively clutched at the rail, and Jake, neatly flipped from his own boat to hers by the force of the impact, wrapped his arms around her legs. If he lost his grip, he'd slide right into the flashing, snapping beak of the male.

The Diatryma clawed one huge talon onto the back of the boat and heaved itself aboard. It balanced itself and stretched its clacking beak to within inches of Evan's face. And suddenly screamed in pain as flames erupted up its back and down its wings.

The great bird leaped and twisted away from the boat, its shrieks more horrible than before. And now the terrified cries of the chick added to the bedlam.

The female, suddenly confused and frightened, spun toward her baby. Fire spat and crackled from the surface of the muddy water in a rapidly widening path toward the shore. She deserted her attack on Charlie and Ralph's boat and raced past her mate, not recognizing him in the middle of the screaming, twirling ball of flames.

Within seconds, the female and her chick were

gone—disappearing with great leaps into the protective shelter of the jungle.

Soon the only sound was the creaking and snapping of the destroyed, sinking boat and the gentle hiss of water finally dousing the flames around the dead male Diatryma.

Ray Wilson stood near the hull of the demolished boat, waist-deep in water, staring at the carnage. An empty gasoline can hung from one hand. The other hand gripped a Bic lighter.

They all sat in the miraculously only slightly damaged second boat and watched Lydia expertly attend to Jake's wounded knee. Once in a while somebody would look at what was left of the other boat and shake his head in disbelief. Then they'd all look at each other and then back at Jake—the only human casualty. They had a decision to make, and nobody wanted to be the first to say it.

"Christ," Jake finally said. "It's only a flesh wound. Relax, everybody!" He grinned around at the circle of grim faces, then over at the wrecked boat. "I sure hope they have disaster insurance."

A little bit of nervous laughter broke the tension, and soon they were all laughing hard, hugging, and slapping each other on the back—survivors of the glorious battle; glad to be alive.

"So now what?" Charlie said after the emotional release had died down a little. "Do we go back, or what?"

"I'm not giving up," Lydia said quickly. She looked around anxiously at the others. Were they going to give up on her?

Charlie stepped forward and sat on the bench next to

Evan. "We have no guns and we're short a can of gasoline." He looked at Ray with respect. "Thank God," he added.

"Since we have only one boat now, the extra gas isn't important," Evan answered. "And I think I know where the rifle went under. Anybody want to help?"

They all waded and rummaged through the wreckage, sliding their feet through the muddy silt of the riverbottom until Evan let out a shout, reached underwater and dragged up a wet, dirty rifle. He held it triumphantly over his head and grinned when Lydia splashed over to him, lifting her knees high in the water for extra speed, and threw her arms around his neck. She planted a wet, slippery kiss on his mouth and everybody cheered.

Spirits were high. The near-catastrophe had drawn the little group closer together in a way that days or weeks of normal proximity to each other could never have done. They talked and laughed with each other as they transferred whatever they could salvage of the supplies from the destroyed boat to the remaining one. The most vital find was the dry, undamaged box of ammunition.

A short time later they were underway again, and Charlie sat on a bench under the shade of the boat canopy, carefully cleaning the retrieved rifle.

Chapter Forty-eight

They'd spent the day picking the tiny, sweet redberries that grew along the ground and through the branches of low-growing bushes. The berry vines twined their fruit and leaves tightly through the limbs of their host plants, attracting the pollinating animals and insects necessary to them both.

Ja-nee's face was smeared with sticky red juice, and Tepi had gently told her more than once that she was putting more in her belly than she was in her reed basket. Ja-nee had only laughed and looked toward her Akuda ma-da for his nod of approval—a nod he invariably gave her. And Tepi's mild warnings of a future ache in the belly went unheeded.

"You're spoiling her, Akuda," she said to him now. But the tone of her rebuke was mild, and she studied his face carefully for the thousandth time that day. There was no telltale sign of pain around his brow or mouth, nor had there been since his confession to her the day before. Had the lost ones' disease miraculously passed him by . . . or was he merely clever at concealing his distress from her? She was afraid to ask.

She'd chosen for herself the easy task of berry picking today, and had asked Akuda to accompany her and Ja-nee instead of making the long trip that some of the men had chosen to make to the swift-moving water where they could find fish of a different taste than usual. He'd accepted her invitation happily, his new love for her making him glad to be in her company for any reason. She did not think he suspected that her main reason for denying him his masculine company was that she wished to keep an anxious eye on him. Ordinarily, as much as she loved him too, and desired his company as much as he did hers, she would not have asked him to perform such a traditional woman's task.

Now they picked berries not far from the riverbank where Akuda and Tepi had seen the waterbeast roar past. It had not looked like any living thing she had ever seen, and it had occurred to her not for the first time while she went about her daily tasks, that perhaps the men who controlled it were not merely members of another tribe, but truly gods. And perhaps these gods had power over the strange malady that brought death to the lost ones. But how was she to ask them? This question had rolled over and over in her head, and still she had no answer.

Now, as they lifted the filled baskets and made preparation to return to the tribe, she listened for any sound that would signify the return of the beast and its masters. Only the calls of the jungle birds reached her ears.

Akuda moaned and thrashed in his sleep. He'd awakened Tepi hours before with his cries, and she'd lain by his side and tried to soothe him with gentle stroking, but the brief periods of peaceful sleep he'd had between periods of discomfort were few.

Over and over again, Tepi told herself it was only a bad sleep story that was responsible for Akuda's distress, but she was afraid to test the truth of her reasoning by awakening him.

Now Ja-nee pressed her body, still warm from sleep, against Tepi's side. She rubbed at her eyes and looked from Akuda to Tepi. "Why does Akuda ma-da make so much noise?" she asked.

Tepi hugged the child to her breast and rocked her gently, but said nothing.

At dawn, Akuda's body radiated an unnatural heat, and his thrashings had driven Tepi from his side. She sat a few feet away from him with Ja-nee asleep in her lap. She had made a decision.

The village elders shook their heads and murmured between themselves in voices low with concern. It was the woman's choice of course—Akuda was her mate. But they wondered if such a bold and frightening plan would not anger the gods instead of gaining their compassion. Such effrontery on the part of a female was unheard of.

The old man who had presided at the mating ceremony smacked his gums together in disapproval and poked a bony finger at Tepi's chest. "We agree that the masters of the strange and noisy waterbeasts must be gods to have tamed such creatures. But we do not know if they are benevolent gods, or even if they are our gods. The risk you take could have evil consequences. And beyond that chance, you must consider the great beasts. You will not enjoy the protection of the many lights at night, nor the safety of a strong, healthy man by your side when the sun is high."

"We may both die if the gods are evil, or a great beast is hungry, that is true," Tepi answered. "But without the risk, Akuda's death is certain. And since I have no wish to continue my life without Akuda anyway, the risk of death for us both is smaller if you will allow me to do as I wish."

"And what of Ja-nee if the gods take you to your death?" he asked.

"I have spoken with Mabeeka. She will gladly take the child. Ja-nee will add prestige to her family since she is well past three summers old."

The pain that flashed in Tepi's eyes at the talk of losing Ja-nee did not go unmarked by the old man, but impressed by the sacrifices she was willing to make for her mate, he said nothing. Instead he nodded and motioned for two of the tribesmen to step forward. He whispered to them and they raced off to do his bidding.

Then he turned his attention back to Tepi. "Our hearts are saddened by the misfortune that has come to your new family, Tepi," he said to her. "Your plan is bold and rings with the mark of desperation, but is not without merit. We will help you."

They placed Akuda on a palette that was lashed to two sturdy saplings, then tied him down to it so he would not roll off and hurt himself. Once during these efforts, he regained consciousness and turned bewildered eyes on his mate. "The baskets," he mumbled. "Do you have the berries?"

"Yes, Akuda. Do not worry," Tepi answered. She smoothed his dark hair back from his face and pressed

er lips to his cheek. His skin was hot and damp, and
ain clouded his eyes again. Tepi closed her hands over
is and prayed to the names of every god she knew.

Four tribesmen grabbed the ends of the saplings, and
t a signal from the elder, they lifted Akuda's palette to
leir shoulders. The old man turned his steps to the path
ading to the river, and they followed him, carefully
alancing Akuda's unconscious body between them.

The entire tribe watched in silence as the small pro-
ession wound its way into the jungle—the old man in
le lead, followed by Akuda and his bearers, then Tepi,
a-nee, and Mabeeka who carried sleeping mats and
nough food to last Tepi for two days.

Akuda could neither hunt nor eat, and Tepi would not
ave his side to hunt for herself. It had been agreed that
fter two days, if Akuda still lived, and the gods had not
et come to cure him, members of the tribe would con-
nue to bring provisions to her regularly. Not many
lought Akuda would live more than four days. Nor did
ley believe that the river gods would miraculously save
im.

They settled Akuda down on the riverbank not far
om where he and Tepi had fished on the day he had
eclared himself to her. The remembering pained her,
nd she was glad that it was not exactly the same spot.
he constant reminder of such a last, happy day would
e too much to live with as she waited for the gods to
ecide Akuda's fate.

And now came the most difficult part. Tepi knelt in
ont of Ja-nee. "You must go now with Mabeeka. Re-
lember what I said. Be obedient and helpful. I will see
ou in a few days." May the gods grant that my words
re not a lie, she thought as she kissed Ja-nee's hands.

Ja-nee pulled her hands away from Tepi's grasp and

stamped her foot. "I will stay here with you and Akud ma-da."

Tepi sighed. She should have left the child back at the village. But the need to have her close as long as possible had clouded her judgment. "No," she said. Her voice was firm.

Ja-nee pouted and forced a tear or two from her eyes. It did no good, and soon Mabeeka tugged her by the hand and they walked together back to the village.

Chapter Forty-nine

A dozen baby reptiles basked under the S.A.D. lights at the shallow end of the pool. Nine of them had tannish, scaly bodies with narrow snouts that tapered to a sharp point. Tiny nostrils, set just below their eyes, flared and vibrated with each searching breath they took.

Three were different. Yellow bands circled their shiny black bodies, and when they wiggled into the water, eyes and nostrils protruded from the surface of the water several inches apart. The biggest one, about ten inches long, clambered over the pile of squirming bodies that were his siblings and rested his broad, flat snout on their backs. Satisfied that he'd acquired a preferred spot in the artificial sun, he shut his eyes and napped.

Dr. Harold Burnham stood at the edge of the pool with Ralph and a curious intern. "Most fortunate," he said. "And very exciting. Those three thecodonts are resistant to the Genesis Gene, and we've been able—"

"They look more like baby alligators to me," the intern said.

"Yes, yes. That's the point. They *look* like alligators, but their DNA parallels Millie's. So they're really thecodonts." Burnham glanced quickly at Millie. She still bobbed, nose in the corner, at the deep end of the pool. Hang on, girl, he begged silently, then turned back to the two men.

"As I was saying," he continued, "the three alligator-types you see there carry the resistant gene that we need to formulate an immunological serum for Millie. Dr. Frankel and I have removed the cells and coagulation factors from their blood samples to obtain a blood serum. Then we drew the immune antibodies from the serum and isolated the immunoglobulin in the protein that will modify the metabolic products of the Genesis Gene—and hopefully destroy it. Dr. Frankel is in the process of synthesizing and concentrating the serum now."

Ralph nodded. "So you think this will prevent the Genesis Gene from spontaneous recurrence after it has been initially immobilized by the synthetic DNA?"

"Exactly. And if it works on Millie, we know a similar procedure using human, resistant blood serum will work on people. A much more reliable testing method than the computers we've been using up to this point. Too many unknown factors there for optimum safety. And we have Mrs. Matthews' blood samples to work with." Burnham rocked back and forth on his heels, obviously pleased with himself.

"What if it doesn't work?" the intern asked.

"It must work," Burnham said. He stopped rocking and looked over at Millie again. She hadn't moved. "It must work," he repeated.

Three scientists splashed their way through the pool toward Millie. She didn't fight the noose over her snout.

She didn't fight their arms around her. She didn't fight the sting of the needle when it penetrated her thick hide.

The three men gently stroked her still body for a few minutes before they left her in peace.

Chapter Fifty

The afternoon of the second day.

Akuda writhed and moaned on his palette. His hands clawed at his scalp and he drew himself into a tight ball, then threw his arms and legs wide and cried out again and again. Tepi continuously bathed his body with the warm river water, and kneaded the tight muscles in his legs and back. She didn't know what else to do.

Twice during the long hours of her vigil, he had seemed to be momentarily free of his worst torture, and had turned pain-blurred eyes on her face. He didn't speak. He would then fall into an exhausted sleep for a while, and for those times Tepi was grateful. She felt the sleep would renew his strength. And it gave her time to rest.

Ja-nee watched Pa sleep. Pa was sucking her thumb, and her eyelashes fluttered as if she were about to wake up, but Ja-nee knew she wouldn't. Pa took a nap every afternoon.

She was supposed to nap too, but she wasn't tired. She missed her Tepi ma-da and Akuda ma-da. What was wrong with Akuda ma-da? Something was happening that she didn't understand, and she was angry that no one would explain it to her. When she asked Mabeeka to explain, Mabeeka had told her she would understand in time. She didn't understand that either.

Tepi ma-da would tell her.

Ja-nee crawled to the far side of the sleeping platform and slid down the post that faced the deepest part of the jungle. No one saw her. She was careful about that. It took only a few seconds to race into the concealing undergrowth.

Now that she was here, she wasn't sure it had been a good idea. She had disobeyed Tepi ma-da's orders to stay in the village with Mabeeka and Pa. Would her disobedience earn her a dreaded slap on the backside? She squirmed uncomfortably at the very thought of it.

They were close enough for her to throw a stone at them. She could hear them near the river—the groans of Akuda ma-da, and the pleading, prayer-chants of Tepi ma-da.

And she heard something else. A low growl, like a beast on the hunt, came from downriver. She skirted a clump of cabbage palms and hid behind a tree trunk. The growl grew louder. It did not sound like any animal she had ever heard. Curiosity and fear struggled in her head. Curiosity won. She peeked from behind the tree toward the bend in the river.

Tepi stopped chanting her prayers. Had she heard it? It was hard to tell over Akuda's moans! She jumped to her feet and hurried to the riverbank. Something. Yes.

But not nearly as loud as she had remembered. Perhaps it was still far away. Her heart pounding with hope and fear, she stared toward the bend in the river.

Charlie saw her first; a small, half-naked woman with long blond hair tangled around her head. "Hey, Doc!" he shouted at Evan and pointed.

They all turned at Charlie's shout.

"BETT! OH MY GOD, BETT!" Ray Wilson leaped from the boat and splashed through the water, stumbling and shouting with joy as he half jumped, half swam through the waistdeep water toward his wife. Tears streamed down his cheeks, but his sobs were mixed with cries of relief and laughter.

The search party cheered.

Tepi stood frozen with surprise. This was a different waterbeast—not as threatening as the other one. But it was the actions of the gods who controlled the great new beast that was even more astonishing. All thoughts and fears of the gods being evil flew from her head—dismissed. They shouted things at her in a strange language, but there was no mistaking that they were words of welcome. The expressions on their faces indicated great happiness!

The short, plump god reached her side. She offered him a shy smile and held her palms up to indicate her friendliness, and show that she carried no weapons.

He flung his arms around her and put his lips all over her face.

Shocked at such familiarity, but fearful of offending him, she stood very still and endured the strange welcome. And why did he shed tears? This was most confusing!

Over his shoulder, Tepi watched the female god leap into the water and wade toward them. This one had a look of great anxiety on her face.

"Bett, Bett, Bett," the male god kept saying to her. Now he held her at arm's length and shook his head repeatedly. He still smiled and cried.

The goddess grabbed Tepi's arm. "Bett! Where is Jenny!" she shouted.

Tepi stared at her. She knew Ja-nee! How could this be! But then, did not the gods know everything?

"JENNY!" The goddess shouted again, but her eyes were on a spot behind Tepi.

Tepi pulled away from the plump god's hands and spun around. Ja-nee stood watching them.

And now the tall goddess repeated the odd form of welcome. She ran to Ja-nee and snatched the child off the ground. Tears soaked her cheeks too, and she pressed her lips all over Ja-nee's face and shoulders. Ja-nee giggled and put her lips on the goddess's cheek in imitation. Then the goddess sat on the ground with the child in her lap and laughed. How strange these gods were, Tepi thought!

The waterbeast was silent now. Tepi stood silently in the middle of the excited babble of voices and watched while the gods tethered the now quiet beast to an oak that grew near the water's edge. She did not understand one word they said. How was she to make her wish known to them? Foolish Tepi, she thought. They are gods. Simply show Akuda to them and they will understand.

She turned and ran toward the hidden spot where he lay, sure they would follow her. They did.

She knelt by Akuda and held her hands up to the gods. Her heart beat faster. Would they help him?

Evan knelt and turned Akuda's face toward them, alarmed at the fever that radiated from his skin. He brushed the man's black hair away from his face. He caught his breath. "Lydia," he said. He waved her forward with one hand.

Lydia, with Ja-nee still in her arms, leaned over to look. "It's Daniel Birdsong," she said, recognizing him from the picture they had. "What's the matter with him?"

"I don't know," Evan answered. "But we have to get him to the Institute as fast as we can. If it's the Genesis Gene working . . ." he let his voice trail off. No need to ruin her and Ray's reunions with Bett and Jenny.

"What about the others?" Lydia asked.

"We know exactly where they are now," Jake said, coming up behind her. "The Park Service can send out more boats. We don't have much room on our one boat for many more. Besides, I agree with Evan. This guy's in bad shape. We don't have a whole lot of time to go searching through the jungle for the others right now."

Charlie examined the palette that Akuda lay on. "We can get him to the boat on this. Everybody grab an end." He followed his own advice and put his hands on one of the saplings that supported the palette.

Evan, Jake, and Ray grabbed the other ends and they lifted on the count of three.

They were going to help! Tepi felt tears sting her eyes as she followed the procession back to the waterbeast.

They had fifty yards to go. Something moved toward them through the underbrush on their left. They stopped, surprised, and listened. More people?

A snuffling sound. Trees snapping. A growl. Not people.

Slowly, they lowered the palette to the ground. Jake motioned them to crouch, hide. Even Tepi understood, and she hunkered down next to the plump god for protection. She knew what was coming. "Kati," she whispered to him. She was glad that Ja-nee was protected by the tall goddess, even though she was just a little jealous of the child's easy willingness to be carried by her.

The Glyptodont crashed through the underbrush and stood shaking its great head and stamping its feet in the sand. It lashed its tail back and forth, agitated at some unseen enemy. The nine-inch spikes at the tip of its tail repeatedly whistled through the air and ended each vicious arc in an earth-shaking thump as the spikes crashed into the ground. It stood between the search party and the boat.

"Jesus fucking Christ," Jake said between his teeth. Anger at his own carelessness and stupidity made him clench his fist and punch it on his good knee. He'd left the rifle on the boat.

"Shh!" Charlie whispered. He poked Jake in the side to shut him up. "Maybe it'll just go away if we keep quiet."

Ja-nee twisted around in Lydia's arms and looked toward the boat. And screamed.

The huge, armadillo-like creature, its thirteen-foot long body trembling in the grip of the killing Genesis Gene, found a direction in which to focus its pain and anger. It charged straight at them.

Evan moved fast. He tackled Lydia and Ja-nee, knocking them off their feet and out of the path of the bellowing giant. Charlie leaped right after them.

Tepi yanked furiously at Akuda's heavy body, screaming for help. Ray and Ralph wasted one precious second in shock before moving quickly to help her drag

Akuda behind the wide trunk of an oak. Ray pushed Ralph and Bett in between the tree and his body, and held them there.

Jake made a decision. He leaped to his feet, wincing at the pain in his knee, and ran directly into the path of the glyptodont's charge, shouting and waving his arms. "HEY! HEY!" he screamed. He dodged sideways, now oblivious to his pain, and smacked the clumsy beast on the snout as it lumbered past him. "HERE, YOU SONOFABITCH!" he yelled, and it stopped, uncertain. "HERE! HERE! COME AND GET ME, YOU BASTARD!"

It lowered its head and turned toward him.

"CHARLIE! THE GUN! GO FOR IT! I'VE GOT ITS ATTENTION!"

Charlie sprinted for the boat.

It turned with unexpected speed and grace. It caught Charlie as his feet hit the edge of the riverbank. His screams were cut off as the beast trampled his head underneath the muddy water.

Jake stood immobile with disbelief. His fault! His fault!

Then Evan was sprinting out into the clearing. "JAKE! RUN, YOU DAMN FOOL! RUN!" He grabbed Jake's arm and yanked him toward the jungle.

The Glyptodont turned. Bellowing a challenge, it charged again. Fast. They weren't going to make it.

The air was filled with screams. And the beast was suddenly overrun with dozens of shouting, running, dark-skinned people. They brandished primitive spears and clubs, and they swarmed toward the glyptodont, shrieking their own chilling war-challenge.

Pointed spears clicked harmlessly off the beast's heavy armor. It swung its deadly tail in a vicious arc, ut the tribesmen simply leaped aside with the agility of monkeys. They moved in toward its head, chanting and shouting the hunting song. The spears pierced the throat and brain of the great animal, and it fell to its knees. In minutes, it was dead.

Silence. The tribe turned toward the search party and waited, proud of themselves for helping the gods. Now surely they would help Tepi and Akuda.

Tepi pulled herself from the short god's grip and ran toward her people. "How brave you are!" she cried.

The old man stepped from the edge of the jungle into the clearing. He was too old to fight and had watched from a distance "It was time to bring your provisions, Tepi," he said, grinning his toothless grin at her. "How fortunate that the whole tribe wished to come along and help you pray to the gods for Akuda's life." He waved his hand toward the trees.

The women and children now stepped into the clearing and peeked shyly at the gods, who still hadn't moved.

The old man leaned forward and whispered to Tepi. "Why did the gods not kill Kati themselves? Was it perhaps a test of our worthiness?"

"It must be so," she answered.

Jake was the first to move. He ran for the riverbank and lifted Charlie's body from the water where he floated face up. A deep gash in the guide's scalp spilled blood over Jake's chest as he held him in his arms.

Charlie groaned.

They settled Charlie and Akuda into comfortable positions in the back of the boat. Ralph dressed Charlie's wound as the guide drifted in and out of consciousness,

339

but he had no idea what to do for Akuda, as Ray's wife called him.

Evan looked around at the tribe as he and Jake untied the boat from its moorings. The smiling people were all small and dark-skinned, and one more child ran up to Jake and touched him for luck before running, giggling, back to his mother.

"The lost tribe," Evan said shaking his head in awe. "Mrs. Birdsong was right . . . they really exist. But I don't see anybody who might even remotely be one of the other people affected with the Genesis Gene. These people are all obviously members of a primitive race."

"Maybe they stayed back at their camp for some reason."

"And maybe they're all dead." Evan frowned as he searched the faces again. "Daniel Birdsong was the last to disappear according to the hospital records. Until Beth and Jenny. If it's the Genesis Gene causing his problems now, the others probably went through its final stages a long time ago." He looked at Jake. "No way they'd have survived it."

Jake tossed the rope onto the deck. "Let's get the hell out of here."

Tepi sat crouched near Akuda's side. She stroked his forehead and told him that he would soon be well.

Ray watched her. He felt sick.

The boat came to life and chugged out into the river. Ja-nee hung out over the railing and waved her hands at Pa and the rest of the tribe. She was riding the waterbeast! How jealous Pa must be! She would tell her all about it when she got back.

Lydia pulled a pair of Jenny's shorts and a red T-shirt out of a backpack. Ja-nee was still dancing and waving at the diminishing lost tribe when Lydia pulled the moss

340

kirt from around the child's waist and struggled the hirt over her head. "I wish I could give you a bath irst," she said. "What *is* that awful smell?"

"Fish oil," Jake said. He revved the motor up to go a ittle faster and grinned down at them. "Keeps the inects away."

"It would keep vampires away," Lydia said. She lopped Ja-nee down on a bench and pulled the shorts p her chubby legs, then lifted her slightly to slide them ver her buttocks.

Ja-nee plucked at the shirt and stared at the strange naterial. It was almost the color of the berries she'd icked! She wiggled off the bench and squeezed past er mother to get to Tepi. "Look at me, Tepi ma-da!" he shouted. She twirled around to show off her new lothes.

Ray had come prepared too. He held out a shirt, eans, and underwear to his wife. She, like Ja-nee, wore nly a moss skirt, and her unashamed nakedness embarassed him.

Tepi looked across Akuda's body at the things the od was handing her, then at the still twirling child. Obiously he meant her to wear similar garments. They ooked hot and uncomfortable, but how could she refuse vithout offending him? She took the things from his ands and examined them. They made no sense to her, nd she looked at him helplessly.

Lydia saw the look and pushed past Ray. "Come," he said, and motioned with her hands for Tepi to get p.

Tepi understood and obediently allowed the goddess o help her, while the male gods turned their heads away rom the ritual.

The underpants were no problem, but by the time

341

Lydia had finished with the straps and hooks of the bra, Tepi had started to giggle. She couldn't help it. And by the time Lydia had her completely dressed, the laughter from both of them had the rest of the search party chuckling too. Except Ray.

Evan put an arm around Ray's shoulders and led him to a semiprivate corner of the boat. "She won't be herself until after treatment, Ray," he said gently. "Right now the Genesis Gene has sublimated who she really is. Her normally dormant, primitive recall is only temporarily dominant. Don't let this get to you. She's going to be okay."

"She loves him."

Evan had noticed. He'd hoped Ray hadn't. A foolish hope. Bett's attachment to Daniel Birdsong was obvious.

Ray turned his back to the rest of the people on the boat, then rubbed the heels of his hands into his eyes to force back his tears. "I can handle that," he said. His voice was low and hoarse, and Evan had to lean forward to listen. "For now, anyway. No, I'm lying . . . it hurts like hell." He jammed his hands in his pockets and shook his head like a wet dog. "The man is *dying,* Evan. What if Burnham's cure doesn't work, and he dies? I'll tell you what . . . my wife and that little girl are next. And look at the pain he's going through!" He looked up at Evan. "I can't handle that," he whispered. "I can't handle that."

For once, Evan had nothing to say.

Chapter Fifty-one

The thecodont babies were thriving. They splashed in the shallow end of the pool and chased after the goldfish and minnows that the Institute staff kept them supplied with.

Burnham, Ralph, and a handful of interested scientists sat dangling their legs over the edge of the pool, watching. There was some lively competition going on over an exceptionally fat goldfish.

"Chee-ohw, chee-ohw," the babies spat at each other, each claiming the prize for his own.

Millie raised her head. "Unk, Unk," she grunted, and blinked twice, listening.

Burnham jabbed Ralph in the ribs and pointed. The chatter between the people stopped. They all stared at Millie.

Millie moved her legs. "Unk, unk," she grunted again. Slowly, she backed herself out of the corner and turned to face the babies. Her tail whipped sideways and she glided forward. "Unk, whunk, unk."

The babies obediently deserted their chase and sped toward their mother. They clambered aboard her head and snout, fighting for choice positions. Millie sat pa-

tiently until they were settled, then glided forward an
in a lightning move, snapped the goldfish up for hersel

She swam toward the people who sat at the edge c
the pool and opened her jaws. She was hungry.

Patients and staff heard the cheers two floors away

Jake had radioed ahead, and when they finally arrive
at Tropical Treasures, two ambulances were waiting fo
them. Jake and Ray went with Charlie, who was cor
scious by now, but had a headache that he claime
would kill a mule. The rest of them piled into the othe
ambulance with Akuda. He was dangerously quiet.

Tepi refused to be more than inches away fror
Akuda, and she held his hands all the way to the Insti
tute.

Ja-nee, frightened now by the commotion and spee
of the thing that carried her through strange places, sa
quietly in Lydia's lap.

Harold Burnham had been notified too. When the an
bulances came screaming up to the Emergency entrance
he was waiting at the door for them. And he was smil
ing.

It took four days. They all kept vigil in the hospital
nobody went home. Even Charlie, now fully recovered
claimed a cot in one of the doctors' lounges. He insiste
on staying until he knew the outcome of the therapy o
his new friends. "Won't even charge you for my time,
he'd said to Evan before he finally went home.

Jenny recovered first. Then Bett. It was touch-and-g

344

with Daniel Birdsong, and he would be weak for months, needing at least fourteen hours of sleep a day, but the Genesis Gene finally gave up its terrible hold on him.

They sat together in a conference room at the Institute. Evan and Lydia shared a couch with Jenny, who sat on her mother's lap playing with a new set of crayons. She held up a picture for her mother to see. It was a collie. Lydia smiled.

Jake sat perched on the edge of a chair. He couldn't stop grinning.

Ray and Bett sat next to each other at the conference table. They held hands.

Dr. Burnham sat next to Ralph at the same table.

"We've notified every hospital and clinic in Florida," Burnham said now. "If any patient comes in with symptoms of the Genesis Gene, they'll send them right over here."

"Can I see Millie and her babies again?" Jenny asked, dropping her picture of the collie and sliding off Lydia's lap. She ran over to Burnham and he picked her up and put her on his own lap.

He bounced her up and down on his knee and she laughed up at him. "Of course," he said with a smile.

"What about Millie and her babies?" Lydia asked. "What happens to them now?"

Ralph answered her. "The babies have been treated with the synthesized DNA and the immunological serum, so they'll be fine, as will Millie, and they'll all stay at Tropical Treasures from now on. We've funded a four-hundred by four-hundred-foot natural habitat to be built for them, and scientists from all over the world can go there to study them. And we hope that when they breed, they'll breed true but pass on the new, resistant gene to their offspring. It will be interesting to watch."

"What about the other throwbacks in the Glades?" Bett asked. The entire story had fascinated her when she'd recovered enough to understand the bizarre string of events connected to the Genesis Gene.

Burnham shrugged. "Without treatment, which is of course impossible to give them, we think the gene will eventually react in them at an earlier and earlier age until it causes death in their descendants before they can reproduce. Judging from the lab tests that Dr. Frankel has done on the rapid progression of the Genesis Gene, it could be happening already.

"At any rate, our theory is, and it's only a theory mind you, since the gene also affects the reproductive organs in the lower orders of animals, it's unlikely that the original parents could reproduce for very long anyway. Perhaps only two or three times. You see, the throwbacks are a sign that something is wrong, and as the reproductive organs continue their decline, they will eventually become useless."

"So we won't have to be afraid of Tyrannosaurus Rex running around the Glades," Jake said with a grin.

"Hardly," Burnham said.

"And the lost tribe?" Bett asked.

"We've decided to keep the secret," Lydia said. "None of saw a good enough reason to disturb their lives anymore." She looked around at the others, who nodded agreement.

A knock at the door interrupted their conversation, and they all turned to see Victor Birdsong and his wife enter the room. Daniel followed at a slower pace behind them.

Mrs. Birdsong walked up to Evan and held out her hand. He took it.

"Thank you for my son," she said simply.

Then they were all on their feet, crowding around the Birdsongs and shaking hands. Soon even Victor Birdsong was smiling.

It was the first time Daniel was on his feet, and against Dr. Burnham's mild protestations, his parents insisted on taking him home immediately. They'd come to say thank you and good-bye.

Daniel looked around, bewildered at all the excitement. Who were all these people?

Evan was the first to understand Daniel's confusion, and he began making introductions and giving short explanations about who each person was. When he got to Bett, he gave her name and nothing else.

Daniel took her hand. They smiled at each other.

It was the smile that strangers give each other when first introduced—a social smile that says, "I'm a friendly person and I hope I remember your name if we ever meet again." Nothing more. Then they turned away from each other.

Epilogue

The Florida panther ran her rough tongue down the length of her squirming cub's body. His sibling growled for attention, so she gave him a lick too.

The twins were as large and as lively as her last four litters, and she was getting used to the way all her cubs looked.

It was time to hunt again, and she stretched her muscles as she rose to her feet. One cub dangled from a teat, but dropped off with an angry snarl as she walked away from them.

They watched her glide noiselessly into the jungle. When they were sure she wasn't coming right back, they slapped and growled at each other for a while, rolling over and over each other in mock battle until they were worn out.

Now it was time for a nap. They flopped down on their soft bed of leaves and yawned. Their jaw-hinges stretched and opened to a ninety-degree angle—it was a wide enough yawn to give clearance to the long, saber canine teeth that grew down from their upper jaws.

Prepare Yourself for

PATRICIA WALLACE

LULLABYE (2917, $3.95/$4.95)
Eight-year-old Bronwyn knew she wasn't like other girls. She didn't have a mother. At least, not a real one. Her mother had been in a coma at the hospital for as long as Bronwyn could remember. She couldn't feel any pain, her father said. But when Bronwyn sat with her mother, she knew her mother was angry—angry at the nurses and doctors, and her own helplessness. Soon, she would show them all the true meaning of suffering . . .

MONDAY'S CHILD (2760, $3.95/$4.95)
Jill Baker was such a pretty little girl, with long, honey-blond hair and haunting gray-green eyes. Just one look at her angelic features could dispel all the nasty rumors that had been spreading around town. There were all those terrible accidents that had begun to plague the community, too. But the fact that each accident occurred after little Jill had been angered had to be coincidence . . .

SEE NO EVIL (2429, $3.95/$4.95)
For young Caryn Dearborn, the cornea operation enabled her to see more than light and shadow for the first time. For Todd Reynolds, it was his chance to run and play like other little boys. For these two children, the sudden death of another child had been the miracle they had been waiting for. But with their eyesight came another kind of vision—of evil, horror, destruction. They could see into other people's minds, their worst fears and deepest terrors. And they could see the gruesome deaths that awaited the unwary . . .

THRILL (3142, $4.50/$5.50)
It was an amusement park like no other in the world. A tri-level marvel of modern technology enhanced by the special effects wizardry of holograms, lasers, and advanced robotics. Nothing could go wrong—until it did. As the crowds swarmed through the gates on Opening Day, they were unprepared for the disaster about to strike. Rich and poor, young and old would be taken for the ride of their lives, trapped in a game of epic proportions where only the winners survived . . .

HAUTALA'S HORROR — HOLD ON TO YOUR HEAD!

MOONDEATH (1844-4, $3.95/$4.95)
Cooper Falls is a small, quiet New Hampshire town, the kind you'd miss if you blinked an eye. But when darkness falls and the full moon rises, an uneasy feeling filters through the air; an unnerving foreboding that causes the skin to prickle and the body to tense.

NIGHT STONE (3030-4, $4.50/$5.50)
Their new house was a place of darkness and shadows, but with her secret doll, Beth was no longer afraid. For as she stared into the eyes of the wooden doll, she heard it call to her and felt the force of its evil power. And she knew it would tell her what she had to do.

MOON WALKER (2598-X, $4.50/$5.50)
No one in Dyer, Maine ever questioned the strange disappearances that plagued their town. And they never discussed the eerie figures seen harvesting the potato fields by day . . . the slow, lumbering hulks with expressionless features and a blood-chilling deadness behind their eyes.

LITTLE BROTHERS (2276-X, $3.95/$4.95)
It has been five years since Kip saw his mother horribly murdered by a blur of "little brown things." But the "little brothers" are about to emerge once again from their underground lair. Only this time there will be no escape for the young boy who witnessed their last feast!

WHO DUNNIT? JUST TRY AND FIGURE IT OUT!

THE MYSTERIES OF MARY ROBERTS RINEHART